EAST INDIA

EPIC ADVENTURE SERIES #12

Colin Falconer

Cover design copyright © Colin Falconer
Skyview Publishing
ISBN 9781542814515

My thanks, as always, to Lise. You're amazing.

Better to reign in Hell than serve in Heaven.
John Milton

CHAPTER 1

Amsterdam
October, 1625

Michiel van Texel leaned on the poop rail and looked for faces he knew. Three hundred and thirty souls, who were to join him on the journey, were making their way up the gangplank from the dock. Half of them were crew, recruited from the dockside taverns in Houttuinnen and the Haarlemmerstraat. 'Seven-week gentlemen' they called them. When they got back from a voyage to the Indies, they had enough money to live the grand life for about that long. Then their guilders would run out, lavished on drink and women, and they would sign up with the Company again, in debt even before they left port.

The fleet commander was helped aboard by some of the younger officers. Ambroise van Himst was a handsome man, with black hair falling around his high white collar, and a neatly trimmed beard. He had risen from the VOC ranks to his present exalted position in just ten years. It helped that his brother-in-law was on the Board of the High and Mighty Seventeen, the council that ran the Company.

Without family connections, this is as high as I will rise, Michiel thought, especially after what happened at Macau.

The undermerchant, and second in command, Christiaan van Sant, followed his commander up the gangplank. He dressed more like a dandy than a clerk, and the way he kept smoothing down his hair in the wind made it seem he was a little overfond of his own appearance. There were rumors that he had somehow become involved with heretics, but his family connections had kept him out of prison.

We all have our secrets, Michiel thought.

He groaned inwardly when he saw the pastor and his family. Michiel was a God-fearing man, like all good Dutchmen, but it didn't mean he liked being around churchmen, and months shut up on a ship this size with a pastor wasn't a prospect he relished.

The pastor had his daughters with him. Two of them were no more than girls, but the oldest was shapely with blue eyes. On cue, some men hanging from the ratlines whistled and laughed. The pastor ushered his family below decks, scowling.

Then Cornelia Noorstrandt came aboard, her maid fussing behind her. Michiel drew a breath. Lord preserve us. The old salts said that beautiful women on a boat were bad luck. They stirred up the devil in a man. When you had three hundred men out from port for months at a time, it could only be trouble.

He was dreading the coming voyage. He had made the trip once before, and he knew that the seas would be blue and the air warm and heavy with spice at the journey's end. But, in between, there would be eight months of monotony, seasickness and the grave risk of scurvy.

Why had he come back? His father had told him he had to rescue his reputation. His brother had warned him that it was the only way to still the wagging tongues and save his career.

But career and reputation didn't matter to him anymore. That wasn't what had made him sign his name for another five years of hell. He knew he would regret it the moment they threw the mooring ropes onto the dock, but if he did not go back he could never lay the past to rest.

He went down to the deck to supervise his soldiers. They were filing down a ladder to the gundeck that would be their quarters until they reached Batavia. His lance corporal, Little Bean, saw the Noorstrandt woman being helped aboard and stopped to stare. He got a boot in the backside from the sergeant, Stonecutter.

Michiel grabbed Stonecutter by the collar and jerked him around. 'Leave the little fellow alone.'

'I didn't see you there, sir,' Stonecutter said.

'I know you didn't,' Michiel said, 'or you wouldn't have done it.'

Stonecutter muttered an oath under his breath. Little Bean looked up and nodded his thanks.

'Get below,' Michiel said and watched them make their way down to the hold. His men had months of sitting idle down there to come. Time enough for them to make plenty of trouble.

CHAPTER 2

They left Holland on a lowering autumn day. The North Sea was grey and bitter. The *Utrecht* sailed at the van of the fleet, under towering sail. She was fifty paces from her stern to her beak and the most magnificent of the *retour* craft ever to sail from Holland for the Indies. Her green and gold hull, carved and scrolled by the finest craftsmen in the Amsterdam shipyards, gleamed in the sun. On the coat of arms that decorated the mirror at the stern were mermaids, tritons, and gargoyles to keep away bad spirits, as well as the more stately likenesses of former Batavian warriors. Her pristine sails were still to be darkened by sea salt.

The red, white and blue VOC pennant fluttered in the stiff North Sea breeze.

Ambroise felt a thrill of excitement as the wind thundered into the canvas. He glanced back over the stern at the two other *retourschepen* – the big merchantmen built for these long voyages around the world and back - the *Verguldige Dolphijn* and the *Gerechtigheid.* They were followed by two small yachts, the *Zandaam* and *Groningen.* There was a warship, too, the *Beschermer.* She was a reassuring sight. He hoped they wouldn't need her.

The spray broke over the scarlet prow, where the lion of Holland snarled at the sea.

Ambroise sat at the head of the dinner table in the Council Room. Cornelia Noorstrandt had been given the seat beside him, on his left. Christiaan van Sant sat on his right. The other company clerks and junior officers sat at the far end.

The ship's skipper, Jacob Schellinger, sat opposite Michiel further down the table. He was a man much vested in his own opinions, and he dominated the conversation with talk of wind and currents.

Ambroise waited for him to draw breath then took the opportunity to turn to Michiel. 'And you, Michiel, I understand this is not your first time in the Indies?'

'No, sir. I served five years under Governor-General Coen in Batavia.'

'And you saw action there?'

'I took part in the assault on Macau.'

There was a long and uncomfortable silence. Michiel was neither surprised nor offended by the general reaction. He was accustomed to it.

Schellinger skewered a piece of beef on his knife and crammed it into his mouth. 'And what takes my lady to the Indies?' he said to Cornelia.

'I am going there to meet my husband,' she said.

'What does he do there?'

'He works jewels, by trade. He has been employed by the Company for his expertise.'

A look came across Schellinger's face that was something like a sneer. 'Right. A man of action, then?'

'Watch your manners,' Ambroise said. The two men stared at each other across the table.

Christiaan came to the rescue. He laughed as if someone had made a joke. 'Let us not be unpleasant with each other,' he said. 'Commander, please, you must tell us about your adventures at the court of the great Mogul.'

'I'm sure I have bored everyone enough with tales of India,' Ambroise said.

Schellinger grunted in agreement.

'Well I should like to know more,' Christiaan said, and there were nods from the junior officers. For many it was their first time out of Holland, or even out of their hometowns. They were hungry for romantic tales of flaming volcanoes and waving coconut palms.

'You leave Holland, you find savages,' Schellinger said, tearing off a piece of salt beef with his teeth.

'On the contrary,' Ambroise said. 'In the court of the great Jahan it was my experience that the lords far surpass ours in magnificence. The walls of the prince's fort at Jumna are cut from a red stone that turns at sunset to the color of blood and at dawn is as pink as a rose. The stone is cut into latticework and the windows gilded with gold leaf.'

The young men's eyes shone. They were enthralled.

'There are beasts called elephants, creatures the like of which you have never seen in your life, each of them the size of a farmer's cottage. The prince watches these creatures fight for his sport. He also has a courtyard with rows of black and white marble tiles, and he makes his servants stand on them, even in the heat of the day, and play the part of living chess pieces. He orders them to move about as he pleases while he sits in some shady spot.'

'The Devil's work,' the pastor muttered.

'Like the preacher says, they are godless,' Schellinger said.

Ambroise shrugged. 'I don't like to say it, but the skipper is right. For all their magnificence, their government is unholy and dominated by avarice. The prince fills his *mahals* with expensive toys and beautiful women.'

'You cannot blame a prince for wanting beautiful women,' Schellinger said.

'Civilized men should remain in control of their base desires,' Ambroise said. 'The prince indulges all his senses and behaves as if public affairs were no concern of his. He reclines on velvet couches and drinks sweetened sherbets, while his subjects squat in fly-ridden hovels without beds or meats to flavor their rice. Wondrous though these lands are, they lack our moral certainties.'

'Do you think so?' Christiaan said. 'I should rather think there is a wolf in all men, no matter where they abide.'

The pastor looked up, eyes wide, as if he had been shot in the back with a pistol. 'It is God that has raised us from the animals,' he said. 'Christian men could not behave so.'

Schellinger finished his wine. Some of it glistened in his beard before he wiped it away with the back of his hand. 'I must return to my watch,' he said. 'I feel an indigestion coming on.'

And he went out banging the door behind him.

The wind whipped at Christiaan's cloak as another black swell rolled under the beam. He struggled along the pitching deck to the stern.

'A filthy night,' he said.

Schellinger grunted. 'Coming up to winter, you have to brave the storms this side of the equator to run with the fair weather in the south.'

Christiaan leaned on the rail beside him. 'It occurs to me that you and the commander are not friends.'

'What do you want?'

'I saw the way he treated you at table. He does not care for you, I think.'

'What's that to me?'

'Our commander is highly thought of by the High and Mighty Seventeen.'

'He'd rather lick ass than eat cheese. I knew him in India.'

'I thought so. I heard there was bad blood between you.'

'Someone been talking?'

'I heard he had you reprimanded on your last trip, and that he docked you two months' pay. Bad luck having to sail with him again so soon.'

'What are you up to, clerk boy?'

Christiaan smiled and put a hand on Schellinger's shoulder. 'Man like you, bowing and scraping to these Company men, ferrying around tailors and Jew boys. What a waste.'

Schellinger shoved his hand away.

Christiaan went back down the companionway, leaving the skipper to his dark thoughts.

That night they ran into their first gale. The *Utrecht* pitched violently, running before the wind under her courses. The passengers, crammed below, groaned in their bunks.

Cornelia fought her way onto the deck, desperate for fresh air. She shrugged aside the thought of being washed overboard. It would be a mercy. The ship heaved as another great wave rolled beneath the keel. The bosun shouted at the night watch, ordering them to lower the course yard.

'It will get better,' a voice said.

She looked up. Michiel was braced under the lantern at the carved rail and seemed as cheerful as if he were out taking the morning air along the canals at home.

'When you find your sea legs, you'll be all right.'

She sat down on the planking and closed her eyes. A drift of spray cooled her burning cheeks.

'You'll ruin your gown sitting there,' he said. The ship lurched and sent her sprawling against the bulkhead. He held out a hand to her. She took it and he lifted her back to her feet.

She heard Schellinger bawling at them to clear the deck.

'He's right,' Michiel said. 'The swell is picking up. We will be safer below.'

'I can't.'

'You must,' he said and led her back to the ladder. She stared into the dark, and the fug made her gorge rise.

'Please,' he said.

She nodded and half fell into the gloom.

CHAPTER 3

They endured two weeks of gales and high seas. Schellinger said it was too dangerous for anyone except the crew to go above decks. Passengers were allowed up only on rare occasions and were met with a heaving swell and lashing rain.

Finally the weather broke, and Michiel came up on deck to find them under full sail, running fast before the wind. The silhouettes of the *Beschermer* and the *Zandaam* stood out against the land. The rest of the fleet had been scattered by the storms. The sea was calmer and they sailed under a sky of broken cloud.

He heard someone come up the ladder and turned around. It was Cornelia.

'Feeling better?' he said.

She nodded. 'You must excuse my behavior that first night.'

'Think nothing of it. There are few things in this world worse than seasickness. I used to suffer from it greatly when I first went under sail.'

'I think I have found what you called my sea legs.'

'You still look pale. Have you been eating?'

'As well as I can. The food is not what I am accustomed to.'

'The captain's table is better than what they feed my men. I wouldn't give it to the pigs at home.'

'Forgive me. I imagine you must consider such privations small suffering compared with what you have been through in your life.' She searched the horizon for landfall. 'Where are we?'

'The skipper says we have rounded Cape Finisterre. We are off the coast of Lusitania, around thirty-six degrees north of the Equator.'

She leaned on the rail. 'Better seas at last.' She looked up at Schellinger at the wheel, and Michiel saw the look she gave him.

'He can be a difficult man. But he's the best skipper in the VOC fleet, by reputation.'

'It seems that he and the commander do not like each other very well.'

Michiel smiled. 'It is difficult for them to hide their enmity.'

'What is the problem between them?'

'Last year, when Ambroise returned from India, Schellinger skippered the vessel that he sailed on. There was some unpleasantness.' He hesitated, unsure how much he should tell her. 'Schellinger was trading under the lap, carrying trade goods over that allowed by the Company. Ambroise found out. Some commanders might have looked the other way but not him. He is a stickler for the rules. He reported Schellinger's conduct to the Company, and Schellinger was reprimanded and lost several months' pay.'

'And the Company saw fit to put the two of them together again for this voyage?'

'I agree it makes no sense, but we have to make the best of it.'

She stared into the water foaming alongside the painted hull. 'I am missing Holland already. I'd give anything to take a bath and eat a proper meal.'

'You must be looking forward to seeing your husband again.'

She turned to look at him. 'Have you ever been married, captain?'

'No, but I once had a romantic expectation of it.'

'I see. Well, that explains it, then.' She laughed. 'I should try to eat something. My maid tells me that the cook has prepared a particularly fine breakfast this morning. She says his porridge might be carved, like a side of beef.' She grabbed at the handrail as the ship lurched.

Schellinger shouted a warning to one of the sailors on the top mast yards, but it was too late. The man lost his footing and fell. There was a sickening thud as his body hit the deck. The man shuddered and died. Blood drained from the back of his skull into the scuppers.

Schellinger leaned on the rail. He looked irritated. 'Get him out of the way!' he shouted to the day watch.

Two of the dead man's fellows went quickly below and returned with a winding sheet. They placed him in it and another man started to stitch the ends together with a large needle and a reel of waxed thread.

'Where's the pastor?' Schellinger yelled.

'He's seasick,' the bosun called up to him. 'He refuses to come out of his cabin.'

'You do it then,' Schellinger said and went back to the wheel.

After they had finished sewing the dead man into the sheet, the bosun said a few words from the good book, and then they pitched the body over the side. One of the sailors sluiced down the planking with a bucket of seawater, and the rest of the watch went on with their work as if nothing had happened.

When Michiel turned around, Cornelia was still staring at the deck.

'Do you think that's all there is?' she said. 'A winding sheet and a bucket of water, and not even a stain of us left behind.'

'The pastor says our soul goes to heaven to meet God.'

'You believe him?'

He smiled. 'It depends who's asking.'

'If the pastor is wrong, I wonder what it's all for?'

'I have asked myself that question many times.'

'And do you have an answer?'

'All I know is that at the end of my life, I would like to be a better man than I was when I started out. It's a humble ambition, but it gives me comfort to think that I might achieve it.'

The young cadet officers on board were barely men; some of them didn't even have beards on their chins. They were penniless blue bloods known as 'jonkers'. All they had going for them was good breeding, a famous name and an innate sense of entitlement. Their families had got them positions as naval ensigns or junior assistants with the Company just to get them off their hands.

The only one old enough to be called a man was Joost van der Linden. Christiaan wondered what he was doing as a cadet. Spent his inheritance, he supposed, and needed money from somewhere. He had hair like a lion's mane and glacial blue eyes. A golden child with nothing in his head, most likely.

He was standing at the rail, watching Michiel deep in conversation with the Noorstrandt woman

'Are you jealous,' Christiaan said into his ear.

The young man looked discomfited at being caught out. 'He shouldn't be talking to her like that. She's a married woman.'

'I was right. You are jealous.'

It never hurts to dream,' Joost said.

'What else do you dream about? Go ahead, tell me. I shan't scoff. A young man like you, it's good to have ambition.'

'I won't be a lackey forever. They say Ambroise rose from a clerk to commander in just ten years.'

'Yes, but his brother-in-law is an Admiral with the Company. You really think he got to be in his position through hard work?'

'The Company needs young men like us.'

'Of course they do.' Christiaan put a hand on his shoulder. 'But eight men out of ten do not survive five years in Batavia. Forget all they have told you about bare-breasted women and coconut palms. It is a death pit, rife with flux and fever.'

'Then why are you going there?'

'I have studied at university, I have French and Latin and I am skilled at apothecary. The chance of rapid advancement is worth the risk.'

They never told them what Batavia was really like before they got on the ship, Christiaan thought. If they did, what fool in his right mind would go? 'Your family has a proud name in Holland,' he said. 'Even I have heard of the van der Lindens, and I lived a long way away in Haarlem. It's a pity the way things have turned out. You were meant for better things. Much better.'

Joost stared at him. 'What better things?' he said.

CHAPTER 4

Only two months out and already Cornelia felt she would go mad. The endless monotony of the days was relieved only by the tolling of the ship's bell, as the helmsman called the hour from the sand in the glass.

She found herself looking forward to mealtimes, though the food was pitiful. Breakfast and supper was gruel mixed with prunes. Lunch was peas or beans with salted pork or smoked herring. They had brought live pigs and chickens with them, but these had almost all been slaughtered and eaten already, and there were maggots in the salted pork.

On fine days they could wander about the deck and take some relief with the cooling breezes. But whenever they ran into a storm, they were all ordered below decks and had to stay there, for their own safety and to stay out of the way of the crew.

Cornelia knew she was better off than most. She had her own cabin and use of one of the two privies with wooden seats projecting over the stern. A long rope with a frayed end trailed into the sea, and she used it to clean herself. Afterwards she tossed it back through the privy into the ocean below to wash it clean. It was as ingenious as it was disgusting.

Still, even this was a luxury of sorts.

The other passengers shared the gun deck and two privies among almost three hundred, along with two hundred sailors. The stink was appalling.

At least the weather had improved and the days were mostly mild. Occasionally they glimpsed the coasts of the Sierra Leone, and there was the promise of fruit and heat on the breath of the sea.

As soon as Michiel went up on deck, he knew that something was wrong.

The sailors were about their work, but they were all stealing glances over their shoulders. Michiel looked up at Schellinger, leaning on the poop. He nodded towards the mainmast.

Little Bean was skewered to it, a knife through the palm of his hand. He was struggling to keep himself upright. He had his other hand on the handle of the knife, but he didn't have the strength to pull it out. If he fell, the blade would tear right through the flesh to the webbing. He was trying to make no sound, but the screams that were in him were coming out in gasps.

'What is going on here,' Michiel said.

'Stonecutter,' Little Bean said.

Michiel nodded and went below.

His men, all eighty of them, were crammed down on the orlop deck. It was Company policy to keep the soldiers separate from the sailors on a long voyage to prevent trouble, so the sailors slept on the gun deck, while his men barracked on the orlop below, crammed in with their hammocks and their seabags. Even a trip to the heads - a pair of plank seats with a hole cut in them, just over the bow of the ship - was allocated to set times, and the men went in groups under Stonecutter's watchful eye.

The air was already thick with smoke, every bastard puffing on pipes as they played *dommelen* or chess. Some men were dozing in their hammocks. Michiel almost gagged at the stench.

'Where's Stonecutter?' he said.

The big sergeant got to his feet and appeared out of the gloom at the far end of the deck. His real name was Joris Jansen, but he was known to the men by the trade he had before he became a soldier, Steenhower

– the Stonecutter. It suited him, too. He was a huge man, a head taller than anyone else, with a face that frightened children and scared off the toughest whores at the docks. Michiel supposed that some men would have chosen to hide from the world and spent their lives in the shadows. Not Stonecutter. He had come out swinging.

'What can I do for you, captain?' Stonecutter said.

'What have you done to Little Bean?'

'He knows the regulations.'

'I didn't ask you about Company regulations. I asked you why he is being punished.'

'He was playing dice with two of the men. They got in an argument and Little Bean pulled out a knife.'

'Which men?'

Stonecutter nodded at two of the mercenaries, Frenchmen.

'Is that what happened?' Michiel said to them.

They couldn't meet his eyes. One of them nodded without looking up and the other mumbled something in French.

'You see,' Stonecutter said.

'You come to me before you mete out punishments. That's also regulations.'

Stonecutter stepped closer and lowered his voice. 'They're all dock scum. They need a firm hand.'

'Next time you come and see me first.'

'I thought you didn't give a damn about the men. Something changed since Macau?'

Michiel grabbed Stonecutter's tunic and bunched it in his fist. It was like shaking a wall. 'Repeat that, and I'll have you flogged.'

'Excuse me, captain,' Stonecutter said but did not take his eyes off his face. 'I meant no harm by it.'

Michiel went back up to the deck. Little Bean was shaking so badly he could barely hold himself up.

'Tell me what happened,' Michiel said.

'I was working scrimshaw on a whale tooth. I swear. I made a joke to one of the others as Stonecutter went past.'

'About Stonecutter?'

Little Bean nodded, gritting his teeth against the pain.

'Are you mad?'

'I didn't think he would hear me.'

Michiel gripped the knife's handle with both hands and wrenched it out of the wood. A spurt of blood splashed onto the deck. Little Bean gasped and slid to his knees.

'Get below,' Michiel said. 'Find the surgeon and have him bind it.' He helped Little Bean to his feet and pushed him towards the hold. When he looked up he saw Cornelia watching him from the quarterdeck.

'I'm sorry you had to see that,' Michiel said.

Cornelia frowned. 'What was it about?'

'It is company regulations. Anyone who draws a knife on a fellow soldier while on board has their hand fixed to the mainmast with their own dagger. They are left there to find a way off it best way they can. It prevents endless bloodshed.'

'But you released him.'

'I didn't believe he was guilty.'

'Yet you weren't there when it happened.'

'I know the man. He was a soldier when I served with the Company in Macau. He isn't capable of such a thing.'

'It was cruel, no matter what he did.' She drew her shawl tighter about her shoulders. 'It is getting chill, I should go back down to my cabin.'

CHAPTER 5

They sailed with fair winds. The *Beschermer* kept close, distinctive by her gun ports, which were painted brilliant crimson. Beyond her was the *Zandaam*, the golden mermaid on her bows glittering in the sun.

Cornelia watched some soldiers throwing lines off the stern, baited with bacon fat. They were trawling not for fish but for seabirds.

She heard Schellinger bawling a string of orders to the duty watch. Most of what he said was incomprehensible to her, but the sailors responded immediately, scampering up and down the ratlines to furl sheets and lower others.

'It is an astounding thing to watch him at his work, is it not?'

She looked around. Christiaan stood close by her right shoulder. She hadn't seen him come up on deck.

'The men down below on the whip staff move the ship's rudder,' he said, 'but ships like this are so big they are steered mainly by the mizzen and sprit sails. It requires great skill on the part of the ship's master. Now we can travel to the end of the world and think nothing of it. Astonishing to live in such times.'

'I am told our skipper has made this journey on three occasions.'

'He is very experienced. We could not be in better hands.'

The way he looked at her unnerved her. He was a strange one for all his high position. She edged away from him. 'And what takes you to the Indies?' she said.

'I look to better myself, as we all do.'

'You are a man of learning, I am told.'

'I have some knowledge of Latin and French. I earned my living as an apothecary for many years.'

'What inspired you to make such a great change in your affairs?'

'Some of us choose our destiny, others have their destiny chosen for them. Take Michiel van Texel for instance. Have you asked him why he would choose to return to the Indies when there was no promotion or advancement offered to him for doing so?'

'Is there something you wish me to know?'

'You have been spending a lot of time in his company. It has not gone unnoticed. But he is not worthy of you.'

'Worthy? What could you mean? I am a married woman.'

He lowered his voice and put his face close to hers. She could smell the taint of his breath. The look on his face was intense; a man either in pain or in ecstasy. 'You deserve better,' he said. 'Ask him about Macau.'

The cabin boys brought in platters of hot, salted pork. The cook had spiced it with cardamom and coriander, but all the spices in India could not disguise the taint. Biscuits sat in copper bowls, arranged like fruit. The commander's butler hurried around with Burgundy wine.

The talk at the table turned again to the commander's adventures in India. The young clerks were always hankering for stories of the Oriental harems.

'So is it true,' Christiaan said, 'that even a common man may have more than one wife?'

'If he can afford it,' Ambroise said. 'Keeping just one may be expense enough for a poor man.'

They all laughed at that.

'Why should a man need more than one wife?' Cornelia said.

She saw a junior clerk, David Krueger, glance at one of his fellows and give him a knowing wink.

'Indeed, some men would count themselves lucky with just one,' Ambroise said. But when his eyes met hers, his cheeks colored and he looked away.

'I have heard that the princes have whole palaces filled with their wives,' Christiaan said.

'I should like to have been born a mogul prince,' Krueger said and received a look of disapproval from the pastor.

'I am sure the princes think the arrangement very fine,' Ambroise said. 'But as a Dutchman I cannot but feel sympathy for these women. Theirs is not such a happy life. Yes, they have the best food, the finest clothes, and they live in the greatest luxury in their *zenanas*, which is what they call their palaces. But they are, I am told, desperately lonely.'

'Yet is it not true,' Michiel said, 'that certain of their women find life without their husbands so unbearable that they follow them voluntarily to the grave?'

'You are right,' Ambroise said. 'I have seen it once with my own eyes. They call it *sati*.'

'What is that?' Christiaan said.

'It is when a native woman throws herself on her husband's funeral pyre and burns along with him.'

The pastor shook his head. 'To destroy oneself is a mortal sin before God.'

'You saw this for yourself?' Cornelia said to Ambroise.

He sipped his wine, and it left a dark stain on his moustaches. 'Yes, though I wish I had not. The woman I saw was most handsome. She had married her husband when she was just thirteen years old and knew no other man. And he, for his part, had no other wives. When he died, she declared she would become *sati*, though her relatives and her friends tried to dissuade her. They even enlisted the support of the governor, but it was to no avail. It is custom there, and she saw she was doing herself great honor in the eyes of her savage gods.'

There was a contemptuous snort from the pastor.

'She dressed in her best clothes and jewels, as if it were her wedding day and then went to sit upon his funeral pyre. When his body burned, her living flesh burned with him. She uttered not a sound when she was consumed. It was the most remarkable thing I have ever seen and the most distressing.'

'Is this situation ever reversed, Commander?' Michiel said. 'Might a man willingly give up his life for a woman, do you think?'

'But of course,' Ambroise said. 'Any man who would not, cannot properly call himself a man.'

'Perhaps no one really knows what is in their heart until they are called upon to act on it.'

'This is godless talk,' the pastor said. 'Those the Lord chooses are exalted by His love and are redeemed, while those who are not chosen will burn.'

'Surely,' Michiel said, 'a man chooses whether or not he burns.'

'Certain persons are elected by God for salvation,' the pastor said. 'The rest are consigned to eternal damnation. Every human action is foreordained by God. There is no such thing as free will.'

'Then what is the point of it all, if God already knows what we shall do and which of us will be sinners?' Michiel said.

'I think my husband knows the ways of God better than any man here,' the pastor's wife said.

'But if you think about it,' Michiel persisted, 'we have all known men who have been brought down by their own actions. God had nothing to do with it.'

The pastor launched into another of his sermons, and Krueger glared at Michiel for giving him cause to blast his holy trumpets again.

Cornelia made it a habit to go up on deck after dinner if the weather and seas were mild, to smell the salt air and stare at the vast panorama of stars. She hated the airless confines of her cabin and the stench of tar and bilge that permeated belowdecks.

She stopped for a moment at the foot of the companionway and looked into the gloom of the gun deck, at the people crammed in there sleeping. She heard a couple coming together in the darkness, fumbling under the bedclothes just a few feet away behind a curtain.

She hurried aloft.

It was a still night and the cold air was better than the crowded fug of the holds. The deck appeared deserted and the night watch were silent at their posts. She thought she was alone with the creaking of the cordage and the gentle swell of the ocean, then she saw Michiel standing at the stern.

'You upset the pastor,' she said.

He turned around and smiled. 'Indeed. I fear I may not be one of the chosen. It seems I am destined for the fire.'

'I should like to think that God is not as rigid as the pastor in his beliefs.'

He raised an eyebrow. 'You should not express such heretical opinions aloud.'

'You do.'

'I spend too much time in the company of common soldiers. They think me already doomed.'

She stood beside him and they stared in silence at the ocean. The wash left in their wake glittered silver against the rising moon.

'How do you know about this *sati* that the Commander spoke of?' she said.

'I served five years with the Company in East India. I am familiar with many of the things that Ambroise speaks about.'

'But you do not talk much about it.'

'I prefer not to,' he said, and there was an edge of disquiet in his voice.

'You have been to Batavia, also?'

'I was garrisoned there for a time.'

'What it is like?'

'For the first few days you find yourself staring open-mouthed at the wonders. There are trees, slender as flowers, that grow to the height of a gabled house. They are utterly different from any tree we have in Holland, for all the branches are on top. And the fruit - well, let us say, you would not want the fruit to fall on you. It would not be quite the same as being struck on the head by an apple. They are the size of cannon balls and almost as hard. The air smells of spice and it is always warm, never a winter.'

'It sounds a paradise. But I know it's not. So many that the Company send out there never come back.'

'True enough.'

'So why would a man go there again?'

A star shot across the heavens and he took the opportunity to change the course of the conversation. 'Did you see it? People believe all shooting stars come from the constellation of Perseus. You see the bright star there? That's the tip of his helmet and the two stars above it are his sword.'

She laughed. 'I think whoever named the stars had a very vivid imagination.'

'No, look, the stars in the shape of a W above it, that's Cassiopeia.'

'I know about Cassiopeia. My father taught me all about the stars. We would stand on the roof of our house on the Nieuwendijk and he pointed them out to me. He said her mother, Andromeda, was a vain queen, always boasting about how beautiful her daughter was. She so offended the gods that they sent a monster to punish her and all her subjects. An oracle told her the only way to save her kingdom was to sacrifice Andromeda. So the poor girl was chained to a rock in the middle of the ocean as a sacrifice. But Perseus saw her, killed the monster, set her free and claimed her.'

'It's always the same in the stories. The princesses are always beautiful and the princes are always brave.'

'And they always live happily ever after.'

'It's just a story. It doesn't happen that way in real life.'

'I liked the stories when I was a child.'

'And when you were older?'

'By the time I was older, my father wasn't there anymore. He died when I was fourteen. My mother died a year later. My uncle said it was a broken heart. I think it might have been pestilence.'

She saw a shadow on the deck. It was the Commander. He was watching them. 'It is late,' she said. 'I should go to my cabin. I shall wish you a good night.'

'Goodnight, *vrouwe*. Remember me to heaven in your prayers.'

'I think it is a little late for that,' she said and heard him laugh.

As she hurried down the ladder she looked back once. He was leaning on the carved rail, his head down. She thought about what Christiaan had said. What had happened in Macau? Whatever it was, she was sure it was no more than malicious gossip.

CHAPTER 6

The days grew hot. It was stinking down below.

The sailors were packed in with the cannon on the gun deck, their hammocks slung between the thwarts, and their sea chests jammed wherever they could find space to stow them.

It was even worse for the soldiers on the orlop. It was airless, black as hell and barely room for a man to stand. They were allowed up on deck for just an hour every day, if the weather wasn't too bad, to be drilled by Stonecutter with wooden swords and pikes. He reveled in it, using his size and strength to bully the younger men.

He was halfway through battering one of the young Englishers. The boy looked terrified.

Finally, Michiel's patience ran out. It wasn't teaching the young recruits anything except to run away from bigger men. 'Sergeant, step back,' he said.

'What's the matter?' Stonecutter said. 'These men have to learn how to fight.'

'I agree. And you're not teaching them anything. You're just showing off.' Michiel took the sword from the Englisher and called the rest of the men around. 'There's two ways you can defend yourself against a heavier opponent. If you just retreat, like this fellow, sooner or later you will get tired and you'll die. You have to look for the other fellow's weakness, not their strength.' He turned to Stonecutter. 'Come at me, sergeant.'

Stonecutter looked wary, but he only knew one way. He swung viciously with the wooden sword, aiming his strike at Michiel's head. In one motion Michiel brought his own sword around to block the blow, two-handed, then spun around in a half circle. He turned his sword around and stabbed backwards, the blunt wooden point hitting Stonecutter in the midriff and doubling him over. He crumpled to his knees, winded.

Michiel stepped away. 'If that were a real sword, his guts would be all over the deck. It takes speed and a little practice but it can be done.' He waited, listening to Stonecutter wheezing on all fours, trying to get his breath back. 'That's how you teach men to fight, sergeant. Not just with brawn but with brains as well. Continue.'

As he turned away, Little Bean caught his arm. 'You've just made an enemy there.'

'As if I give a damn,' Michiel said, but he knew Little Bean was right. It was small justice for what he had done to Little Bean and there was little satisfaction in it. He would have to control his temper better next time.

In Holland it would be winter. There would be snow in the fields and ice on the rivers. Hard to imagine, when there was sweat running inside your ruffed collar and the sun baked the back of your neck.

The pastor's family had put up an awning on the quarterdeck. They were crowded in the shade beneath it, listening to his wife reading from the Bible.

When Joost van der Linden stepped onto the deck, the pastor's daughter, Hendrika, glanced up from her sewing. Joost gave her a secret smile. Hendrika would have smiled back, but she saw her mother glaring at her and put her head down again.

'You don't have a chance,' Christiaan said.

Joost looked around. 'What was that, undermerchant?'

'I said, you don't have a chance with that girl.'

'Is that a fact?'

'The pastor won't let her out of his sight for a moment, and he's promised her to a provost's son in Batavia.'

'How do you know all this?'

'I make it my business to find out.'

Joost shrugged. 'You could be right,' he said and lit his pipe. 'Pastors don't have much use for the Company, I suppose, except when there's fighting to be done in the name of the Lord. For myself, I have no use for pastors either. Does that shock you?'

Christiaan shook his head. 'Not at all.'

'What's the name of those other girls?'

'That one with the blonde curls is Elisabeth Post. Her father's a soldier. He's been fighting in Batavia, gone two years now. The skinny one's her sister, Alida. She is just married. That milksop whose arm she hangs off is her husband. But you don't care about them - you have your eyes on Hendrika.'

Joost stared at the ocean.

'Big handsome boy like you,' Christiaan said. 'It must rankle to lose the best ones to pansy boys and provost's sons. If only you had a bit of money, hey?'

Joost shot him a venomous look.

Christiaan smiled. 'I'm not making fun of you if that's what you think. In fact, I'm a lot like you. What I want, I can't have.'

Joost looked back at Hendrika. 'I can't stop thinking about her.'

Christiaan slapped him on the shoulder. 'As I said, right now you don't have a chance. But that could change if you want it bad enough.'

'What are you suggesting?' Joost said.

And Christiaan told him.

Ambroise walked alone on the deck. He had known in his bones that he should not take this voyage. But the Company had made him President of the Fleet, and if he continued to work hard and do as he was asked, they would one day make him a Commissioner. It was everything he had worked for, these last ten years. How could he refuse?

He had only returned from his last journey to India a few months before, and he had not fully recovered. The tropical vapors had drained his health and taken his vigor. When he had asked for time to consider, his brother-in-law had pressed him to take this golden opportunity.

But from the moment he stepped onto the boat, he knew he had made a terrible mistake. Was it when he saw Schellinger or when he saw Cornelia Noorstrandt?

He had tried to avoid her during the voyage, for the sake of his mortal soul and his peace of mind, but she was always there at mealtimes. It seemed to him that he saw in her eyes a spark from a kindred fire. When he spoke of the women of India, the clerks winked at each other and the preacher frowned. She alone seemed to share his anguish for their position. While others asked him about the mogul's toys, she wanted to know of the people.

That a woman so exquisite should be possessed by a diamond polisher both astonished and tormented him.

He took out his astrolabe, preparing to take the day's reading. The fixing of their position was Schellinger's responsibility, but he liked to keep his own record of latitudes for his journal.

'Commander. May I have a word?'

He turned around. It was Cornelia, looking radiant in an uncut bodice; cream velvet bordered with grey.

'Of course, *vrouwe*.'

'I am not disturbing you?' she said and nodded at the instrument in his hands.

'Not at all. How may I help you?'

'I have a question about Captain van Texel. Something Christiaan said has troubled me.'

'What was it he said?'

'He made reference to a place called Macau.'

Ambroise frowned. 'A bad business.' He seemed reluctant to say more.

'How so?'

'Two years ago, the Company sent an expedition against the Portuguese fort that has been built there. We were resoundingly defeated. There was an enquiry afterwards in Batavia. Michiel was charged with cowardice, but the charges against him were never proved. Christiaan should not be talking about such things.'

'Cowardice?'

'He ran away. That was what was said.'

'Yet he is still a captain.'

Ambroise shrugged. 'As I said, the charges against him were dropped.'

'But you disapprove of him?'

'No, I do not. Nor do I trust him. The fact remains that, with the exception of one man, all the men in his charge that day are dead. Michiel is still alive. As an officer of the Company, I know what I should have done in his position. I should rather lay down my life than continue with such a stain on my character.'

'I see. Thank you for telling me.' She turned to go.

'It's called an astrolabe.'

'Commander?'

He held it up for her to see, dangling it from his thumb by a ring, anxious to keep her talking. 'The sun is over my left shoulder. If I hold it this way, the edge of the disc faces the sun. We move this arm here, which is called the alidade, until the sun shines through both these peepholes.'

'To what purpose?'

'It tells me how far to the north or the south we have travelled. It is accurate to around one nautical mile. It is called the latitude.'

'But how do you know how far we have travelled east or west?'

He shrugged. 'That is a different problem. For that we rely on something called dead reckoning.'

'You mean guesswork?'

'I should not like to state it quite so baldly.'

'Is there another way?'

Her questions discomfited him. He heard himself stammer out an answer. 'You have seen the leadsmen drop a block of wood over the side, with a line attached?'

She nodded.

'As he does so, he keeps note of the time through an hourglass, and counts how many knots run out of the line, to calculate how fast the ship runs.'

'That works?'

'As I said, it is not exact. The sea currents, a badly tied line, even moisture in the hourglass can interfere with the calculation. That is why it is important to have an experienced skipper.'

'And *Heer* Schellinger is a good skipper?'

Ambroise looked up at the poop. 'He knows the sea as well as any man,' he said.

He was painfully aware of her closeness. His mouth was dry. 'The angles are marked on the wheel rim here. They give us our position either north or south of the center of the earth, which is called the equator.'

A swell moved under the boat and she fell against him. He put out an arm to steady her and, for a moment, their bodies pressed against each other. She moved away, her face flushed.

'I'm sorry, *vrouwe*,' he mumbled.

There was a high color in her cheeks. 'The wind is getting stronger. I should go below.'

His hands were shaking. He looked around to see if anyone had noticed what had taken place.

Schellinger leaned on the gilded rail, his lips drawn back in a sneer. Look at that pansy boy, he thought, holding the astrolabe as if it were a purse, showing off to that fancy doxie who would not know a real man if she was presented with one by Lord God Almighty Himself.

What the Commander knew about seamanship he could carve on a clay pipe with a sea anchor.

He knew what that bastard was after; what every man on the ship was thinking about right now. And fair enough too, after two months without a woman. He'd fuck an albatross if it flew close enough.

But that pansy pretended he was so refined.

You're no better than us, he thought, standing there in your padded doublet, that thick gold medallion around your neck and acting like you're the Prince of the World. I'll never forget what you did to me. All you Company bastards with your fine clothes. There's not a man among you I couldn't drink under the table or kick to death with both my hands tied behind my back and a whore in my lap.

He gripped the rail, his knuckles white, and swore he'd get even one day.

CHAPTER 7

The *Utrecht* sailed south through warm seas, the ship's bell counting cadence of the endless hot days. At night, the men tossed in restless sleep below decks, their dreams peopled with whores and brown ladies. The dark coast of Africa brooded below the horizon, drawing them further from the certainties of the *Kerke* and the comforts of their good Calvinist homes, towards new and uncertain shores and godless kingdoms.

Every Sunday, the ship's company gathered before the main mast, and the pastor delivered a sermon and warned them about the ways of the Devil. Then they sang hymns and prayed for the success of their voyage to India. Hendrika read a passage from the Bible.

After the service, the pastor fell into conversation with Joost, who kept glancing in Hendrika's direction. She kept her eyes lowered, as a maiden should.

Schellinger smiled to himself. Clear enough what was happening there. He saw Cornelia, her maid in tow. 'Looking for the commander?' he said to her. 'He's not well this morning. Lying in his bunk puking his guts up.' He shouted an order to his understeersman, who made correction to the rudder to hold their course. 'Don't look so worried. The commander may be President of the Fleet but it's me who will see you to Batavia safe and sound.'

'You have all our confidences, I'm sure,' Cornelia said. 'I hope the commander is soon returned to health.'

'I dare say he'll be well enough soon. But if it's male company you're missing, I shall be happy to oblige you.'

'I think I shall return to my cabin,' she said.

'I can stay here, *vrouwe*,' her maid said. 'Perhaps I might afford the skipper some company if that's what he wants.'

'I think you'll be in the way,' Cornelia said.

'Not at all,' Schellinger said. 'I might even find some tasks for her. There are some things on a ship I find are best done by a woman.'

Cornelia glared at him. 'Come below,' she said to the girl, who grudgingly followed her mistress down the ladder.

Schellinger watched them go. When he turned back, he saw Christiaan standing behind him.

'It seems Sara has taken a liking to you,' Christiaan said.

'Who?'

'The Noorstrandt maid. Her name is Sara.'

'Sara,' Schellinger repeated, rolling the name around his tongue. 'Pretty little thing. There's a girl who could put some tobacco in your pipe.'

'And aren't we all dying for a good smoke?'

Schellinger laughed. 'You and me both, *Heer* Undermerchant. You and me both.'

Cornelia waited until they got back to her cabin before she rebuked her. Ever since they had left Amsterdam, the girl had been making eyes at the sailors.

'What do you think you're doing?' she said.

Sara had the impertinence to raise an eyebrow.

'You were flirting with him. Everyone heard you. It will be the scandal of the whole ship.'

'I can do what I like.'

'Not while you are in my employ. You will not say another word to him, I forbid you even to look at him.'

All she got was a sulky look. If the girl weren't careful she would end her days selling herself down by the dockside.

'The Company has rules about such behavior and how women conduct themselves on their ships. Do you understand?'

'Yes, *vrouwe.*'

She left it there and hoped that would be the end of it.

CHAPTER 8

They had been favored with good winds and the *Utrecht* was a month ahead of schedule by the skipper's reckoning. Seaweed floated on the waves, and speckled gulls circled, screaming. It was no more than two days' sailing to the Dutch colony at Good Hope.

Michiel checked on Little Bean. His hand was wrapped in a filthy bandage and the wound was oozing. He was in good spirits despite the pain. Some men always found a way to see the bright side of things, no matter what, and he was one of them.

He didn't know how his men endured it. Company rules allowed them just an hour on deck out of every twelve. The rest of the time they were cooped up like chickens. Today, at least, the hatches were open and there was good weather above. In foul seas it was dark as the devil's ass and men couldn't keep their dinners down.

He went back up on deck, hoping to see Cornelia. He was not disappointed. They talked for a while about Batavia and he tried to explain to her about the seasons, which were nothing like Holland.

Her manner changed when she saw Christiaan come from below and fall into conversation with Schellinger.

'Is something wrong?' Michiel said.

'The undermerchant,' she said. 'He frightens me. He has no love for you, you know.'

'What has he said about me?'

'He wanted me to ask you about Macau.'

Michiel sighed. He supposed it was only a matter of time before someone brought it up in polite conversation. 'There was a full enquiry at the time. My name was cleared.'

'Forgive me. You don't have to talk about it. I do not even know where Macau is.'

'It is a port city in Cathay. The mandarins have allowed the Portuguese a permanent settlement there. It has proved a lucrative acquisition for trade with the Japans.'

'Why were you there?'

I don't have to tell her anything, he thought. I could let her listen to the gossip and believe whatever she wants. Instead he said, 'Governor Coen in Batavia wished to acquire Macau for the Company. He hoped to steal the trade with the Japans and use the port as his base to assault a great city called Manila, in the east. I was part of the expedition that sailed there to invade.'

'I take it from your voice that it did not go as planned.'

'The Portuguese fort there was only half completed, and they had barely a hundred and fifty men able to defend it. We arrived there with thirteen ships and a landing force of eight hundred soldiers. It should have been easy, but the Portuguese defended fiercely. We lost forty men, and our admiral was shot in the belly just taking the beach. As we marched into the city, a cannon salvo from the fort landed on a barrel of gunpowder in the middle of our formation. It turned the tide of the battle. We lost a lot of men, including our commander, and most of our ammunition. We had to pull back. But the Portuguese gave us no time to rest. They came at us. They gave their black slaves copious amounts of rum to fight for them, and they are as fierce an enemy as I have ever faced. Even their women. There were hordes of them screaming the name of John the Baptist. Every one of us they killed, they cut off the head and kept it as a trophy.'

He fell silent, lost in the memories of the night time slaughter.

'You were lucky to escape with your life.'

'Luck had nothing to do with it. Little Bean was wounded in the head by a musket ball. I put him over my shoulder and ran. I did not stop running until we were back in one of the boats in the harbor.'

'I think most men would have done the same.'

'No, *vrouwe*. Every man under my command, except Little Bean, died that night. So not every man did the same.'

'If you had stood your ground, would the outcome have been different?'

'That is not the point.'

'It seems to me that is exactly the point. If you had not left the battle, you would have died and so would the soldier whose life you saved. And it would have been for nothing.'

'Yet that was my duty.' He felt her hand on his. He snatched his away. 'I am not deserving of sympathy.'

'Why have you come back to the East Indies?'

'Isn't it clear?

'You want to prove yourself to the world.'

'To prove myself to *me*. I was cleared of fault by Governor Coen. In my heart, I do not agree with that judgment. Every night when I close my eyes, I see the faces of the men who died. What I long for is the chance to do it all again. To do it differently.' He looked away. The sun was sinking low in the sky. 'It is getting late. I shall go to my cabin.'

'Thank you for your candor.'

He gave her a grim smile. 'Think nothing of it,' he said. 'Candor is all I have left.'

It was dusk and most of the passengers were below deck. There was just the night watch on top. Schellinger saw Sara emerge from the companionway. He supposed her mistress was at dinner with the officers. He called out to her to join him on the poop. He could be free with her there. Anything he said would be carried away with the wind.

'Hello, little Sara,' he said. 'How's your mistress tonight?'

'Down there making calf eyes at the captain,' she said.

Schellinger spat into the sea.

'You can't blame him, I suppose,' she said. 'How can any poor girl compete with her?'

'You're more of a woman than she'll ever be.'

'You don't mean it.'

'I mean it well enough,' he said, his voice husky. A long time at sea without a woman, and this Sara wasn't a bad sort of a piece. 'If I dressed you in lace and jewels, all the men would be looking at you instead of her.'

'How's a poor skipper with a wife at home in Holland going to give a girl lace and jewels?'

He felt her wriggle against him and reached out to grab her. She twisted away. So that was how it was going to be, was it?

She let her cloak fall open and gave him a glimpse of her plump breasts tied up tight inside her bodice, screaming to be set free. 'The commander,' she said, 'now there's a man. I bet he has jewels to give a girl.'

'I'll be a richer man than him one day,' he said. 'You think I'm going to pilot these old tubs around the ocean all my life. A man like me? I could do anything.'

She turned her back on him but he caught her by the wrist and spun her around. He held her against him and kissed her hard on the lips. He thought she might fight him but not a bit of it. Her mouth was hot and dirty-sweet. He felt her thigh rubbing against his groin. God's death!

She pushed him away and darted off down the ladder .

He thought the little tease was going to leave him like that, but she stopped halfway down and whispered, 'Look for me when you finish your watch,' and then she was gone.

Among the *Utrecht*'s other innovations, the shipwrights had roofed in the gallery overlooking the stern and had built privies there in addition to those in the beak. These were for the exclusive use of the commander and the ship's officers. A real luxury compared to some of the other old tubs he'd sailed in.

When he came off the watch that night, Sara was waiting for him, good as her word. He took her to the gallery, shut the door and lifted her off the floor. Without a word, he pulled up her skirts and pulled his breeches down to his knees. He wet himself with his fingers and pushed his way inside her. She bit into his shoulder to stifle a cry of pain.

'I'm going to make a great lady of you,' he whispered, and he fucked her hard and quickly, right there in the commander's privy.

CHAPTER 9

Table Bay, Cabo de Bono Esperanza
December, 1625

The *Utrecht* laid anchor in Table Bay. The Dutch East India Company flag hung limp at the foremast peak. There was scarcely a breeze. A musky foreign odor drifted from the shore and the great hump of the Table Mountain blushed with pink.

Ambroise went to find victuals for the second leg of their journey. They needed fresh meat, fruit and water.

Michiel watched boats ply back and forth between the ships of the anchored fleet, their lamps glowing in the quickening dusk. Schellinger had put on his cloak and was striding about the deck, giving orders. Cornelia's maid was up there on the poop with him. A yawl was lowered off the starboard side and he headed towards it.

'Are you leaving the ship?' Michiel said.

'Five months I've been drinking this putrid water and sissy wine. I want something a little sweeter in my throat. We are a month ahead of schedule and never a word of thanks from our damned Commander. He's gone ashore to drink his fill and left me here.'

'He's getting provisions for the fleet. Do you have permission to leave?'

'The undermerchant says I can and that's enough for me.'

'Who's in charge of the ship then?'

'My understeersman. We're safely anchored. You don't need me here.' Schellinger turned to Sara. 'Are you ready?'

'The mistress says I may not leave the boat.'

'Miss High and Mighty says that, does she? Well, I say you can.' He turned and made his way down the main deck in his big knee-length boots. 'Are you coming or not?'

Michiel saw her hesitate. The she gathered up her skirts and followed him.

The bosun rowed Schellinger and Sara over to the *Zandaam*, which was anchored just a few cable lengths away in the harbor. They climbed aboard and went straight down to the steerage, to spend the evening drinking and gambling.

Sara was the only woman on board, and Schellinger kept his arm around her, plumping her right breast in his palm, and grinning at the other men. He liked what it did to them, how it tormented them. The way she wriggled, he guessed she liked it, too.

He was good and drunk by the time they left the *Zandaam*. The bosun wanted to go back to the *Utrecht,* but he was having none of it.

'We're going over to the *Beschermer*,' he said. 'I've got some old debts to settle.'

The bosun rolled his eyes at him. Schellinger ignored him. He made him set to with the oars, while he leaned back in the prow, Sara cradled under one arm, a Beardman jug of raw *genever* under the other.

When they reached the warship, he could barely manage to make his way up the cleats. Sara, in her long skirts, needed help and he told the bosun to help her. He noticed he managed to get a good feel as he was helping her up from the yawl. She giggled and let him.

Van Schenk, the skipper of the *Beschermer,* didn't look too pleased to see them, but Schellinger was past caring what anyone thought. He knew most of the crew and joined a game of dice on the main deck. He grabbed a jug of wine from one of the sailors and helped himself. Sara hung on his arm, while he made lewd jokes about her to the men and called her his *soetecut* - sweetie cunt.

'How are things going with the commander?' Barrel, the ship's constable, asked him. Everyone knew about the bad blood between them.

'That pansy bastard!' Schellinger shouted.

The bosun shook his head. 'Keep your voice down, skipper.'

'He orders me around like I'm a cabin boy. Here's him, couldn't row a boat across a canal.'

'Better watch what you're saying, skipper,' the bosun said. 'He could make a lot of trouble for you.'

'He'd better watch out I don't make trouble for him.'

'You're all talk,' Barrel said.

Schellinger started to rise, ready to fight him, but the bosun put a hand on his shoulder and pushed him down again, so he took another pull at the gin bottle.

'Does he know about the girl you've got there,' Barrel said.

'He better not say anything about it,' Schellinger said, 'considering we all know what he's been doing, how he's passed the long days at sea.'

'Let's leave it now, skipper,' the bosun said.

'The pansy bastard's fucking her mistress,' he said, nodding at Sara. 'Isn't he, *soetecut*? And she's a married woman, too. Miss High and Mighty has money, and a house on the Leleistraat. Don't tell me that bastard doesn't know what he's about.' He nudged her. 'Tell them. That's right, isn't it?'

Sara licked her lips, hesitating. She glanced at Schellinger and nodded. 'I've seen them doing it,' she said, and he gave her a squeeze and a little kiss as reward.

Van Schenk heard the loud talk and came over. 'You better get off my ship,' he said. 'You talking like this, it's not going to do any of us any good.'

'Go fuck yourself,' Schellinger said.

Everyone fell silent, thinking there would be a fight. But instead van Schenk turned and strode off towards his cabin.

Schellinger took another swill of *genever.* It leaked down the side of his face. 'Where's the dice?' he said.

The moon was low over the land, and there was a month's pay in the pot, almost forty guilders. It was all at stake on one roll of the dice between Schellinger and Barrel. Schellinger let the dice fly. A six and a four. He guffawed, delighted.

It was Barrel's turn. He threw two sixes.

As soon as the dice fell, there was a moment's quiet, and the men standing around watching got ready for trouble.

As Barrel reached for the coins in the pot, Schellinger grabbed his wrist. 'You cheated,' he said.

'Fuck you,' Barrel said.

Schellinger picked him up as easily as if he were a child and threw him against the mast. He held him upright with his left hand and pummeled him with his right. Sprays of blood splattered on the decking.

Two of Barrel's shipmates jumped onto Schellinger's back, but he shrugged them off and started laying about with his fists. In no time there were three bodies on the deck, and van Schenk was calling for the provost.

Schellinger pulled out his knife. 'Bring on your provost. I'll have his liver for fish bait!'

He felt the bosun's arms go around him, dragging him towards the cleats. 'That's enough now, skipper. We've had our fun. Let's get off this tub.'

When they were back in the yawl, Schellinger put a hand down Sara's dress and scooped out one of her breasts. She laughed as he landed a wet kiss on her throat. She enjoyed all that, he thought. Nothing like a little blood to get a woman going.

'There's going to be trouble over this,' the bosun said.

Sara giggled. 'That was the best night I have had in my whole life.'

CHAPTER 10

The Great Cabin was the finest on the ship. Indeed, it was the most luxurious of the whole Indian fleet, or so it was said. There was even room enough to stand upright. It was ten paces across at its widest point, and a large window looked out over the stern.

The walls were paneled, and the dark wood glowed in the golden light of the gimbal lamps hanging from the roof beams. There was a gilt-framed mirror and a large Indian carpet. In one corner was an immense carved chest that held the commander's personal belongings.

The commander himself sat behind a desk of polished mahogany, the ship's council seated on either side of him. Schellinger stood in the middle of the room, facing them.

He looks awful, Michiel thought, and he smells like pork rotting in the sun. Don't heave your guts all over the commander's fine Persian rug, skipper, or it will be the worse for you.

The bosun, Jan Decker, was there too, looking like a schoolboy caught cheating at his lessons, though he had not as yet been called to account.

Ambroise's hands rested on the smooth arms of his chair, his fingers beating a tattoo. He was trapped, Michiel suspected, between the thorny ways of his duty and a niggardly desire for revenge.

It was bad enough, the fighting and drinking. He wondered if Ambroise would also confront Schellinger over what he had been saying about him and Cornelia. Or perhaps he would not want it repeated a second time. It didn't matter that it wasn't true. What good was the truth? An entertaining lie was always preferred to a dull truth.

'What have you to say for yourself?' Ambroise said.

Schellinger looked as if he had been basted in cold grease. 'It shall not happen again,' he muttered, his eyes fixed on the window above the commander's head. Gin poisoning and public humiliation, Michiel thought. A fine breakfast.

'Is that it?' Ambroise said. He shuffled some papers on his desk. 'This morning, at first light, I have the commander of the *Zandaam* knocking at my cabin door, saying that you were on board his vessel last night, and that you were roaring drunk and fornicating below decks with...' Ambroise decided to leave the girl's name out of it for the present, out of respect to her mistress. '...with a certain lady. Shortly after, I have the skipper of the *Beschermer* here, claiming that you boarded his ship in the company of several of your sailors and this same lady, and that you beat one of his crew so soundly he cannot rise from his bunk this morning to do his duties. It was only his personal intervention that prevented murder, he said. He furthermore complains of your blasphemies and that you made various calumnies against me before the whole ship.'

'I was drunk,' Schellinger said, his face a mask. 'Nobody takes seriously what a man says when he is drinking.'

'You are the captain of the *Utrecht*, not some whoring sailor on leave in an Amsterdam bawdy house. What you say is always taken seriously.'

Schellinger continued to stare over the commander's head. His pride will not endure this lecture, Michiel thought.

'This could be a matter for the Broad Council,' Ambroise said.

For a moment, Michiel saw real fear in the skipper's eyes. The Broad Council was made up of every high personage in the entire fleet, and was convened only for the most serious infractions of discipline. They had far more power than Ambroise. If the commander brought the matter to them, Schellinger could find himself held in chains in the guts of his own ship all the way to the East Indies. The humiliation would drive him mad.

The muscles in Schellinger's jaw worked. 'We have had long months at sea,' he managed, finally. There was some conciliation in his voice at last. 'It was just a bit of fun. I shall see it is not repeated.'

'I shall bring your behavior before your betters in Batavia,' Ambroise said. 'You are a drunkard and a fornicator, and it is my opinion that you should never again be placed in command of any vessel of the Honorable Company. Perhaps we would be better served to have the upper steersman find our way to Java.'

Schellinger swayed on his feet. Ambroise had the power to do it; whether he had the stomach for it was something else. Such an action would reflect badly on him as well, for letting the situation deteriorate so far.

Michiel saw Christiaan smirking. Now what in God's name can be going through your mind, he thought.

'By your leave,' Schellinger mumbled, 'I humbly ask your pardon if I gave offence. It was not my intention.'

Ambroise dismissed him with a flick of his hand. 'Worthless fool that you are, you can't conduct yourself with the dignity your rank merits. You've behaved like the lowest of ordinary seamen. Go to your cabin and sleep it off! You're confined on board until we sail.'

Schellinger stumbled out of the door.

The others filed out of the cabin. Michiel remained. He looked out of the great window, thrown open to the morning. The clouds were piling up over Table Mountain. A storm was coming.

'You wish to say something to me?' Ambroise said.

'With all respect, Commander, I wonder if that was the wisest course of action. You've put him in his place, made him grovel, and not one of us believes he doesn't deserve it. But will he still be of a mind to crawl when we sail over the horizon? If you cannot deal gently with such a man, then perhaps it is best to put him in chains.'

Ambroise regarded him with contempt. 'I think you are in no position to lecture me on how to command men.'

'I did not mean to give offence.'

'I have made my decision. You may leave if that is all your business with me.'

It was tempting to persevere, but Michiel knew it was useless. Ambroise thought himself infallible in his judgment. He bowed and left the cabin.

Schellinger leaned over the carved rail, quietly retching into the sea. He heard footsteps and wiped his mouth with his sleeve. He frowned when he saw Christiaan. 'What do you want, undermerchant?'

'He went hard on you in there. I didn't think anything would make a big tough fellow like yourself turn pale.'

'It's the gin that has done this, not that pansy bastard.'

'It's plain he has a grudge against you though, skipper.'

'I've eaten shit from that pigeon-toed bastard for the last time,' Schellinger said. 'God's death, if the *Beschermer* were not lying off there, I should treat that miserly dog so that he would not come out of his cabin for a long time. And if I were younger, perhaps I should do something else.'

Christiaan looked around to make sure no one had heard. But Schellinger's words were carried away on the breeze. He drew closer. 'There are many men on this ship of a like mind, skipper,' he said.

Schellinger frowned at him. 'What are you talking about?'
Christiaan smiled. 'You know what I'm talking about.'

CHAPTER 11

They spent a week at the cape before continuing the journey. After the *Utrecht* rounded the Cabo de Bona Esperanza, she would sail eastwards with the trades across five thousand miles of empty ocean, only turning north when they reached the Great Southland.

The Governor of Batavia in Java had warned them that existing calculations of the distance between the cape and the Southland might be incorrect by up to nine hundred nautical miles. He had also reiterated the dangers of Houtman's Rocks, a coral barrier of treacherous reefs that guarded the coasts there. But Ambroise was confident in Schellinger's knowledge and seamanship. No one else might have behaved as he did in Table Bay and come away with little else but a sore head and a reprimand.

They still faced two more months at sea, with rotting food, stinking water and hot, endless days. But Ambroise was just happy to be on the last leg of the voyage.

By day, the dinner table in the Council Room did service as a desk for the two clerks, David Krueger and Salomon du Chesne. One night, after the evening meal had been cleared away, Krueger sat there, carefully copying letters in his painstaking script by the light of the oil lamp.

Christiaan watched him. His work did not have the flourish or the beauty of his assistant. He was slow and he lacked style. Like the man himself, really.

Krueger sensed Christiaan watching him and looked up, unnerved. 'What is it, *Heer* Undermerchant?'

'I am sorry. Does my presence trouble you?'

'Not at all,' Krueger lied.

Christiaan leaned on the table. 'Do you enjoy your work?' he said.

The young clerk looked scared. 'Do you find fault in me?'

Christiaan raised an eyebrow and continued to stare.

'*Heer* Undermerchant?'

'What moved you to go to the Indies?'

'I suppose I was looking for adventure.' Krueger's pen jerked across the document, spoiling it. He would have to start again and that would mean another hour more before he would be able to climb into his bunk.

'You think you're going to find adventure in Batavia? You'll be lucky to see the sunlight. You'll spend all day, dawn till dusk, hunched over a desk.'

'But I would do the same in Amsterdam.'

'Who got you this job, Krueger?'

'My father wanted me to…'

'I thought so.'

'You are unhappy with my work?'

'You copy one of the commander's letters. The next day you have to make seven more. You write reports about the Company's victories against the Mataram or the Spanish or the Specks, but you're never there to see it for yourself. You're just a clerk. No one respects you; no one is afraid of you. And where does it get you, eh Krueger? We sail across the known world and what do you see? An inkpot and a piece of paper. All the while you know you were meant for better things. Isn't that right?'

Krueger stared back, his face pale.

Michiel ached to be off this painted pigsty. He was exhausted by the monotony and the stench of bilge and unwashed bodies. There was green scum floating in their water barrels and you had to hold your nose to drink it. The food was as bad; the salt meat was rotten and there were weevils in the biscuits. Everyone had boils and the itch.

Several of his men had scurvy. Some were spitting out their teeth, their gums raw and bleeding. At this rate, a number of them wouldn't make it to Batavia.

Little Bean had not risen from his hammock for days. Weakened by the wound to his hand, he had taken sick again. Michiel brought him some of his own water ration, but as he brought it to his lips it spilled down his chin. Poor bastard, he thought. They would see the red coasts of the Great Southland any day, and from there it was just two weeks sailing to Batavia, but it looked as if even that might be too far for Little Bean.

Cornelia was surprised to see one of the clerks on deck. He came out of the Great Cabin, blinking in the sunlight.

'*Vrouwe*,' he murmured. He wouldn't meet her eyes. 'May I speak with you?'

'It's Salomon, isn't it?'

'Yes, *vrouwe*.'

'What is it you wish to talk to me about?'

His lips worked silently. Whatever was troubling him, he looked as if he was choking on it.

'Come on, I don't bite.'

'I don't know how to say it.'

'You have a problem I can help you with?'

'I don't know if I should be doing this.'

'What could be so bad?'

'I am worried about Krueger. You know him? He works alongside me.'

She nodded.

'It's about him and the undermerchant. They are spending a lot of time together this morning, whispering. Whenever I walk into the stateroom, they stop talking and *Heer* van Sant pretends he is merely collecting copies of his letters.'

'If you have concerns, you should report it to the Commander.'

'I will only be making trouble for myself if I do that. I thought perhaps you could raise the matter with Captain van Texel. He is more likely to listen to the complaint, and as you and the captain are on such friendly terms…'

She stared at him, horrified. She had not behaved improperly. Her dealings with the captain had been entirely innocent. Besides, since his confession to her about his actions at the battle of Macau, he had avoided her company.

But everyone likes to talk, she supposed, and on a long journey like this, with so many people crowded together, every word, every small action, was magnified in its importance a hundred times. She had been indiscrete and that was enough for the crew and crowd.

'I think you should take your concerns directly to the commander,' she said again.

Salomon looked miserable. 'I don't think it will do me any good. And I fear what the undermerchant will do if he hears of it.' He shook his head and went back down the ladder to the Great Cabin.

CHAPTER 12

The mast head swung through the heavens, and the wake rippled phosphor in the light of the moon. The long swells of the ocean retreated towards the African coast.

'A fine night,' Christiaan said.

Schellinger shook his head. 'There's a storm waiting out there somewhere. I can feel it in my water.'

Someone came up the ladder, wrapped in a long black cloak. The wind blew back the hood, and Christiaan realized it was Sara.

'What are you doing up here?' Schellinger said.

'I've just had words with the mistress. I shouldn't be up here. She told me I can't talk to you anymore after what happened at the cape.'

'You don't want to take notice of that one.'

'She's threatened to make a complaint to the commander.'

'She can complain all she wants. Don't you worry, no one lays a hand on you while I'm master of this ship.' He turned to Christiaan. 'Isn't that right, undermerchant?' He searched the dark horizon. 'Storm coming for sure,' he said, as the breeze luffed in the courses.

He is right, Christiaan thought. Even he could smell rain on the wind and he was no sailor.

Cornelia went up on deck to get some air. It was on twilight, and spray rushed over the bows. The dark clouds at the stern were stained a dirty orange from the sunset. The pastor stood at the rail with his wife. He looked like a predatory black bird, with his cloak flapping behind him in the wind.

Michiel was on the quarterdeck. He had barely spoken a word to her since Cape Town. She made her way towards him, clinging to the ships' rails.

'*Vrouwe*,' he said and bowed his head.

'I was hoping I would find you up here,' she said. 'I need to talk to you.'

'I am at your service,' he said.

'It's about one of the clerks, Salomon. He came to me a few days ago and asked me to speak to you.'

'Why did he not come to me himself?'

'He is afraid of repercussions. He wished to use me as his conduit.'

Michiel shrugged. He seemed perplexed. 'What is his concern?'

'He says he has seen Krueger and the undermerchant whispering together.'

'That is all?'

'Do you not wonder what secrets Christiaan is keeping?'

'I have little to do with him, aside from Company business. The clerk should take his concerns to the Commander. Or you can.'

'Salomon thought you might give him a better hearing.'

'I would still have to take it to the Commander and I doubt that he would listen to me. He has a high opinion of the undermerchant. Unwarranted, I believe, but who am I to say?'

'I do not like the way he looks at me.'

'Yes,' Michiel said. 'I have seen it.'

'I wonder if you truly understand what it is like for the women on this ship. To most men, beauty is a provocation. They look at us like a wolf regards his dinner.'

'I hate to sound like the pastor, but all men have faults. For some it is lust, for others it is greed, or cowardice.'

'And you think yourself a coward.'

'I know it.'

The wind took the hood of her cape and blew it around her face. She set it back and crossed her arms in front of her. 'You were candid with me that night before we reached the cape. So now I shall be candid with you. Before I married Boudewyn I was in love with a man from a family as poor as my own. He wanted to marry me, but my family instead arranged a match with Boudewyn. I had to choose between love or comfort and wealth. I chose wealth, and every night I am haunted as much by my cowardice as you are by yours.'

She regretted the words as soon as she had spoken them and turned away so that he could not see her face.

'Is there a way back?' he said finally.

'Not for me,' she said. 'But I hope you will find yours.'

On the way back to his cabin, Michiel bumped into Christiaan in the companionway. He nodded and was about to squeeze past him, but Christiaan seemed intent on making conversation.

'A bad business,' he said.

'What is?'

'I don't like the way Schellinger is behaving since we left the Cape. I'd be happier if we had sight of the *Berschemer* again.'

'What are you saying, Christiaan?'

'Just that I'm uneasy.' He nodded over his shoulder, towards the Great Cabin. 'I heard he has a Rubens locked away in his chest. He's going to trade it under the lap when we get to Batavia. He has more besides.'

'That's not my business.'

He tried to go past him, but Christiaan took hold of his sleeve. 'I've been watching you. I don't believe a word of what they say. Don't look at me like that. Everyone on board knows what happened in Macau.'

'I was cleared by the board of enquiry.'

'Of course. But you know what some men are saying about you behind your back. It must make you angry.'

'There's nothing I can do about it. Now please, I'm tired. I want to get to my bunk.'

'Let's face it, captain, you're never going to get another promotion now, no matter what you do. Your career is over and it hasn't even started.'

'None of us knows what fate has in store.'

'Do you really believe in fate or do you think a man makes his own future?'

'It's a little late at night for philosophy.'

'You want her, don't you?'

Michiel stared at him. 'What?'

'Come on now, I've seen the way you look at her.' Christiaan tapped him on the chest with a forefinger. 'I know what is going on in your heart.'

'Nothing goes on there, *Heer* Undermerchant.'

Christiaan smiled. 'In this world a woman like that will always marry a Boudewyn, not a man like you. You know that don't you? His family are rich and they have a good name. It's not right though, is it? It's not just. Sometimes you think about how it might be if things were different.

Michiel wanted to pick him up and throw him against the bulkhead, not for his impertinence, but for knowing too much. He bit down his temper. 'I never think about things like that.'

Christiaan sat at his desk and brooded. It was tiny, his cabin, but he shared it with no one and that alone emphasized his status as an important man of affairs. Still, right above him the commander had a stateroom the breadth and width of the poop. He did not have to live cramped up like this.

He tried to console himself by admiring the luxuries he had surrounded himself with; the tapestries on the walls and the fancy gimbal lamp that hung from the ceiling. He had arranged his little bottles of potions and secret herbs on a shelf, next to his books of apothecary. They had all been carefully transported from his shop in Haarlem.

He thought about Cornelia Noorstrandt. He took his pen and idly drew a picture of her, naked. He imagined large breasts under that tight bodice, just as he liked them. He drew her on her knees, a man's penis in her mouth. He added some little details to the man's appearance, to make him look more like an undermerchant.

There was a knock at the door. He quickly held the paper to the flame of the lamp on his desk and watched it burn. Then he took it to the porthole and let the wind take the burning scraps.

He picked up his Bible and opened it at a page. 'Come in.'

It was Sara. He shut the Bible with a noise like a musket shot. It startled her and made her jump.

'Sara, what can I do for you?'

'Never been in here before.'

'Of course not.'

'It's not as grand as my mistress's.'

'Well she's a paying passenger. What is it you want?'

She came in, closing the door behind her. 'They say before you joined the Company you were an apothecary.'

'If that's what people say, then it must be true.'

She stared at his books. Only a few of them were written in Dutch, though he doubted she could even read her own language.

'This is nice,' she said, running a finger down one of his earthenware Bellarmine jugs. They were common enough in the taverns and alehouses; they had a bearded face engraved on the neck in a caricature of Cardinal Bellarmine. Men drank their beer out of them and, when they were empty, they smashed them in the hearth, cursing the cardinal's name.'

'And what's this? Is it a witch bottle?'

'You put a twist of human hair or nail parings in it. It can ward off evil spells.'

She picked it up and peered inside. 'Does it work?'

'Why, do you think you need one?'

She set the bottle back down. 'There's been a lot of talk about you on the ship.'

'Has there?'

'About the way you dress. So fancy. The skipper told me he thought you most likely preferred boys but I thought, no, not this one. I can see it in his eyes. I know what this one likes and it isn't a tight little bottom, well, not a boy's anyway.'

'Very astute.'

'Whatever that means.' Her eyes were drawn to his brass chemist's mortar. The words AMOR VINCIT OMNIA were inscribed on it in Latin.

He saw her staring at it. 'Do you know Latin?'

She shook her head.

'It means *Love Conquers All.*'

'I don't know about that.'

'Why are you here?'

'The skipper sent me,' she said. 'He said you have something to stop a woman from getting with child.'

He smiled and opened his medicine chest. Glass bottles and vials were neatly arranged inside. He took out one of the bottles and handed it to her. 'One draught should be enough. You must take it within a day of conjugation or it will not work.'

She looked blank.

'It means swallow it as soon as you can after you've fucked him.'

'I don't have any money,' she said.

He waved his hand dismissively. 'It is a favor for the skipper. Tell him I said so.'

She nodded, pleased.

She was about to leave, when he said, 'Does your mistress know what you are doing when you are not at her bidding?'

'It's no business of hers.'

'Oh, she'll make it her business.'

'She told me I wasn't to talk to the skipper for the rest of the voyage.'

'What does the skipper say to that?'

'He told me to defy her.'

'Poor Sara. You make up her hair, but who makes up yours? You help her put on her dresses and her jewels, but how many dresses do you have? Who gives you jewels?'

'I'm not a great lady, like her.'

'What's a great lady? It's just an accident of birth. Your mistress was a cloth merchant's daughter once. It's money that makes a lady; money and chance.'

'The skipper says I'm more beautiful than she is.'

He got up and opened the cabin door. 'There are better things ahead for you,' he said, and gave her a squeeze as she went out.

CHAPTER 13

Maria de Groot was annoying everyone. While the other children were content to sit on the deck and play with their knucklebones, Maria ran around screaming and crying.

Joost and his fellow *jonkers* strutted about the deck, amusing themselves with secret glances at the women sitting under the awning. In fact, Joost was so preoccupied that he was taken completely unawares when Maria ran into his legs, winding him. The other *jonkers* laughed, but Joost did not share the joke. He clutched at his groin, furious.

Maria had dropped her toy, a spinning top. It was her favorite. Joost picked it up and when the little girl tried to grab it back, he held it out of her reach.

'What have we got here?' he said.

'Give it to me!' Maria leaped into the air, hand out-stretched.

'What shall I do with this?' Joost said to his friends, taunting the little girl with her toy, holding it out to her then moving it away again.

'Give it *back*!'

'Perhaps I should toss it to the fishes!'

He looked over at Maria's mother, Neeltje. She was clutching her baby, wide-eyed, afraid to speak up against one of the *jonkers*. Even the pastor held back, sensing the mood the young men were in.

Joost's friends enjoyed the sport. Joost pretended to toss the toy into the sea and each time he did it, Maria howled. When she saw it was a trick, her efforts to retrieve her toy became even more desperate.

After a while, the other young men grew tired of it. 'Give it back to her,' one of them said.

But Joost kept up his little game.

'Give it back to her,' Michiel said. 'Or do you want the commander to know you have been tormenting a child on the main deck?'

They stared at each other.

'It's just a game,' someone shouted from the poop. It was Christiaan, up there with Schellinger. They were laughing. 'You don't mean anything by it, do you, Joost?'

While the adults were arguing, Maria saw her opportunity. She leaped as high as she could to try to get a hand on the toy. Joost shouted angrily and wrenched it back from her. With one movement he tossed it into the ocean.

She screamed in anguish.

Joost and Michiel stared at each other. Joost smiled. Then he turned his back on him, his friends crowing with laughter.

Michiel looked up at Christiaan, furious.

The top was made of wood, so it floated for a while on the surface, and Maria stared after it until it was a speck on the horizon. Her mother tried to console her, but she was having none of it. She sat curled up on the deck under the awning for the rest of the day and wouldn't let anyone come near her.

The winds had strengthened to gale force and waves broke in fountains of spray over the bows. The passengers huddled in their bunks, moaning, while the crew clambered aloft to reef the sails. Cornelia heard Schellinger bellowing commands to the men at the whip staff. It required three of them to steady the huge rudder.

She was thrown from one side of the passageway to the other as she made her way to the Great Cabin. She was surprised to find Christiaan there, with Salomon and Krueger.

It was the first time she had seen Ambroise unkempt. There was sweat on his upper lip and his skin was grey. He did not rise from his bunk. She clung to the rafters as the ship heaved violently in the heavy seas.

'What can we do for you, *vrouwe*?' Christiaan said.

'It is about my maid,' she said. "I want the commander to speak with her.'

A wave hammered into the bow and made the *Utrecht* lurch. Christiaan grasped at the bulkhead. 'This is not the right time to speak of this,' he said.

'Something needs be done about her and Captain Schellinger.'

'What would you have us do?'

'She is causing a scandal about the ship by her behavior. After what happened at Cabo de Esperanza, she was supposed to keep away from him. Now she is bolder than she was before. Something must be done.'

'You wish to have her disciplined by the provost?'

'It may not come to that if the Commander can talk some sense into her and Schellinger.'

'When the storm passes, we will see what we can do.'

A shudder went through the ship as the bow slammed into another breaker. Christiaan gasped and whispered a prayer.

Down on the gun deck, the fug of tobacco fumes, sour breath and bodies was stupefying. The hammocks nudged each other as the ship rolled. It was a sweat-stinking gloomy place, filled with snores and the shouts of men playing dice or checkers.

Michiel thought he saw Christiaan in the shadows talking to Stonecutter, but when he looked again he was gone.

Gerrits, the chief gunnery officer, was playing dice with his deputy, Ryckert. Little Bean was lying in his hammock. He was a tough fellow to kill, Michiel thought. His hand had healed finally, though he could not use two of the fingers.

'How is it?' Michiel said.

'It's all right. Would have been worse if you hadn't come and pulled out the knife.'

'Is Stonecutter still riding you?'

'Some.'

Michiel lowered his voice. 'Who was that he was talking to? It looked like the undermerchant.'

Little Bean nodded. 'He's down here all the time, the two of them muttering to each other. It gives me the creeps.'

'I wonder what that's about,' Michiel said.

'Is it true about you and the fancy lady?' Little Bean said. 'Stonecutter says you've been visiting her cabin every night. Says he got it straight from the undermerchant.'

Michiel felt the stirring of real alarm.

He made his way to the Commander's cabin. The oil lamps had been lit, and Salomon and Krueger were standing outside talking in whispers to the surgeon, *Maistre* Arentson.

'I have to speak to the commander,' Michiel said.

'I'm afraid that won't be possible,' Salomon said.

'Why not?'

'It is the fever,' Arentson said. 'He brought it with him from Surat. I have seen it before. It is the kind of malady that lies sleeping in a man and can strike again at any time.'

'Is it serious?'

Arentson didn't answer. Clearly, it was.

'Let me see him,' Michiel said.

Arentson led the way inside. Ambroise lay in his bunk, under an embroidered coverlet. His face was wreathed in sweat, but he was shivering as if he were freezing to death.

'I shall bleed him,' Arentson said. 'Perhaps it will be as well to drain away some of the foul humors.'

It was all these butchers knew how to do, Michiel thought, with their foul leeches and their bleeding bowls.

'Then an infusion of herbs perhaps. After that, all we can do is pray for him.'

A sudden squall shook the boat and they were all thrown staggering across the cabin.

'The storm is getting worse,' Krueger said.

On cue, another huge swell passed beneath the hull and Salomon put a hand across his mouth and ran for the companionway.

Arentson shook his head. 'You would have thought the boy would have grown accustomed to the sea by now,' he said.

CHAPTER 14

Schellinger prowled the ship in his cloak and high boots. His face was dark. He growled at the uppersteersman and ordered ten lashes for one of the sailors over some trivial offence. He was never such a tyrant when the commander was there to rebuke him, but Ambroise was still in his bunk, thrashing around and moaning in delirium. Arentson feared he might even die in the next few days unless the fever broke.

Schellinger smiled at the prospect. From his lips to God's ear.

They gathered in the steerage, a dozen of them crowded in. There was Jan Decker, Stonecutter, Krueger and Joost along with the rest of the *jonkers*.

And Christiaan.

Decker kept watch through a knothole in the door, while the others huddled together, in whispered conversation. A flask of *genever* gin passed from hand to hand, the oily fumes filling the cramped cabin. A candle leaked grease onto the table. The only sound was the creaking of the rudder post.

'He's going to die,' Christiaan said.

'He was supposed to have died two days ago,' Joost said.

'He's just bones and rags. To look at him, you'd think he was dead already.'

There was silence, each man alone with his dark calculations.

'Do any of you know how much treasure there is on this ship?' Christiaan said.

Krueger swallowed some more gin and wiped his mouth with the back of his sleeve. 'Treasure?'

'There are a dozen bound chests of silver coin in the hold, worth a quarter of a million guilders. Even our commander, who lives like a prince, would not see so much money if he lived ten lifetimes. There's also a casket of jewels under lock and key in the Great Cabin, intended for the treasure house of Moghul Jahangir himself. Their worth is beyond imagining.'

'What are you telling us?' Krueger said.

'That we have a choice,' Christiaan said, and his voice was as sweetly reasonable as if they were discussing who should have the last crust of bread at table. 'For myself, I know I shall never see such riches again in my lifetime. And you, Joost. What good has your noble blood been to you without real money?' He looked at Decker, still crouched by the door. 'You, Jan. How many guilders do they give you every month to sail this stinking tub to the end of the earth and back. You are helping to make some fat burgher in Amsterdam a fortune, while you live on the crumbs.

'When the commander dies, we shall have untold riches in cash and jewels in our trust. As undermerchant, I will take over command. When this happens, what would you all have me do? Shall we continue to Batavia so you may finish your short and miserable lives, or do you wish me to deliver your dreams into your hands?'

'What about the skipper?' Decker said.

'Leave him to me. I know how to sway him.'

'And van Texel?'

Christiaan shook his head. 'He has virtue oozing out of every pore. A man might think Macau never happened.'

He could see them all thinking it through; how much could they trust each other? The black robed judges of the Company showed little sympathy to mutineers - *muyters*. None of them fancied the rod and the wheel.

And yet life could turn on such moments. They all knew that if this opportunity slipped them by, they faced a lifetime of drudgery in the Company's service, eating stinking food on tubs like this one. Most likely they would end up in a damp grave somewhere in the Indies, far from home.

'You have a plan?' Krueger said.

Christiaan narrowed his eyes. 'Let us suppose the *Utrecht* does not arrive in Java,' he said. 'How long before she is reported missing in Amsterdam? A year?'

'Most likely,' Decker nodded.

'More than enough time for us to disappear. We might even add to our riches in the meantime.'

'How?'

'The flag at the top of the masthead could be as precious to us as the caskets of silver. With the Company flag flying, we can come close up to Indiamen stragglers who will suspect nothing until it is too late.'

'Why don't we do it now?' Joost said. 'Why do we have to wait until the commander is dead?'

'Because we don't have enough to follow us,' Christiaan said. 'When I am in command I'll get rid of the provost first. All the sailors are terrified of him. I'll arrest him for trading under the lap and lock him in the hold. I'll throw van Texel in there with him. When they are both out of the way, we'll only have Gerrits in our way, then we may do as we please. How many soldiers do we have, Stonecutter?'

'Ninety-seven. We lost some to scurvy. But we can't count on them. They're too loyal to van Texel. If we do this, we'll have to lock them in the orlop.'

Christiaan turned to Decker. 'What about the crew?'

'Those ratline monkeys are whores' brats from the docks. They'd shit on their own mother's head for a silver guilder.'

'And the gunners?'

'Ryckert is a friend of mine,' Decker said. 'Get rid of Gerrits and I reckon I can sway him. We have twenty-eight cannon, seven of them bronze pieces large enough to batter down the walls of Batavia Castle itself.'

'Let's hope it doesn't come to that,' Christiaan said, and they all laughed nervously at the joke. 'There are muskets, cutlasses and pikes in the arsenal. We can raid from Coromandel to Madagascar then sail through the Straits of Gibraltar to the Barbary Coast and live like kings!'

Krueger and Decker nodded. They could see it now - how easily it might be done if they had the nerve to follow through.

'You each know who can be trusted and who cannot. But you must tell no one about our plans until the commander is stitched in a sheet and over the side with the preacher's prayers.' Christiaan looked around, making eye contact with each of them in turn. 'If you don't have the balls for this, you might as well be maidservants or cabin boys.'

'All right,' Krueger said. 'Let's do it.'

The gin bottle passed again from hand to hand. Oaths were foresworn.

Once Christiaan had recruited Schellinger, as he promised he would, all they needed was for the commander to die.

The sky was clear and a quarter moon hung over the horizon. Schellinger reeked of raw gin.

'No sign of the *Beschermer*, then?' Christiaan said to him.

'We lost sight of her in the storm,' Schellinger said.

An interesting accident. Christiaan thought. There was no sign of the *Zandaam* or the *Groningen* either, or any of the fleet. A man might wonder how an experienced skipper could allow such a thing to happen. Without the *Beschermer's* cannon trained on them, a man might more easily find his own destiny.

'You have been below?' Schellinger said. 'How is that bastard?'

'Arentson says his condition worsens.'

There was a long silence between them, measured by the rhythmic beating of the swell against the hull.

'If he dies, I suppose you shall be commander of the vessel until we reach Batavia.'

'I fancy I should,' Christiaan said.

'A great honor for you, *Heer* Undermerchant.'

'Both of us have been entrusted with a great deal.'

Schellinger nodded.

'How much do they pay you to bear such responsibilities? Thirty guilders a month?' Christiaan spat into the sea. Not expertly done, to be sure, for spitting was sailor's work.

'I get by.'

'With a little private trade on the side? Wasn't that the cause of the argument between you and the commander in Surat harbor?'

'The bastard does more under the table trading than I ever did.'

'And still at it, too. Did you know he has in his trunk a cameo that once belonged to the Emperor Constantine himself? It is twelve hundred years old. It is of inestimable worth.'

'How do you know all this?'

'You'd be surprised what I know. The cameo belongs to Paul Rubens. It was given to the commander to trade under the lap to the great Moghul of East India, but the Honorable Company knows about it and will take a commission, though smaller than they are accustomed to. It is a bauble fit for some Eastern prince, and what will you see out of the business, skipper?'

'Well it's one rule for them and one for us, isn't it?'

'It doesn't have to be that way,' Christiaan said.

There, it was said.

Schellinger looked around. It was the night watch, and there was no one around to hear them. Still, a whiff of mutiny could condemn a man to agonies that eclipsed the imagination.

He lowered his voice. 'What did you have in mind?'

'When Amboise dies, you and I will be in command of our own fate. We may do what we will.'

'These are dangerous thoughts, *Heer* Undermerchant.'

'These same thoughts have never occurred to you?'

'What exactly do you propose?'

'First I have to know if we are of a mind.'

'If your plan is a sound one.'

Christiaan stepped closer. 'If we do not arrive in Batavia, we will be thought lost, along with the twelve chests of cash in the hold. The *Utrecht* has a bank of guns we could use to add considerably to our fortunes, picking off stragglers on the way to the Indies. It would be a year, perhaps two, before the Governor learns that he has competition from our own dishonorable Company.' He smiled at his own joke. 'Enough time to earn our weight in gold and live like sultans in the Coromandel.'

'You fancy yourself as a pirate then, do you, Undermerchant?'

'The men in Amsterdam who run the Company are pirates. They have the sanction of the *stadtholder* and do it from the safety of a big table in Amsterdam. But they kill Englanders and Portuguese, and whoever else gets in their way, in the name of profit. All trade is done with the sword in the end, is it not? It is only a matter of scale.'

'You are persuasive.'

'According to Arentson, the commander will be bait for the fish this time tomorrow. Then I shall be sitting in the Great Cabin, and you shall be here at the wheel. Do we go to Batavia or do we go looking for gold and women?'

Schellinger nodded, slowly. 'Gold and women sound good to me, undermerchant.'

CHAPTER 15

The *Utrecht* sailed alone on a vast ocean. She was a different ship now to the one that had left Amsterdam, though the timbers and cordage were the same. There were whispers and gossip in the passageways, averted glances on the decks, and little laughter from the women gathered under the awning on the quarterdeck.

Everyone was waiting for news from the Great Cabin, wondering what would happen if the commander should die.

Michiel checked on him a dozen times a day. The fever had wasted him. At times, he shivered so violently with cold that his teeth rattled in his head. Then, suddenly, his face would turn red as beet and he sweated as if he were in a steam bath. He tossed in his bunk, fighting off invisible demons.

Arentson said this day would be his last.

Michiel looked around the orlop. Most of his men were sleeping, their hammocks strung between the guns. Stonecutter was snoring like someone sawing through the main mast. The noise he made all but drowned out the groaning of the timbers as the great ship pitched on the swell.

Little Bean had taken his bandage off. There was a livid pink scar on both sides of his hand, and he could not grip anything with it. But it was his left hand and the right could still hold a sword or a pike, though it was impossible for him to load a musket. Stonecutter though, had kept off his back, unusually quiet of late.

Michiel went up to the gun deck. It was hot as hell and noisy as a dockside tavern. Babies were crying and a woman was giving birth in the corner. The midwife was burning seagull feathers under her nose for the pain. The shrieking she made was like someone was torturing her, but no one was taking any notice.

He stepped over a dozen sleeping bodies and made his way up to the deck. He saw Ryckert blow his pipe smoke in the direction of one of the women and make some remark to his comrades that caused ribald laughter. Everyone knew what a clay pipe represented when waved in a lady's direction. It seemed to Michiel that the provost, who was supposed to be in charge of law and order on the ship, was losing control.

He sat with his back against the stern castle, out of sight. He could hear Schellinger on the poop, shouting commands to the uppersteersman. Sara was with him, flaunting her skirts and curls. The women sitting under the awnings shot her dark looks.

'Look at that tart!' Neeltje Groot hissed.

'It is a mortal sin,' the pastor's wife said.

'They say she sleeps in his cabin every night now,' Neeltje said.

'What is *Vrouwe* Noorstrandt doing about it?' the pastor's wife said. 'That's what I want to know.'

'Has your husband spoken with her?' Neeltje asked.

'Of course he has, and sharply, too. She told him that it is a matter between the skipper and the provost now. But the provost is scared to go against him and so he lets it continue.'

The two women shook their heads and muttered darkly at such goings on.

'It's no wonder she can't control her maid,' the pastor's wife said. 'She can't control herself.'

'Whatever do you mean?'

'Everyone is talking about it, her and Captain van Texel. They are being far too familiar with each other and her a married woman!

Perhaps it is God's will if the Commander dies. The undermerchant won't stand for such goings on.'

So that's the way it goes, Michiel thought. They were still thirty days from Batavia. It might as well be thirty years.

That night a child called out among the huddled shapes asleep on the gun deck. Rats scuttled in the hold, and devils chased each other through the black dreams of the sailors. Somewhere, men were whispering. The coasts of Christian men receded in the darkness.

CHAPTER 16

The next morning, Michiel came to the Great Cabin expecting to find the commander dead.

Arentson was in a great excitement. 'He's better!' he said. 'The fever has broken. It is a miracle!'

Michiel went in. Ambroise was sitting up. He looked like a corpse, but he was breathing.

'Commander,' Michiel said. 'We thought you were lost to us. Everyone has prayed for your recovery. You must get well.'

'It was bad this time,' Ambroise said. His voice was so soft Michiel could barely hear him.

The fever had left him painfully weak, and he spent the next few days in his cabin reading passages from the Bible.

The plotters regathered in the steerage, where the creaking of the rudder drowned out their voices. They crammed in with the gunpowder and gin fumes, while the ship pitched and rolled in the trades.

Schellinger and Ryckert had joined them, and Schellinger had brought Sara with him.

'He got out of bed for the first time today,' Christiaan said.

Krueger put his head in his hands. This was not the way it was meant to turn out. 'You told us he was dying.'

'He's tougher than we thought,' Schellinger said.

'Now what's going to happen to me?' Sara said. 'She'll have me whipped.'

'We have to end all talk of taking over the ship,' Schellinger said. 'Nothing can happen now.'

Christiaan pretended to agree with him. It was hard to credit that the commander would rally this way. Even harder to believe that Schellinger would turn out to be a milkmaid beneath his bluster.

'Of course, it may already be too late,' he said. 'The provost has told me he has heard whispers about the ship and intends to investigate them further when we get to Batavia. You know what that means.' He looked around at their faces. They were all pale with fear. It was heartening to see the effect one little lie might have. 'Which one of you will break first if they put you to the rack, do you think?'

'They won't do that,' Decker said.

'Sure about that, are you?' Christiaan let the silence hang. Finally he said, 'There is only one way out of our predicament now.'

'What do you suggest?' Krueger said.

'It occurs to me that if I cannot remove van Texel and Gerrits from their posts, then we must get the commander to do it for us.'

'How are we going to do that?'

'Imagine, all of you, what might happen should someone take the Noorstrandt woman unawares and violate her.'

Even Schellinger gaped at him, astonished at his audacity. 'What?'

'Think on it. The commander will be outraged, and he will have to act. He will order me to investigate, and I will report to him that it was van Texel, and that Gerrits helped him. That will leave Ryckert in charge of the cannons and Stonecutter in command of the soldiery.'

Decker shook his head. 'It is too dangerous.'

'That's why you're just a bosun,' Christiaan said. He turned to the rest of them. 'It is an opportunity that might come once in a lifetime. Which of you is man enough to take it?'

'I need time to think on it,' Schellinger said and walked out. Sara ran after him.

Ambroise went up to the poop deck, though it took all his strength. He might as well have been climbing to the top of the tower in the Westerkerk.

There was still no sign of the rest of the fleet.

'Where is the *Beschermer*?' he said.

Schellinger gave him a lazy smile. 'We shall come upon her soon enough. But it is a wide sea and we are a small ship.'

'We should have come upon them days ago,' Ambroise said.

Schellinger shrugged, his eyes fixed on the horizon.

'There is a matter we must discuss,' Ambroise said. 'It concerns *Vrouwe* Noorstrandt's maid.'

'What about her?'

'While I have been unwell, your behavior with her has caused scandal about the ship.'

'One rule for the officers and one for the rest of us, is that it?'

Ambroise could not believe what Schellinger had said. For a moment, he was too stunned to speak.

'It's all round the ship,' Schellinger said. 'How the captain has been spending his nights. It's driving you mad, isn't it? I have seen the way you look at her.'

'That is scandalous gossip and there is not a word of truth to it.'

'I could say the same about me and Sara.'

'Let me make myself clear to you, Schellinger. You are not to speak with *Vrouwe* Noorstrandt's maid again, nor go near her. Do you understand?'

They stared at each other.

'I will be making a full report of your behavior to Governor Coen when we reach Batavia.' Ambroise turned away and went back to his cabin. His hands were shaking.

'He looks desperately weak, doesn't he?' Christiaan said. 'The surgeon says he can't keep his food down.'

'You heard that pretty little speech, did you?'

'I did. It's good to see the commander in such good spirits.'

Schellinger didn't look quite as jaunty now, Christiaan thought. For all his bold talk about what he'd like to do to the commander, now he was up and about again he looked as fidgety as a virgin in a whorehouse.

'Do not dismiss his talk as idle threats, skipper. He means what he says.'

'He's all milk and water.'

'Is he? I am privy to many things that happen in the Great Cabin that you are not. From what I hear, your mistress may soon find herself tied to the main mast to earn herself some stripes from the provost.'

'He wouldn't dare.'

'He might. As soon as he was well, the pastor himself was banging on his cabin door, pleading with him to have her disciplined. He might do it just to get himself some peace and quiet.'

'Not while I live and breathe.'

'Well, I'm on your side, you know that. But he's a powerful man. You don't want to tangle with him when we reach Batavia. Of course, right now he's so weak he can barely stand up.'

Schellinger stared into the dark. 'All right,' he said. 'You've made your point. I'm in.'

CHAPTER 17

The ship's timbers creaked in the following swell. Rats scampered in the shadows and the candle beside the bed guttered. Cornelia woke in the semi-darkness to find a cockroach scuttling across her pillow. She knocked it away with the back of her hand and tried to get back to sleep, but her nerves were shaken.

There was a knock. She thought she heard Sara's voice. She opened the door a crack and peered out. Suddenly, the door was kicked open and a hand clamped across her mouth. She couldn't breathe. Someone grabbed her hair, pulling her head so far back that her eyes filled with tears.

She kicked out in panic, but someone else held her feet and dragged her back to her bunk.

How many of them were there? She had no idea. One smudged out the candle while another tore off her nightdress. Fingers probed inside her. Then one of her assailants was on top of her, his weight crushing her. His breath was hot on her face, and it stank like a dog's.

The hand on her jaw relaxed its hold for a moment, and she bit down as hard as she could. The man yelled out in pain, and she tried to scream for help. A clout around the side of the head knocked her senseless before she could make a sound. One of them stuffed a filthy rag in her mouth and it made her gag.

After that, they hit her every time she struggled, and by the time they finished she was barely conscious. They smeared some foulness on her, tar and ordure, and then they were gone.

She didn't know how long she lay there. Finally she managed to sit up. Her hands were shaking so badly she could barely pull the rag from her mouth. She put a hand between her legs. Her fingers came away dripping with blood and muck.

She fumbled in the darkness for her nightdress but couldn't find it, so she pulled the coverlet up around her shoulders and curled up under it. She was too weak to wipe away the filth they had smeared her with. It dried to a crust on her body.

The door yawed open on its hinges. Then a massive swell passed under the hull and sent the ship pitching to starboard. It slammed shut.

The fever left Ambroise feeling so exhausted that he found it hard to concentrate. He sat in his chair in the Great Cabin, a sheen of sweat on his forehead. He wanted only to lie down and sleep.

'There has been godless behavior on this ship,' the pastor said. 'The skipper uses oaths against our Lord in the most scandalous manner. I urge you to take action.'

'What would you have me do?'

'The Company has legislated a punishment for such behavior.'

It was true, Ambroise thought. Under VOC rules it was not permissible for any man 'to call loudly or with familiar vanity on the name of God.' But if they were to enforce the letter of the law every day, there would not be a man left standing to crew the watch.

'You wish me to order twenty lashes for the skipper?'

'It is the law.'

'I shall think on what you've said.' The law, it seemed to Ambroise, was whatever was reasonable on an unescorted ship, halfway between the known world and an isolated outpost four months' sail from the Netherlands. He waited for the pastor to leave.

'Also the ship is unruly. You should be more careful of your underlings.'

'What do you mean?' Ambroise said.

'I mean Christiaan van Sant. Did you know he was a follower of Torrentius?'

Torrentius van der Beeks was a celebrated painter who was also notorious for being the leader of a group calling themselves 'spiritual libertines.' Back in Holland, there had been rumors of orgies and other scandalous incidents, and Torrentius had finally been arrested and interrogated. He had been put on trial, just before they left Amsterdam. It was all anyone there could talk about.

'I don't believe a word of it,' Ambroise said. He had heard the rumors, of course, everyone had. But he refused to believe that an undermerchant in the Honorable Company could be allied to such devilish societies.

'I have it on good authority,' the pastor said, persisting. 'His family paid a small fortune to keep him out of prison. That's why he's been sent to the Indies. They hope to keep him out of trouble.'

'Who told you this nonsense?'

'I overheard Joost van der Linden say it to one of his *jonker* friends.'

'There you are then. Tittle tattle.'

'He is impious.'

'Oh impious, is it? Very well, I shall have him keel-hauled.'

'That seems excessive.'

'I was being ironic, pastor.' Ambroise sighed. 'What makes you cast this calumny against my undermerchant?'

'He smirks during the Sunday sermon.'

Ambroise would have laughed if he did not feel so desperate. 'Thank you for bringing these matters to my attention. For myself I find my undermerchant an amusing and capable young fellow. He may seem a little strange in his demeanor at times, but he shows great promise. I foresee a bright future for him in the Company. Now, will that be all?'

'There is the matter of *Vrouwe* Noorstrandt's maid.'

'I am aware of that matter. Good day, pastor.'

'You must act!'

'I will give everything you have said full consideration. Now if you do not mind, I have urgent matters to attend to.'

The pastor took his leave with ill grace.

Ambroise went to the window, threw it wide, and watched the great ocean swells marching towards the coasts of Africa, far behind them. The sky was like lead.

Easy for the pastor to lecture him about his duty. If the *Beschermer* were off the starboard, with the *Zandaam* and the *Groningen*, he might more easily bring Schellinger to heel. But the mood on the ship had changed while he had been sick, and it had nothing to do with oaths or with blasphemy.

The truth of it was, he was frightened for his life.

CHAPTER 18

Cornelia used the water in the ewer by her bed to wash the filth off her body as best she could. She put on a new nightdress and lay down, staring at the timber decking above her head. She felt as if she was watching herself through a gauze curtain.

Ambroise was solicitous at her absence and, thinking she was seasick, sent the pastor's maid to her cabin with dried plums. But Cornelia wouldn't open the door to her. He sent Arentson to visit her, but she refused to see him as well. Sara didn't even look in on her. She spent all her time in Schellinger's cabin now, all pretense gone.

On the third morning, Cornelia scrubbed at her skin until it was red and soaked herself with her most expensive perfumes. Finally, she put on her finest dress, with a white coif, and a lace ruff to hide the bite marks on her neck, and knocked on the door of the Great Cabin.

'*Vrouwe*,' Ambroise said when he saw her, 'what has happened to you?'

He called for his chief steward to fetch wine to fortify her, and then he sat her down in the great chair and waited for her to speak. But she could not find her voice.

'I heard you have been sick.'

She shook her head.

The steward returned and poured wine into a pewter cup. Her hands were trembling so badly that when she tried to pick it up she spilled most of it on her dress. Ambroise took the cup from her and set it back down on the table. He sent the steward from the room with a look.

'You're hurt,' he said. Her left eye was swollen, and there were livid bruises on her cheek.

'I was attacked,' she said, so softly that he did not hear her at first. 'I was attacked,' she repeated.

He stared at her. 'When?'

'Two nights ago.'

'Two nights!'

She nodded.

'Why did you not come to me straight away?'

'I could not face... I could not.'

'Who was it? I'll make them sorry they were ever born!'

'I do not know. It was dark. They did not speak.'

He sat down, then stood up again. 'This is an outrage.'

An outrage. Was that what it was? Until now it had been this obscene, evil and unspeakable thing, something too terrible to say aloud. Now it was simply an outrage.

'What hour did this take place?'

'I don't know. There was no moon.'

'What were you doing abroad at that hour of the night?'

It was not meant as accusation, but she understood that should the story ever be retold, it would become one.

'Someone knocked at my door. I thought I heard my maid's voice. I cannot be sure. I looked out and someone grabbed me.'

'You don't know who it was?'

Cornelia shook her head. She believed Sara was somehow behind it. If she was right, Schellinger must be in on it. She remembered all his lewd looks since they left Amsterdam. She suspected that even if he was not part of it, he had ordered some of his lapdogs to do his bidding.

She wondered what Ambroise would do. What could he do? Nothing would ever set this to rights.

'Tell me again what happened,' Ambroise said. 'Everything.'

She told him how they had stripped her, violated her, smeared her with pitch and human ordure and left her there. How she had laid there for two days, too ashamed and frightened to leave her cabin.

'And no clue as to who these men were?'

'All I know is that I fought them as best I could and that I bit one of them on the hand. Whether he still bears the wound I do not know.'

He put his head in his hands. 'This is beyond words. What can I say?'

When she did not answer he looked up, but she was already gone.

Christiaan watched Ambroise sweat. His pallor was a sickly green. He was as pompous as a duke strutting around the deck in Amsterdam, he thought, but now we are out here on the wild sea, we can all see the man beneath the fine clothes.

He and the provost stood side by side in the Great Cabin as Ambroise stammered out the story of Cornelia's assault.

When he was done, Christiaan contrived to look appalled. 'We must get to the bottom of this immediately,' he said. 'The offenders must be arrested and face the Governor's wrath as soon as we reach Batavia.'

'I am not yet fully recovered from my malady,' Ambroise said. 'I entrust you with the task.'

'Of course,' Christiaan said. 'We will start immediately. Before the sun sets, every one of these devils will be in chains.'

CHAPTER 19

The ship was in uproar. Michiel caught snatches of gossip among the passengers and crew, but everyone told a different story. Ambroise had locked himself in the Great Cabin and would see no one. His clerks said they had been sworn to secrecy, while Christiaan and the provost barged about the ship interrogating the crew in whispers.

All he could discover was that something terrible had happened and it involved Cornelia.

He went to the orlop to find Little Bean. Stonecutter was nowhere to be seen.

'Do you know what's going on?' he said to him.

'They say *Vrouwe* Noorstrandt was attacked last night in her cabin.'

'What?'

'The undermerchant is talking to everyone, asking them what they know about it. Stonecutter said someone has given him names. One of them was you, captain.'

'Me?'

'It's what he said. I said, well the captain wouldn't do anything like that, and he threatened to fix my other hand to the mast for insubordination.'

'What the devil is he playing at?'

'I don't know. But you'd better watch out. If Stonecutter has the chance, he'll do you down. No doubt about it.'

Christiaan presented himself in the Great Cabin. The provost was with him, holding Jan Decker in check with an iron fist around his upper arm.

When Ambroise saw the prisoner, his face fell. 'What's going on?' he said. They might as well have arrested Schellinger himself. There would be hell to pay for this.

'One of the sailors told me he was up and down all night,' Christiaan said.

'I had the gripe,' Decker said. 'I spent half the night in the heads.'

'So you say.'

Decker was close to tears. 'I didn't do anything! Who was it gave you my name?'

Christiaan shoved him forward. 'Show the Commander,' he said. There was a filthy piece of cloth wrapped around Decker's right hand.

'Caught it in a halyard, Commander,' Decker said. 'Rope burn, that's all.'

'Let me see,' Ambroise said.

Decker took his time taking off the filthy bandage so Ambroise could examine the wound. There was a half-moon tear on the palm, another on the back of the hand.

'That doesn't look like a rope burn to me,' Ambroise said.

Decker turned to Schellinger, hoping he would back him up.

The skipper was standing in the corner with his arms folded, looking around with wry contempt at the carpets and the Bible open on the table by the great window. He stepped forward and glanced at the wound. 'Rope burn,' he said. 'Any real seafaring man can tell. I was there when he did it. Now get back to your duties, bosun.'

Decker scuttled off.

Ambroise and Schellinger stared at each other.

'You can't do this,' Schellinger said. 'Me and the bosun have sailed together for years. I trust him with my life.'

Ambroise looked away first. 'No one is above the law on this ship.'

Schellinger gave a slow smile. 'So you say.'

'This unspeakable crime will not go unpunished.'

'Anything happens to the bosun, the crew could become unmanageable.'

'The crew are rabble. They will do what they are told or face the consequences. That will be all.'

Schellinger went out.

Christiaan pushed a piece of paper across the desk, written in his own neat hand. 'These are the names,' he said.

Ambroise looked at what Christiaan had written. 'How did you come by this?'

'Ryckert is convinced and several of his men backed up his claims. They all say they saw Gerrits leave the gundeck that night and he didn't return until at least six bells.'

'And Captain van Texel?'

'His sergeant, Stonecutter, told me he saw him and Gerrits whispering on the deck that night and then go down the ladder leading to the lady's cabin together. He has been very friendly with her during the voyage. Everyone knows it.'

'That in no way proves his guilt,' Ambroise said.

'Yet the whisper has already gone around the ship that these are the men responsible.'

'You have confounded me with this. I thought the perpetrators must be just common sailors. But these men are key to the running of the ship. If I arrest the bosun and captain van Texel, I will make an enemy of the skipper and lose the loyalty of the soldiers as well. It may instigate a general revolt.'

'We cannot sit by and do nothing.'

'Thank you, Christiaan. Leave me.'

'But what are you going to do?'

'Put the bosun in Hell for now. I shall think what to do with the others.'

'Just the bosun, then? Is that wise?'

'I said, leave me!'

Christiaan and the provost turned for the door. 'How is the lady?' Christiaan said over his shoulder.

'She refuses to come out of her cabin.'

'And you, Commander? You are quite recovered now?'

'Quite, thank you.'

A lie, Christiaan thought. Throughout the interrogation, he had shivered and sweated by turns. They were still a month from Batavia. He would not last that long.

As Christiaan walked up onto the poop, Schellinger looked up from the wheel. He sent the uppersteersman below so they could talk privately. 'What game are you playing, undermerchant?' he said. 'You were supposed to keep Jan out of this.'

'Decker has the lady's teeth marks on his hand. Any fool can see it.'

'What's going to happen?'

'We have orders to arrest him.'

'And the other two?'

Christiaan shrugged.

'He intends to break him,' Schellinger said.

'He knows what to say. He won't give anything away.'

'Every man talks in Hell, undermerchant. You'd better stay on your toes. If this goes to shit, I'll take your throat out.'

Michiel looked at Ambroise, shaking and sweating, then at Christiaan, and knew he was in terrible danger. And not just him; perhaps the ship itself was lurching out of control.

'Your name has been given to us,' Ambroise said. He couldn't look him in the eyes.

'What are you talking about?' Michiel said.

'The attack on *Vrouwe* Noorstrandt,' Christiaan said.

'What exactly happened to her?'

Ambroise fussed with the papers on his desk. 'She was most vilely assaulted.'

'You mean she was raped? Here on this ship?'

'That is what she claims.'

'You cannot believe that I am capable of such a thing?'

'We have made extensive enquiries,' Christiaan said. 'The provost and I have taken evidence from everyone on board.'

'Gossip means nothing. Did the lady say it was me?'

'It was dark,' Ambroise said. 'The only man we know for certain was involved is the bosun.'

'He said I was with him?'

Ambroise shook his head. 'He still appeals his innocence.'

Michiel looked from one man to the other. 'You believe Stonecutter over me?'

'There were others,' Christiaan said.

'Two of the Frenchies, I don't doubt. He wants to sully my name and put two of the mercenaries up to it. Paid them good money too I'm sure. And you fell for it?'

'Ryckert too,' Christiaan said. 'He says he saw you with Gerrits just before the attack.'

'So Ryckert takes over from Gerrits when he is arrested. That's not evidence, it's self-interest.' Michiel turned to Amboise. 'Why are you listening to these slanders?'

Ambroise stared at the desk. 'I have to think about this.'

'I have no ill will towards the captain here or to Gerrits,' Christiaan said. 'But what happened to *Vrouwe* Noorstrandt is grotesque, unthinkable. It is a stain on our honor and the honor of the Company. Something must be done.'

'I said I will think about it,' Ambroise said. 'Now leave me, both of you.'

CHAPTER 20

Christiaan felt the eyes of the soldiers on them as he, Schellinger and the provost made their way across the orlop. The provost found the hatchway in the decking and opened the padlock with his keys. He threw it open.

Decker blinked in the light. His skin was crusted with filth, and there were weeping sores on his wrists and legs where the chains had opened the skin. The sailors called it Hell. There was no room to lie down or to sit up, and you had to crouch down there in your own filth and vomit until it pleased the commander to let you go.

'Now you can piss off,' Schellinger said to the provost.

'The commander...'

'Just fuck off.'

Christiaan nodded to him, confirming the order. The provost hesitated then shrugged and backed off. 'I won't be far away,' he said.

They waited until he was out of earshot.

Decker was sobbing. Christiaan drew back at the smell of him. He had been in there for three days. He wouldn't make it to Java, in his opinion.

'Get me out of here. Please, skipper. Please.'

The wound on his hand was infected. It was swollen and purple, like the bite of a dog.

'You stupid bastard, Jan,' Schellinger said. 'You let her leave her mark on you.'

'Please...'

'Stop your sniveling. Grow some balls.'

'*Heer* Undermerchant, please, get me out of here or I'll tell them what you made me do. You too, skipper.'

'I didn't have anything to do with it,' Schellinger growled. 'God's death, don't you drag my name into this.'

'You've got to help me, skipper!'

'I'll do what I can, as long as you keep your mouth shut.' He slammed the hatchway shut behind him. They heard Decker start his weeping again as they walked away.

'When I was an understeersman,' Schellinger said, 'I saw one man kept in Hell for a month. By the time they brought the bastard out, he was raving like an idiot, and he could never stand straight again.'

'Maybe better he dies in there,' Christiaan said. 'Better for all of us.'

'No way for a man to behave,' Schellinger said, 'no matter what they do to you. Better if he does go crazy before we reach Batavia. Even this torture will seem like a paradise with willing virgins compared to what they'll have waiting for him in the fort.'

'And if they break him, he'll give up all our names.'

'The fuck he will,' Schellinger said.

When they got back on deck, Christiaan took deep breaths to clear his head and get the stink out of his nostrils. This wasn't working out how he'd planned. What was the Commander thinking? Why didn't he have van Texel and Gerrits in chains already?

It was taking too long.

Ambroise blinked and tried to focus. The sickness was on him again. The words in his journal seemed to melt down the page. It was hard even to think.

Recent events on the ship had unnerved him. Now he wanted only to see the fever coasts again and know that good Dutchmen were at hand. A fortune in *rix-dollars* and German *thalers* lay in the hold, while his authority over the crew felt ever more fragile.

There was a knock on the door. Christiaan looked in. 'You are unwell again, *Heer* Commander?' he said.

'It is nothing. It will pass.'

'You are very pale.'

'Come in. Sit down.'

Ambroise had once thought Christiaan to be a man of fashion and learning, with no real stomach for the job. But he had misjudged him. Christiaan's moral certainty had been a comfort these last few days. If he had fault, it was that he was too rash. Left to his own devices, he would have thrown half his officers in chains, and there would have been mutiny.

The bosun was certainly guilty. No matter what Schellinger said, the wound on his hand was made by a human bite. And besides, he had been on watch the night Cornelia was attacked and claimed to have seen nothing.

And where was Cornelia's maid when the assault had taken place? He had no doubt she was fornicating with Schellinger in his cabin. He was guilty of a dereliction of duty, at least, and would have to answer for that to Governor Coen. But he needed Schellinger's good graces right now, more than Schellinger needed his.

Any day now they would sight the Southland coast and turn north for Java. Three weeks' sailing would bring them under the walls of the fort. On that happy day he would leave Schellinger's fate - and that of Sara de Ruyter - to the tender mercies of the judges in Batavia.

He set aside his journal and replaced the pen in its stand. 'I want you to speak to Schellinger for me, Christiaan. Remind him again to set lookouts on the masthead tonight in accordance with the Governor's directive on the Houtman Rocks.'

'He says we are still six hundred miles from the Southland.'

'It will not hurt to remind him.'

Christiaan leaned in, as if even the bulkheads might be listening. 'I think we should have him put in chains with the bosun,' he said. 'We cannot be seen to be doing nothing. That poor woman. What she must have suffered.'

'No one is more concerned for her plight than I.'

'Then why do we hesitate?'

'If this had happened before we reached the Cape, then I most certainly would have done so, but we need his expertise in these latitudes. This is the most dangerous part of the journey.'

'Then let us at least take action against van Texel and Gerrits. The pastor is telling everyone that you are weak. Many of the sailors are thieves and rapists anyway. What if they think they can do what they will with any of the women without reprisal? We will lose control of the ship.'

'We have spoken about this before and you know my mind on it.'

'We have God and the law on our side.'

'Even God cannot help us as much as the *Beschermer*, but our escort may now be anywhere between here and India.'

'Be assured, whatever course you decide on, you shall have my utmost support. But this is a terrible, obscene crime that has been committed here.'

Ambroise put a hand to his forehead. It came away greasy with sweat, yet he was shaking with cold, like he had just been pulled from a canal in the middle of winter.

'Commander?'

'I think I shall take to my bed, *Heer* Undermerchant. Remember what I said. Talk to Schellinger if you please.'

'Shall I send for the surgeon?'

'He will only concoct one of his foul herbal potions and try to bleed me again. Rest is the best medicine. I shall take to my bunk. I hope to feel better in the morning.'

'It is our fondest wish.'

After Christiaan left, Ambroise lay down, shivering with cold, and pulled the blankets over him. I am a future Councilor of India, he thought. One day I will be President of the Fleet. I have a glorious future ahead of me.

If only I can bring the Company's irreplaceable cargo to Batavia.

They arrived singly to the steerage; Christiaan, Schellinger, Krueger, Ryckert, Joost, Stonecutter. They spoke in whispers. A single candle flickered on the table, throwing shadows on the tarred oak walls.

The commander was still sick with the fevers, and Cornelia Noorstrandt was locked away in her cabin and refused to come out. Nerves on the ship were at breaking point.

'So what's to be done?' Ryckert said.

'I say we forget about all this,' Krueger said. 'That bastard was supposed to die.'

'I don't see how we can forget about it,' Schellinger said. 'Not now that my bosun is in chains in the hold. If he doesn't break before we get to Batavia, they'll wring the truth out of him there. There's no going back now.'

Ryckert chewed on his knuckle. Krueger looked like he wanted to cry and Joost was grey as a corpse. They all knew there was only way out now.

'Why doesn't the Commander do something? What's he waiting for?' Joost said.

'It doesn't matter,' Christiaan said. 'If he won't act, then we have to. Are we ready? Tomorrow night, we do it.'

Slowly, one by one, they nodded their heads.

'Christ in Heaven,' Schellinger said. 'What have you led us to?'

CHAPTER 21

The scarlet lion of Holland dipped through the swells, its wake as bright as phosphorus. Schellinger strode onto the deck in his cloak and high sea boots, leaned over the lee rail and spat into the sea. The scrolled stern gleamed in the moonlight, and the yellow glow from the window of the great cabin was reflected in the wake. Somewhere down there, he thought, that little pimp of a commander lay snug in his bunk, moaning like the weakling he was.

The Great Southland was over the horizon. Soon they would be in Batavia. Landfall meant trouble for all of them. How could Jan have been so stupid to let her bite him?

The provost struck the mainmast with his ceremonial mace to mark the turn of the watch. 'All's well!'

All's well for now, Schellinger thought, but not for much longer. He went through Christiaan's plan in his head one more time. All this talk about overpowering the provost and the soldiers sounded all right when he was explaining it, but when a man thought about in the cold light of reason, there was a lot that could go wrong.

He put his telescope to his eye and searched the horizon. Was that surf out there? He called to the lookout, who was hunched forward on the bowsprit, silhouetted against the night stars. The man shouted back that it was only moonlight on the water.

These were dangerous latitudes, coming up to twenty-eight degrees, but according to his charts he was still six hundred miles west of the Great Southland, and running north east before the wind. He told himself there was nothing to worry about.

The commander had sent him a message to post mast lookouts. He thought he was a skipper now, the pompous bastard. Well, he would see to him when the time came.

He thought he heard a sound, like distant thunder. He put the telescope back to his eye. Just the wind, perhaps.

He felt a shiver along his spine. No, there it was, that sound again, thunder in a clear night sky. That's not moonlight, he thought.

He saw the danger in time to brace himself for the impact. He heard the grinding of timbers as the *Utrecht* touched the reef and imagined the rudder bolts tearing away, as the great ship lurched out of the water with a shriek like a wounded animal. He heard a scream as one of the crew fell from the yards and bounced on the deck, his head pulped.

A shudder passed through the length of the ship. The prow rose into the air and then the *Utrecht* canted to port in a tower of spray.

Ambroise was thrown from his bunk. He scrambled for a hold as he slid across the deck of his cabin, then lay on his back, hard against the bulwark, stunned. He heard the ship's keel grinding across the reef, followed by a sudden and deathly silence. The *Utrecht* listed onto her side, and he thought they were about to capsize.

The passengers started screaming on the gun decks.

He got to his feet, blood leaking down his face where he had hit his head. He steadied himself on the bulwark and climbed out of the cabin and along the companionway, still in his nightshirt.

The *Utrecht* fought her way back from her list. Another swell crashed into the hull, sending a wall of spray over the decks. The courses flapped useless from the yards.

Ambroise found Schellinger standing under the great lamp, hunched into his cloak, his knuckles white around the rail. He was screaming orders, while sailors poured from the hatches to help the night watch.

'What have you done?' Ambroise shouted.

'It's just a sandbank,' Schellinger said, as if this catastrophe was some inconvenience for which he bore no responsibility.

The boom of surf around them in the darkness mingled with the screams of the passengers pouring onto the decks. The sailors cursed at them, shoving them out of their way.

'How can it be a sandbank? By your reckoning we are six hundred miles from the Southland.'

'Some unknown reef. We are on the tail of it.' Schellinger pushed Ambroise aside and grabbed one of the sailors by his shirt. 'Only the crew on deck. Get that rabble of passengers back down below!'

Ambroise took him by shoulder and spun him around. 'I warned you about this. Did you not keep a proper lookout, as I advised?' The ship lurched, broad-sided by another roller. Ambroise staggered sideways. 'What counsel now?'

'I'll get us off. It's not the first time I've been on a ship that's touched ground.'

'If you had followed my instruction this would not have happened at all.'

Schellinger turned away.

I cannot stand here in my nightshirt arguing, Ambroise thought. He hurried back below. He hoped Schellinger was right and this was just a sandbank.

God help them all if he was wrong.

It was the first time Cornelia had been on deck for days.

It was difficult to stand upright as the ship had listed to windward. Spray drifted in the glow of the stern lamps, and the ship groaned with the impact of each comber. Down on the main deck, the press of people was crushing those standing against the starboard rail. One of the crew was trying to herd them all back down into the orlop deck, but it was hopeless.

Two men unlashed the painter, but a gust of wind picked up the smaller boat and hurled it across the deck as if it were a scrap. A man screamed and toppled into the water. Schellinger shouted more orders from the poop as the sailors scrambled to secure the boat. But another gust of wind took it, and in moments it was gone.

They lowered the yawl next, and Schellinger and several of the crew clambered in. The pastor tried to get in after them. One of them knocked him roughly aside.

This must be the Houtman Rocks, Ambroise thought. The reefs were at twenty-eight and a third degrees off the Southland, and Governor Coen's directive had clearly said they should approach no closer than a hundred miles before turning north for Java. Schellinger had ignored it. The arrogant gin-soaked bastard had led them right onto the rocks. So much for dead reckoning, so much for his much vaunted expertise.

Schellinger had taken soundings around the ship in the yawl. Now he scrambled out, climbing up the cleats and shoving his way across the crowded deck. He came back up to the poop, the leadsman behind him.

'Seven fathoms at a musket shot astern, shallows from the bows,' he said. 'What did I tell you? It is a sand bank not before known. I'll put out a kedge anchor astern and we can wind ourselves off with the capstan. If we are at low water, it will be easy enough with the rising tide.'

'You put us on the Houtman Rocks,' Ambroise said.

'It is not the Houtman. What do you know of the sea?'

The moon sunk below the horizon. From the main deck came the sound of mothers calling out their children's names, while the pastor led his family and the devout in a hymn. The ship shuddered again.

'We must overboard the cannon,' Schellinger said.

'What?'

'The Company would rather lose the cannon than the ship.'

'You just said it is only a sandbank.'

'I still cannot float her off with the cannon weighing her down. Get me the bosun up here.'

'The bosun will remain in chains until we reach Batavia.'

'We will not reach Batavia unless you do as I say. You want me to save this ship? Then give me my bosun. He's the most experienced men I have.'

Ambroise hesitated.

'I need my bosun!'

Ambroise called to the provost and gave him the order. Where was Christiaan, he wondered. He needed his cool head right now.

The gun deck was chaos. It was pitch black and everyone was screaming and trampling on each other in their panic to scramble up the ladders.

Michiel saw the gunners heaving the bronze pieces from their mountings and pushing them through the ports into the sea. Gerrits held a lamp and screamed at them to work faster. He had tears running down his face. He had made his men polish those pieces every day since Amsterdam, buffing them till they shone. The crimson paint was still fresh on the muzzles.

Michiel climbed down to the orlop and found Little Bean. 'Where's Stonecutter?'

'I don't know. Him and two of the Frenchies are gone.'

Michiel wasn't about to leave his men to drown. They would have a better chance to save themselves up on deck, if that's what it came to. It would be more difficult without Stonecutter, but Little Bean knew what had to be done, and at least he could trust him.

'Stay together and stay orderly!' he shouted at him. 'I'll get you all out of this.

A wave of spray soaked him as soon as he came through the hatch. He looked around and was shocked at what he saw. The passengers were corralled on the starboard side by the listing of the ship. The sailors were fighting with them, trying to get them back below. Schellinger was roaring orders but no one could hear him.

The ship jarred with every wave. She canted so hard onto her beam that he couldn't stand upright. The timbers sounded as if they were going to burst apart.

Ambroise gathered the ship's council on the quarterdeck; Schellinger and the three steersmen, along with Decker, who was mad-eyed and hunched over, his wrists still raw from the shackles. What use would he be to Schellinger now?

'Where's Christiaan?' he said.

'Who knows?' Schellinger spat on the deck. 'Who cares?'

Schellinger had taken repeated soundings, fore and aft. They were on a falling tide, and winching themselves off the reef would not be as simple as he had first thought. Even jettisoning the precious cannon had not helped them. There was thirty-eight tons of stone in the hold as ballast, meant for the façade of the sea gate of Batavia castle. Compared to that, the cannon were nothing.

The ship had listed even further to starboard, and the sea foamed around them, each roller lifting her and threatening to drive the mast through the keel like a nail through wood.

'We have to lose the main mast,' Schellinger said.

Ambroise frowned. 'How can we reach Batavia if you do that?'

'That is my concern, not yours.'

'Your concern was seeing us safe to the Indies and look how miserably you have failed at your commission. I shall hold you responsible for this disaster with the Company.'

'Do what you will. But unless we lose some weight off the ship, you'll be taking your complaint to the fish.'

The uppersteersman nodded. 'We've no choice if we want to float her off.'

Cutting the main mast was such a drastic action that Company regulations said the ship's captain had to wield the first blow himself. When Ambroise set off across the main deck with axe in hand, there was a collective moan from the passengers. It emphasized to all of them how dire their situation must be.

After his first strike, the sailors took over and set to work with their axes. Ambroise could not bring himself to watch. Instead he turned his gaze on Schellinger. I should have replaced you at the Cape when I had the chance, he thought. Your arrogance has finally outstripped your talents as a seaman.

He closed his eyes and tried to pray, but no words would come. All he could hear in his head was the hammer of the axes over the rush of the wind.

There was a crack like cannon fire and the mast started to fall. Just at that moment, a swell passed under the boat and sent it pitching forward into the sheets and lines of the foremast. A man screamed as he was pinned against the bulwark. Another lost his fingers to a wet and coiled rope.

Instead of lifting her, it made her cant even further to the wind. A broken section of the t'gallant thumped like a battering ram against the port side. Schellinger and the steersmen screamed themselves hoarse, but the crew could not shift it. A wave washed across the decks, dragging more men over the side.

'Can you do nothing right?' Ambroise shouted.

'Go to hell!' Schellinger shouted back at him, but his words were lost on the wind.

Cornelia crouched on the deck, sodden and trembling. After this longest night, light was finally leeching into the sky. She thought at first that the smudge she saw on the horizon was ocean swell. But as the light grew stronger the crabbed silhouettes became more distinct.

'Land!' she shouted.

An eerie stillness fell over the boat as everyone turned to stare.

'God be thanked,' the pastor said, and his cry was taken up by others. Their prayers had been answered. Their good Calvinist god had come to their aid.

CHAPTER 22

The Houtman Rocks

A high island loomed from the grey horizon, too far distant to be of help to them. But there were exposed reefs closer to hand, and Ambroise sent Schellinger to investigate them in the yawl. On his return the skipper assured him that the shoals would not be covered by the high tide. Ambroise decided to land the passengers there, with the money and treasures, while they went about the business of saving the ship. He would send the soldiers to keep guard over the Company's goods.

He pushed through the press of people on the main deck. They grabbed at him, demanding to be saved. Why are they yelling at me, he thought. I'm not the one who put us on this cursed reef.

He found Michiel and told him to come with him. 'Bring some of your men,' he said.

As they went below, Ambroise was astounded to hear singing coming from the hold. Some sailors had broken open one of the brandy casks and were reeling around, drunk. Another was attacking one of the money chests with an adze.

'Get away from that!' he shouted.

Michiel wrestled the axe out of the sailor's hand and threw him bodily to the floor.

Ambroise went to fetch the small wooden box he had hidden in his private chests. He told Michiel to have his men bring the money boxes up onto the deck to take with them to the islands.

The soldiers were climbing down into the yawl, taking the treasure chests with them. Waves were breaking over the gunwales, and Cornelia heard screams as several men fell into the sea. The sailors were trying to load barrels of biscuits and water, while they fought off the terrified passengers with their fists. Men started fighting with women and children to get into the boat, which slammed against the hull with each surge of the swell. The pastor was one of the first aboard. It seemed God had seen fit to preserve him.

Cornelia heard the bosun and Schellinger arguing over what to do.

'I'm not sitting on some reef to die of thirst with this rabble,' Decker shouted. 'We have to get in the longboat. Look at these cattle! Let's leave them.'

'We can't,' Schellinger said.

'We must. Let's get away from here.'

She was carried along in the surge of desperate people. Someone clawed her in the face, then a man's elbow took her and she almost went down.

Michiel peered through the grey light at the uncertain silhouettes scattered on the horizon. Just a few scraps of reef, by what he could make out, perhaps not even that when the tide rose.

The passengers were wide-eyed and panicked, like horses trapped in a fire. He saw one God-fearing Dutchman push a child against the bulwark, and send him sprawling, in a panic to save his own miserable life. Another child, separated from his mother, went over the side into the foaming water.

He saw Cornelia caught in the throng and fighting with the sailors lined against the bulwark. She would be crushed or drowned for certain, for all that the bravehearts around her cared.

He shoved his way among them and found her hand.

'This way,' he said.

He had worked on farms as a boy and was accustomed to shouldering his way among the milking herds. It was no different to that. You used your elbows, your weight and a rough voice. 'Look after the *vrouwe!*' he shouted to one of the sailors as he lifted her off her feet and over the side.

She scrambled down the cleats and into the yawl, her fingers scrambling for purchase on the wet timber. A breaker slammed her into the hull and she fell, screaming, expecting to land in the water. Something or someone broke her fall, but her ankle turned under her weight as she landed. She saw a bright flash of pain and passed out.

She came to as the yawl rowed clear of the wreck. The greasy morning light revealed the full extent of their disaster. They must have struck at high water, for now the *Utrecht* lay hard on her beam, her main mast athwartships in a tangle of lines.

It was impossible to stand or walk on the wet and sloping deck. Ambroise found himself climbing the great ship as if he was rappelling a wall, holding onto lines or the upper works to keep balance. He scrambled along a ladder into the hold and saw the provost down there, with his jacket off, screaming instructions to a knot of soldiers toiling at a capstan. Michiel was with them.

'Get that chest secure, then get to the boats!' Ambroise shouted. 'Leave the rest. We need you and your soldiers on the islands to keep order. There are reports the passengers are fighting over the water already.'

Michiel nodded. 'Just this one last chest to secure away.'

Ambroise made his way down to the Great Cabin. A mountain of a man loomed out of the darkness and blocked his way. It was Michiel's sergeant, the one they called Stonecutter. He had a piece of silk plundered from the chests around his waist. He smirked when he saw Ambroise and wiggled his hips in poor imitation of a Mogul concubine. The two Frenchies he had with him roared with laughter.

'What are you doing?' Ambroise said. 'Get out of here and back up on the deck.'

'Look at me, I'm Cornelia Noorstrandt!' Stonecutter flounced through the bilge, wiggling his backside outrageously; the parody of beauty with his ugly, boil-scarred face.

Another wave hit the ship broadside and sent them all tumbling. It only made the drunken soldiers laugh harder. Stonecutter cursed as the jug of brandy he was holding shattered against the bulwark.

'Get out of here!' Ambroise roared. His hand went to his sword.

There was a moment of stillness and the laughter stopped. The three soldiers put their hands to their own weapons. These men were mercenaries, Ambroise thought, and paid to kill for the Company, but they would just as well kill for themselves if they had to. They thought they were all about to die, and the law and Company rules meant nothing to them now.

He fled, hauling himself through the door of the council room. He found Salomon du Chesne gathering up documents and placing them in a leather satchel.

'Leave all that,' he said, 'come with me.'

They had to climb into his cabin. His papers littered the floor. Even his heavy sea chest was hard up against the starboard bulwark. He unlocked his desk drawer and took out the casket he had hidden there.

He gave it to Salomon along with the key. He entrusted him also with the small wooden crate he had brought from the forward hold.

'Salomon, you must guard these with your life. They are the property of the Company. Wrap them in cloth so no one can recognize them for what they are. Should anything happen to me, you are to ensure that they find their way into the hands of Jan Pieterszen Coen, the Lord General in Batavia. Do you understand?'

Salomon looked sick with fear.

'I will see you safe onto the yawl. And may God be with you.'

'You also, Commander.'

Dear God. He already feared for the bullion. If he lost the jewels as well, he might never show his face in Holland again.

He crawled back up the companionway. The bullion chests had been lashed to the deck; eight so far. The other four were still down in the hold.

The yawl returned from the island. Michiel got the rest of his men aboard her. Ambroise made sure Salomon went with them. The clerk sat huddled at the stern, clutching his cargo to his chest like it was an infant.

Someone threw open the door to Christiaan's cabin.

'Who's there?' he said.

'It's me,' Schellinger said. He held up the oil lamp he was carrying. 'Is that you, *Heer* Undermerchant? The commander has been looking everywhere for you.'

'Is it bad up there?'

'Of course it's bad. We're on the Houtman Rocks.'

'Can't you float her off?'

'You're welcome to go up and see for yourself.'

Christiaan shook his head.

'The ship is finished. The mast is down, and it's pinned us to the rocks like a butterfly. Her back's broken.'

'Is there no chance?'

'You'd have more luck floating a hearth brick now. She's going to sit here until she breaks up. The Commander's trying to get as many as he can to the shore but they're fighting each other over the water already.'

'What about the money chests?'

'Easy, we put one under each arm and swim to the islands with them.' Schellinger went off, laughing.

Christiaan heard the screams from the main deck through the open door. Water streamed down the companionway as another wave hit them broadside.

It didn't seem to him like the ship was breaking up. She might be stuck fast but that wasn't any good reason to leave her. He liked his chances better here, especially if the people were fighting each other already. He decided to bide his time and sit tight with the wine and the treasure.

CHAPTER 23

The *Utrecht* shrieked with each roller that smashed into her. The seas washed over her decks.

Schellinger watched from the stern, white-lipped. They had lost the painter, and a second yawl had been crushed between the hull and the reef.

What a gutless bunch, he thought. His crew had been hindered at every turn in their attempts at an orderly evacuation. The passengers tussled with the sailors and each other every time the yawl came alongside.

The soldiers had been sent to keep order on the islands, but a handful of them had refused to go. They had broken open all the brandy and wine barrels and were given over to their own amusements. He could hear their drunken singing down in the holds.

The sun rose over the meagre outcrops of grey sand, where the yellow-bellied tailors and shopkeepers were crying for their mothers. Salvation for some, he supposed, though it looked to him like a graveyard.

There were decisions to be made here. Pastors who droned on about honor, morality and the esteem of other men had never found themselves shipwrecked in the middle of the ocean with a scurvy bunch of drunks and cowards.

Their best chance, it seemed to him, was to take the remaining longboat and make for Batavia. It would be months before anyone in the Company realized they had foundered - months more before they sent a ship to look for them. They did not have enough food and water to sustain them for a few days, never mind the long months they might wait for rescue.

Best chance? It was their only chance.

The low island

Cornelia opened her eyes.

It looked like a battlefield. Wreckage from the *Utrecht* littered the beach, washed up by the fast-running current. Broken spars from the toppled main mast were angled into the sand like battle flags, and a flotsam of timbers lay along the half crescent bay. Those saved on the yawl lay sprawled and groaning in the ghost grey light among the brushwood.

The morning's events had proved to her that for all the pastor's talk of God-fearing Christians, it did not take a great deal for men to become animals again. Most of the water barrels had been broken open before Michiel and the soldiers landed on the beach. It had started with a few men claiming they needed it for their women and children. Then some others, thinking they had been duped, considered this justification to take whatever they wished. Before long, the pilfering became a general assault. If the provost and Michiel had not arrived with the soldiers, there would be no water left at all.

Up and down the beach, men were nursing blackened eyes and bleeding lips. Even the pastor had a bloody nose from the carpenter.

Michiel had posted a cordon around the remaining water barrels. They stood guard, pikes and swords at the ready.

As the morning wore on, the wind grew chill and clouds raced across the sky. Another storm was driving in from the sea, and there was no shelter among the sparse bushes and stones.

Cornelia huddled into her cloak, her limbs stiff with cold. Out on
the reef, the *Utrecht* leaned drunkenly on her side. The sea broke over
her, each roller throwing up a great mountain of spray.

'Are you all right, *vrouwe*?'

She looked up. It was Michiel. 'Thank you for helping me off the
ship,' she said.

'Panic does strange things to most men. Do not judge it. I have
experienced it myself, as you know.'

'Not today.'

'Have you had a ration of water?' He called for one of the soldiers
to bring over a pannikin.

'How much do we have left?'

He shook his head. 'Not enough. But take it anyway.'

She took the tin cup from him, her hands shaking. It tasted like the
best Madeira. Odd that something so very commonplace could become
so precious. They were at the end of the world, without hope or haven,
so she supposed one pannikin of water would make no difference now.

'It is good to see you alive, if not unharmed.' He hesitated. 'I heard
what happened. I'm so sorry.'

She turned away. She felt her cheeks burn, even in the cold. 'I don't
think I can talk about it. But thank you.'

'It's unspeakable that it should have happened, and no one there to
protect you. They accused me of it, did you know?'

'You?'

'On Stonecutter's word. He has it in for me. The undermerchant
too, by the looks of it, though God alone knows why, I have never
given him cause to hate me.'

'You are the last man I would have accused. But I doubt that it
matters now. At least my shame will never become common gossip in

Batavia. Despite what you say, I fear we shall never see rescue. I wonder if even God himself knows these wretched islands exist.'

'Do not even think it,' he said. 'We live; we breathe; we face every day as it comes. It is only hopeless if we give up hope.'

CHAPTER 24

The understeersman emerged from below decks to report that the holds were broken and most of the remaining water barrels were ruined with seawater.

Schellinger scowled. 'We should have brought them up before the bullion.'

Ambroise leaned on the rail. All he could think of was the Company's reaction to the loss of so much silver. In his mind, he argued his case before Governor Coen. In every one of his imaginings, Coen remained unmoved.

He needed to lie down and rest. The fever was back. The rain lashed down, but he felt like he was burning up. He tried to blink the sweat out of his eyes.

The yawl returned from the island. All the passengers were off the ship now. Decker, standing in the bow, cupped his hands to his mouth and shouted something up to Schellinger at the quarterdeck rail.

Schellinger turned around. 'The provost is unable to keep order.'

Ambroise stared at him.

'You have to go ashore and take charge. There is nothing more you can do here.'

'I cannot leave the ship,' Ambroise said. 'The bullion is my direct responsibility.'

Schellinger narrowed his eyes. 'What's more important, silver or people's lives?'

'You go to the island,' Ambroise said.

'They will not listen to me. You are the Commander.'

'Where's Christiaan?'

'Who cares? You must go to the island and restore order. We are all dead men without the water.'

Schellinger was right; he did have a responsibility to the people. He looked around and saw Joost clinging to the rail beside him.

'Van der Linden, you and your cadets must watch over the bullion.'

'You are leaving us here on the boat?'

'There is no choice. I have to go to the islands and make sure there is order. I will come back for you as soon as it is done.'

'You can't just leave us here!'

'Don't worry, boy,' Schellinger said. 'I'll be here to hold your hand. We have to look after the Company's precious silver.'

The seas were getting higher and it was dangerous to clamber down the fallen lines. They had to wait for a moment's respite between the breakers to drop down into the yawl. Hands clutched at Ambroise and carried him safely aboard. The boat pitched dangerously in the surf, and he fell face first into the bilge at the stern.

Schellinger and Decker scrambled into the boat after him, then the Noorstrandt maid, Sara, who seemed to come out of nowhere. Ambroise realized that he had been outmaneuvered.

'You are not staying with the ship?' he said.

'It serves no purpose now,' Schellinger said.

Ambroise looked up at the stern and saw the *jonkers* lining the rail. 'I am not abandoning you!' he shouted. 'I have to attend my duty. We will be back!'

Schellinger smirked, as if he knew something better.

Ambroise realized they couldn't hear him anyway. His words were lost in the wind and spray. The little boat pitched again and he nearly fell into the foaming sea.

Schellinger let the wind take them over the reef towards the crouching islands. Ambroise looked back at the broken ship and experienced a sense of dread. He hoped he had made the right choice.

Schellinger was right; the people were more important than silver bullion. But he wondered if Governor Jan Pieterszen Coen would see it that way.

Christiaan clung to the bulkhead. He could barely stand up. He managed to clamber into the hold. It reeked of brandy fumes.

Joost was there with two of the other *jonkers*. There were piles of silver cash on the deck, from a chest they had looted, and they squirmed among the metal coins like puppies in dirt. Joost threw a handful of silver *thalers* at the others. 'There, I told you one day I'd be rich enough to throw money around,' he said and laughed at his own wit. He let a pile of *rix-dollars* slip through his fingers like sand. 'More than I could make in a whole lifetime for this god-rotting Company,' he said and took another swig of the Commander's best brandy.

'Where's the skipper?' Christiaan said.

'He's abandoned us,' Joost said, 'left us here to drown on this tub, the lying, yellow bastard. And the Commander has behaved like any fine lord, only thinking about his own scrawny neck. They're all gone.'

Christiaan staggered back to his cabin. Ambroise and Schellinger gone? Well, that changed things.

'We cannot make it to the island,' Schellinger shouted over the rush of the wind. It was almost impossible to see the land - the spray from the waves breaking over the rocks almost obscured the islands from sight.

'But that is the only reason I agreed to leave the ship!' Ambroise shouted. 'You have to put me with the people.'

'Can't be done!' Schellinger shouted back, wrestling with the tiller.

'Then what are you going to do?'

'We'll make for that island there,' he said, pointing out a scrap of land scarcely larger than the *Utrecht* herself.

Ambroise stared at the grim speck. 'You said we were going to the island.'

Schellinger shrugged his shoulders.

Ambroise looked around the boat, counting how many friends he had here. There were forty men, perhaps fifty, but they were all Schellinger's.

CHAPTER 25

Christiaan reclined in the Commander's carved chair in the Great Cabin, resplendent in one of Ambroise's splendid silk-lined cloaks. He had a bottle of finest Burgundy at his elbow.

Crowded in around him were the drunken, the frightened and the mutinous. They had all been thrust into a skewed, topsy-turvy world, with the port side for a ceiling and the starboard for a floor. It was a world where apothecaries were king, and ordinary seaman drank the finest brandies straight from a crystal decanter.

Schellinger had miscalculated, Christiaan decided. Their castle of Baltic Oak was beached, most assuredly, but he felt in no more danger here than if he were in some island fortress. From time to time the swell rolled across the reef, and a wave broke against the hull of the ship, sending foam and spray hissing around her, but she was firmly wedged and moving hardly at all anymore.

He had spent his time emptying out Ambroise's desk and upending the contents onto the floor. Wet boots trampled letters and family portraits, and the company seals lay in the saltwater slop.

Joost had put on one of the commander's jackets and, with a bottle of French wine in one hand, was doing a passable impression. 'You men!' he squeaked. 'Away from those bullion casks or I shall slap you with my glove!'

The gathered assembly roared with laughter.

Ambroise's sea chest was opened and Stonecutter put on the commander's frock coats and hats.

Christiaan banged on the desk with his fist and called the others to attention. 'I have here the commander's journal,' he announced.

The men whooped and whistled and then fell expectantly to silence.

'I read you an entry from March,' Christiaan said. '*There is on board a very lovely young woman by the name of Cornelia Noorstrandt. She is a woman of great virtue and intelligence, and she has shown me much friendship...*'

'I bet he fucked her!' someone shouted, and they all roared.

'*...she has much interest in my experiences in the East...*'

'That means he did it to her from behind!' Krueger shouted.

'*...and I have tried to share with her my knowledge of the court of the great mogul, such as it is.*'

'I know what he shared with her!' Ryckert said and made a gesture with his hips.

Christiaan read several more passages concerning Cornelia and then he reached the entry for the twenty-seventh of May.

'*I am still no closer to discovering the names of those responsible for the Most Terrible Outrage on Vrouwe Noorstrandt. So far the only man whose guilt is incontrovertible is that of Jan Decker, the bosun. Christiaan van Sant, the undermerchant, has made exhaustive enquiry about the ship. We both share outrage at what has occurred.*' There were cheers at this and Christiaan looked around the room and gave a slight bow of his head.

'*However,*' he went on, '*suspicion has also fallen on the chief gunnery officer, Frederick Gerrits, who was seen going below at six bells on the night of the offence by Ryckert, the gunner's mate.*'

'You bastard!' Gerrits shouted. 'I had nothing to do with it. I should cut your bloody throat.' He reached for the knife at his belt. Stonecutter grabbed him from behind in a bearhug, clamping both his arms to his sides.

'Get him out of here,' Christiaan said. Stonecutter dragged him out, still shouting curses and threats.

When Gerrits was gone, the journal was placed in the middle of the room, and those that felt the need urinated on the open pages. Then Joost picked it up, dripping and stinking, and tossed it out of the stern window. The others cheered.

They took to looting the commander's chest. Joost excelled himself. He found a medallion, cut from agate and bearing the likeness of the *stadtholder*, Prince Frederick Henry. God alone knew how many thousands of guilders it was worth, but before anyone could stop him he had tossed it out of the window after the journal. 'There goes the rest of the rubbish!' he shouted. Then he saluted and fell down drunk.

Christiaan felt a glow of pleasure. God had led the way to the kingdom. These men had all gone too far in this now. You made a woman pregnant, she had no choice but to bear the pain of childbirth; you made a man a mutineer, he had no choice but to cut throats.

The seal island

A mile away, Ambroise crouched over a tiny fire of green sticks. They had spent the afternoon sheltering under a scrap of canvas, whipped and harried by the wind, and soaked through from the storm. He gazed out at the reef. A pinprick of light burned in the stern cabin, a mere firefly in this grim horizon.

What were they doing out there?

He calculated that twelve chests of silver *rix dollars* and German *thalers* were still on board the ship. Tomorrow, he thought, I must go back and salvage them. I must rescue, too, those good young cadets who protected them. As for Stonecutter and the two mercenaries who had defied him, well, justice would have to wait for now, but he would see them punished for their perfidy.

The wind howled, setting the tiny embers glowing in the fire. The reef sounded like cannon fire.

Each time the wind abated he prayed that it would be the last of the big gusts. Perhaps tomorrow they would wake to seas blue and calm. He would restore order among the people and retrieve the bullion from the *Utrecht*.

Only then might he worry over his own survival here on this accursed rock.

CHAPTER 26

Clouds chased the moon. The lanterns on the poop threw an eerie light over the sloping deck and the ragged stump of the mainmast. Another breaker lifted the ship and crunched her down again on the reef.

One of the Frenchies was trying to salvage the biscuit barrels from below decks. Stonecutter watched him. The boy had seen him leave the orlop deck the night he had taught that stuck-up Noorstrandt witch a lesson. He had sworn he wouldn't speak of it to anyone. But a man like him, how could you be sure? He had cheated him at dice once, and there had been a lot of money in the pot. Never had settled with him for that.

He took a couple of paces across the sloping deck, and the knife slipped between the Frenchie's ribs easily as testing the flesh of a suckling pig. A little nudge and he was over the side, just like that, good riddance. He rinsed the blade in the scuppers and went back to the Great Cabin to drink a few more quarts of the commander's good brandy.

'You think he'll come back for us?' Joost said.

Christiaan studied the anxious faces around the table. The effects of the wine were beginning to wear off along with the bravado. They were all starting to think about survival now. Hope was a dangerous beast, and guilt and brandy wine made for the worst kind of hangover. Only Ryckert didn't seem to care, bullying the commander's butler to fetch more of the Company's best cognac. The cabin boy staggered along the sloping deck with plates of cold salted pork and beef.

Christiaan had dressed for dinner by placing one of the Commander's gold medallions around his neck. 'He'll be back for us,' he said.

'The seas are rising,' Stonecutter said. 'I don't like it.'

Through the oaken doors they heard the drumming of the surf on the reef. But the *Utrecht* was solidly built and Schellinger had said she was firmly fixed on the rocks. Christiaan told himself there was nothing to worry about.

'Where's that bastard Gerrits?' Ryckert said.

Christiaan glanced over at Stonecutter, who shrugged his massive shoulders. 'I heard he went missing during the night,' he said. 'He probably tried to swim for the island.'

'I wish him luck with that,' Joost said. 'It's risky, with the currents and the shark fish.'

'He was a sulky bastard,' Ryckert said. 'He won't be missed.'

The low island

Michiel had set his soldiers to work, building makeshift tents from sailcloth and salvaged timber. He had even made them set out their camp in orderly rows, as if they were on campaign.

Now he stood on the shingle beach and watched the provost make his way towards them, muttering to himself. His sea boots crunched on the coral and his cloak flapped in the wind. His imperious bulk was intimidating on a ship the size of the *Utrecht,* but here on this God-forsaken island of clinkered limestone and scrub he just looked clumsy and slow.

'Captain van Texel.'

'Yes, *Heer* Provost.'

'We have a problem.'

Michiel smiled. 'I would say we have many.'

The man ignored him. He had no sense of irony. 'I have made an inventory. We have supplies for just a few days. Even with what we have, I will need your men to keep close guard in case there is another outbreak of lawlessness. There must be no more pilfering.'

'Don't worry, my men know what to do.'

The provost pointed across the water. They could just make out the yawl, beached on the cay on the other side of the channel barely a cannon shot distant.

'He has to come back for us. He's not going to leave us here.'

'Unless he has casks of water and provisions, what difference will it make?'

'His place is here with us,' the provost said. 'To maintain order.'

'My men will do that. But I ask myself, how much order will there be when we are all dying of thirst?'

'I've made a count. There are two hundred and thirteen of us. I've worked out a water ration.'

'A dewdrop a day?'

'It is no laughing matter.'

'And I am not laughing. My men will make sure there is no more trouble.'

The provost nodded. He looked back towards the cay and their errant commander. 'He'll be back in the morning, you'll see.'

The island was not much larger than the *kerke* in Michiel's village. It was just an outcrop of coral, with a few gnarled salt bushes that were home to sea birds. The shoreline was a flat reef that hung over the water in jagged ledges. The lonely cry of mutton birds and gulls accompanied the gathering of the dark. The relentless wind moaned and gusted.

He took his tinderbox from his pocket. Inside was a flint stone, a bar of steel and some linen impregnated with saltpeter. He built a pile of twigs over some of the dried fibers and used the flint stone and the steel to make a spark. He fanned the flame with his breath until he had a small fire going.

He did the same thing up and down the beach, so that there was a fire between every half dozen men. The soldiers huddled around in their groups, but the brushwood they had collected burned through quickly and turned to ash. Not much choice after that but to shiver inside their sea cloaks.

At last he fell into a black, numbing sleep but woke in the middle of the night with the gritty sand stinging his face and the cold so fierce that his whole body shook. Unable to get back to sleep, he lay there listening to the hollow boom of the breakers on the reef.

There were no more blankets. The few that had been rescued from the wreck had been requisitioned by the pastor for his family. So much for sacrifice in the name of the Lord.

Somewhere in the dark two men were fighting with their fists, squabbling over ownership of a biscuit.

He lit an oil lamp and went to check on the sentries he had posted by the water barrels. Then he walked along the beach, trying to keep warm. He almost stumbled over Cornelia, curled up in a depression among the bushes and hard shale, shivering with cold.

'Who is that?' She sounded panicked.

Michiel took several steps backward in the darkness. 'I am sorry, *vrouwe*. I did not see you.'

'Stay away from me, I shall scream!'

'It me, Michiel. I am on patrol. You are in no danger.'

She was panting like she had run a mile through the sand.

'I'll leave you to your sleep,' he said.

'No, don't go. Stand here a while. I am frightened.'

He waited, huddled into his cloak. After a while he got down on his haunches, so he was not as exposed to the wind.

'I'm sorry,' she said. 'I have nightmares. I wake and don't know where I am. I jump at every little sound.'

'You should come and sleep nearer to our camp. No one will harm you there.'

'All right,' she said. He helped her to her feet. 'What is happening,' she said. 'Do you think Schellinger and Ambroise have plans for our survival?'

He could say yes, he supposed, tell her that everything would be fine. But that would insult the lady's intelligence. 'I don't know. I would say Ambroise has largely lost control of things.'

'Why has he not come to our island himself?'

'The seas are too rough for landing, and there is sharp coral everywhere. But I don't think that's the reason. If you ask me, those boys over there; their thoughts run only to their own salvation.'

'You don't trust Schellinger.'

'Do you?'

'Whenever he looks at me, it makes my skin crawl. Dear God, why did this happen to us?'

'Bad luck happens to a lot of people. I don't suppose fate chose us in particular.'

'What about God?'

'Look, as I see it, if a man has good luck he says it's God. If he has bad luck he says it's the Devil. But it's all the same thing. I'm a simple man. I'll pray to God if that's what someone wants me to do, but really I don't mind either way.'

'That's blasphemy,' she said.

'To me it's just the hard truth, as I've learned it. There's good luck and bad luck, and who has one and who has the other, well I've never seen any design to it.'

'You don't think God is punishing us then?'

'What for?'

'For the things that happened on our voyage.'

'Then why are you here freezing to death with the rest of us? Where is the retribution in that? I've been a soldier for many years now, and I've seen men do unspeakable things in wars. Some of them were punished and some of them are still walking around today, like it was nothing. God's not watching.'

'So, who do you pray to, on nights like tonight?'

'I don't. I just try to keep warm and make sure my sword is sharp. I'm a very practical man.'

'You shouldn't let the pastor hear you talk like this.'

'Well, I don't, you see. That's practical too.'

They reached the camp and he could hear the sounds of another fight further down the beach. He shone his oil lamp into a shallow depression not far from his sentries. 'Keep an eye on her,' he said to them and waited until she had settled herself under her cloak. 'Now I'd better go and sort that out. I'll be along to check on you in a while.'

He picked his way carefully along the beach. The wind picked up, wilder now and very cold.

CHAPTER 27

The seal island

The next day there was a gale blowing. It seemed to Ambroise that God was conspiring against him and the Honorable Company.

He stood on the beach, staring out at the wreck of the *Utrecht*. A miracle she had held together as long as she had. It was testament to the Amsterdam shipwrights who had built her and to the strong Baltic oak of her timbers.

Beside him, Schellinger's weather-burned face was twisted into a mask of resentment. Let her sink and be done with it, his expression said. The sailors with them seemed to be of like mind. They were all dark looks and muttering this morning. They just wanted to save their own skins now.

'You should forget about going back out to the ship,' Schellinger said, finally giving voice to what was written plain on his face.

'Forget, how can I forget?' Ambroise said. 'We have a duty to salvage the rest of the Company goods.'

'We have a duty to ourselves first. Look around you. We have eighty *kannen* of water among forty of us. Over on the other island there are another two hundred people with even less than that. If we don't find water soon, we're all dead.'

'Our first duty is to get the Company goods.'

'Who cares about some Mogul's playthings now? We are stranded here at the end of the world. We will be lucky to survive even a few more days. God rot the Company.'

'What did you say?' Ambroise said.

'My men won't sit around on this God-forsaken rock and wait to die.'

Decker joined in, backing his skipper. 'He's right. The men are demanding we take the yawl and find some water, while we still have the strength for it.'

Ambroise pointed a finger at him. 'You will not dictate to me. You should be in irons.'

Schellinger hesitated, then shrugged his shoulders. 'All right,' he said, 'better do as our Commander says.'

'The Commander returns!' someone shouted, and everyone crowded onto the sloping deck, among the tangle of lines and canvas.

Christiaan joined them, watching the yawl battle to make headway against the wind and rising swell.

He prayed for its progress with dread in his heart. He doubted that he was alone in feeling so torn. Those who had snubbed their noses at Death, when they had the commander's fine brandy inside them, were not displaying the same bravado this morning. What would the Commander say when he discovered that the Great Cabin had been looted and despoiled? Their salvations lay with that one small boat, but so did retribution. Perhaps they could blame the destruction on the storm.

He clung to the rail, watching the yawl battling the sea. The wind had picked up again, hurling immense breakers against the hull. The water had risen alarmingly and, desperate as they were, no one would venture into the swirling waters in the holds to plunder the rest of the brandy.

The minutes turned to hours, and his fingers froze around the timbers. The yawl made no headway, no matter how hard the sailors rowed. Finally, he watched them hoist the sails and retreat through the surf.

Well, that was settled then. They were on their own.

'What are you doing?' Ambroise shouted over the wind.

Schellinger shook his head. 'We have to turn back!'

'Your men are not trying!' Ambroise screamed, though he had seen for himself the muscles in their backs and shoulders knotting from the effort. The morning was almost gone, and the rowers had exhausted themselves just holding their position a cannon's shot from the wreck.

'Damn you,' the skipper said. 'We can make no headway in this without sweep oars.'

'Put up the sail!'

'In this wind? We have no room to maneuver. There's reefs either side of us.'

'We have to get to the ship!'

'We can't, damn you.'

Ambroise stared in agony at the wreck of his ship. 'I should never have allowed you to persuade me to leave her,' he said.

His words were lost on the wind.

CHAPTER 28

The seal island

Ambroise had made a thorough scouting of the islands with his eyeglass. Their island, which was home to a colony of seals, was to the north of the wreck. The closest island to the *Utrecht*, where they had landed the people, was no more than an islet of sand, just a few feet above the level of the sea.

There was a longer island on the other side of a fast-running channel. It had shallow limestone cliffs, a few feet high, and there were certain times of day when it took on a strange mushroom-like appearance as if some invisible hand were holding a mirror to it, making it look upside down and twice the size.

When Sara saw it, she announced that the place was bewitched. They had all stared at her in shock, for with her long hair loose and awry and her skin coarse and red from the wind, she was beginning to look much like a witch herself.

There were higher islands on the other side of the lagoon, but Schellinger said because of the wind and currents it would take them most of the day to get there in the yawl. 'The best course is for me and my men to search for water there,' he said, 'for there is none here.'

'We cannot abandon all these people,' Ambroise said.

'We do not abandon them. But water must take precedence over everything else.'

'Very well. But I will come with you. On the way, we will stop at the low island and tell the others what we plan to do.'

Schellinger stared at the sky, sniffing at the air like a wild animal. 'I can smell more weather coming,' he said and slapped his hand against his thigh impatiently. 'We do not have the time for this.'

'I have to explain to them our plans,' Ambroise said, 'so they know they are not abandoned. We cannot just leave them without assuring them of our good intentions.'

'Good intentions? You go back there, that scabrous rabble will steal the yawl for themselves.'

'They would not dare.'

'You planned to put the captain in irons. Do you think you still have his loyalty?'

'I have to take them a barrel of water at least.'

'This is no time for fine scruples. One barrel of water will make no difference to so many. If we do not find good water, and plenty of it, we are all of us dead men and your conscience means nothing to anyone.'

'It is an order.'

Schellinger stepped closer, towering over him. 'You can't give me orders now. We're stuck on an island in the middle of God knows where and I'm your only chance, so don't be so high and mighty with me.'

'Disobeying my order is tantamount to mutiny.'

That word. Schellinger changed tack. 'We shall only be away a day, two at the most.'

'I cannot leave them without explanation.'

Decker came over, the other men standing in anxious knots behind him. Ambroise saw Sara there too, what a sorry sight she looked now.

'What's happening?' Decker said.

'The Commander wants to go over to the island with a barrel of water and get their blessing for our plans,' Schellinger said.

Ambroise saw the look Decker gave him. Two weeks in Hell had sent him over the edge. He would stick me here and now, he thought, if it weren't for Schellinger.

'We need all the water we have,' Decker said. 'Why give it away to those dogs?'

'We can spare one barrel,' Ambroise said.

'See if you think that when your tongue has fur on it like a dead dog.'

Schellinger stepped between them. 'All right, enough. Let's do like he says, Jan. One barrel. He's the commander, after all.'

Ambroise sat alone in the bow, staring at the backs of the sailors as they rowed the yawl across the channel towards the far cay. The precious barrel of water had been placed in the middle of the boat. Decker stared at it as if it were a chest of silver guilders. Perhaps it was more precious than coin now. Where on these forsaken islands would a man spend guilders?

They rowed the whole way in silence, the wind buffeting the little boat, salt spray drenching their coats.

Suddenly, Decker stood up at the tiller and pointed. 'Look at those fools,' he said. Knots of people had gathered on the beach. As they came closer in, some of them started splashing into the shallows towards them. 'They mean to capture us.'

Ambroise could hear their shouts carried on the wind. 'They are just desperate for water.'

'Turn about,' Schellinger said. The men at the oars immediately beached their oars and ran up the sail.

'What are you doing?' Ambroise said.

'Look at those idiots. If they reach the yawl, they'll swamp us.'

'I order you to go to the beach.'

Schellinger shook his head. 'No, it's too dangerous.'

Ambroise hesitated. The waters around the boat were shallow and he could easily wade to the beach. But if he did not stay with Schellinger and Decker, what chance was there that they would return with water, even if they found any?

There was a moment, before the sail took the breeze, when he almost plunged into the shallows and made for the beach. Instead he sat down again by the bow as Schellinger set a course back the way they had come.

He turned around and watched the people's cay disappear into the haze. He stared long after their curses and screams were carried away on the wind, until they were just specks on an angry, grey sea.

CHAPTER 29

Ambroise went down to the beach at first light to find that the yawl had been loaded to her gunwales. Schellinger had told his men they must take all their provisions with them, though the islands they were about to explore were, by Ambroise's reckoning, no more than a few hours' sailing distant.

The mood was sullen. The sailors kept their eyes downcast. Schellinger was shouting orders, supervising the loading of the remaining biscuit and water barrels.

'I did not give the order for this,' Ambroise said.

Schellinger shrugged his shoulders.

'The aim of our expedition is merely to search for water. We should lighten the yawl and leave our provisions here on the beach.'

'If there is a storm, and we are stranded on the islands without food or water, you will thank me for this.'

'You will unload the boat.'

Schellinger shook his head. Ambroise saw Decker touch the knife at his belt.

Finally, he got into the yawl and sat by the bow in fretful silence. He had the fever again this morning. He felt weak with hunger and cold to his bones. As the sailors pushed them out through the shallows, he tried to blow some warmth into his hands.

Perhaps Schellinger is right, he thought. We have to find water first. Once the people are saved, we will set our minds to salvaging the Company's property.

They made slow progress, drifting with the current, the sail furled. Schellinger took his time negotiating the maze of reefs that guarded the higher island from the lagoon. Ambroise slumped in the bows, miserable. Even Sara was silent this morning. She was not as brazen as she had been on the ship and clung to Schellinger's arm at every opportunity.

They drifted past islands thick with bird droppings, their limestone outcrops undercut at their base by the sea. Every channel seemed to be guarded by sand bars and mud flats. They saw a seal basking in the sun. It opened one docile eye and then returned to its slumber.

The islands on the outer reef were no more hospitable than the cays they had left behind. They were just sand and salt bush, inhabited by huge flocks of gulls and cormorants that took to the air and darkened the sky when they passed. Sandpipers and herons waded among the mud shallows. Once, Ambroise saw a huge sea eagle's nest on one of the headlands.

As they came closer to the high island, he saw it was not one island but two. The highest point on both of them was no larger than the dunes at Texel. The southernmost island was larger; perhaps two or three miles long.

Schellinger barked an order to the men at the oars, and they glided through the shallows towards a long beach, as white as any Ambroise had ever seen.

Two of the men jumped out in their bare feet to drag the yawl towards the shore, and immediately one of them howled in pain. He had to be pulled back on board the boat, blood streaming from his foot. Moments afterwards, the other man met the same circumstance. The thick mud was infested with razor sharp shells.

The two men groaned and writhed in the scuppers and Schellinger spat into the water. 'This place is accursed,' he said.

The high island

Almost as soon as they landed, they discovered rain pools among the limestone outcrops, but they were tainted with seawater and proved undrinkable. After this disappointment, Schellinger ordered his men to dig holes at various places on the island, but they found nothing. They spent the whole day searching, though it seemed to Ambroise that no one looked very hard, unwilling to wander out of sight of the yawl. They didn't trust Schellinger and they didn't trust each other.

He saw secret glances between Schellinger and Decker. He noted the new leeboards Schellinger had fitted to their yawl overnight; extra planking fashioned from flotsam. It would make the craft seaworthy if they took her on the ocean.

It seemed to him that Schellinger had already decided on what he would do, and it had nothing to do with finding water for the others stranded on the cay.

That night they gathered around a meagre fire and Schellinger told them all his plan. 'There's no water here,' he said. 'If we stay, we're going to die.'

'One day more of searching,' Ambroise protested. 'It may be all that stands between the people and death. We cannot give up so soon.'

'The weather is getting worse. If there is a storm out there, we may never get away.'

'That could work in our favor,' Ambroise said. 'A tempest may bring rain.'

'Then the people will be saved anyway,' Schellinger said. 'But with just twenty gallons of water left we cannot afford to find out.'

There were murmurs of agreement from the sailors.

'If it rains they will live,' Decker said. 'If it doesn't they will die. It doesn't make sense for us to die with them.'

'You are making too much haste in this,' Ambroise said, hoping for at least one voice of support from the crew. He knew it was a vain hope. Some of these men had been press-ganged into service; the rest were cutthroats whose only loyalty was to themselves.

'We don't owe the soldiers anything,' Sara said. 'Or the passengers.'

Schellinger silenced her with a glance.

'But it's true,' Decker said. 'We all saw how they behaved when we were trying to load the lifeboats. They would have trampled on their own mothers to get to land. Such people don't deserve special treatment.'

'They set about the provost when he tried to guard the water barrels,' someone else said. 'If they have no water left, whose fault is that?'

'I still have a responsibility to them,' Ambroise said.

Schellinger jerked his thumb in the direction of a knot of sailors huddled together for warmth by the beached yawl. 'And I have a responsibility to us.'

'I say we make for the mainland,' Decker said. 'How far are we?'

'No more than forty or fifty miles to the west,' Schellinger said.

So, finally we have the truth from him, Ambroise thought. It was not some unknown sandbank. They were on the Houtman Rocks.

Schellinger went on, 'If we find any water, on the Southland or any island in between, we shall bring it back here for them. We are not abandoning them. On the contrary, we are their only hope of salvation.'

Ambroise shook his head. 'I must have time to think about this.'

'You don't have time to ponder,' Schellinger said. He tossed another twig into the small fire of salt bush. 'May I speak with you privately?'

They walked a little way from the fire, out of earshot of the others. The wind bruised their faces and they battled just to stay on their feet in the gale.

Schellinger leaned in close. 'Would you sacrifice us all so that you can die with an easier mind?' he said.

'My conscience is not at issue.'

'Isn't it? Hard decisions have to be made, Commander. There are some skippers who would leave you here, sail straight for Batavia and report everyone lost.'

'All right, we will go east as far as the Southland,' Ambroise said. 'We will find water there and come back for the people.'

Schellinger clapped Ambroise on the shoulder. 'Good,' he said. 'I knew you'd see it my way in the end.'

The next morning Ambroise woke stiff and cold. A black depression settled on him when he remembered where he was and how he had come to be in this stark and lonely place. He got up, stamping his feet, and made his way down the beach to the yawl.

An hour later they set out. In the grey dawn light, the skeleton of the *Utrecht* was now no more than a speck.

Schellinger shouted commands from the tiller, steering them through the jagged maze of reefs and crouching islands towards the open sea.

I have done all I can, Ambroise told himself. What is there left to do, if others do not have the fortitude to do their duty alongside me?

But deep inside, the voice of his conscience gnawed at him. The screeching of gulls sounded like the jeering of a mob.

CHAPTER 30

The low island

The water barrels had been left unguarded, for there was no water left to preserve. Michiel's lips were cracked and bleeding from thirst and from the wind. He took shelter under a canvas awning and tried to rest to maintain his strength. Most of his men were already too weak from thirst to move.

He watched one of the younger recruits dribble urine into a metal pannikin and hold it to his lips with trembling hands. His Adam's apple bobbed in his throat as he upended the cup. But he couldn't do it. He spat the liquid out and threw the cup away. He collapsed gagging and weeping onto the ground.

Little Bean had crawled halfway to the water's edge, and now lay on the coral beach, already dead, or near enough to it.

There were so many ways for a man to die, Michiel thought. He could drown, or die of thirst or fever or cold. A murderer or mutineer might be broken on a wheel, and a good man might die in battle by inches, with a musket ball in his belly, suffering every bit as much pain as the common criminal.

There never seemed any sense to it in the end, no matter what the pastor said. You took it as it came, and you were a fool to resist, for in the end you had no choice.

Christiaan settled himself in the Commander's carved chair. He ran his hands along the smooth wooden arms and supposed himself a councilor of India and President of the Fleet. It required imagination, of course, with the contents of the commander's chests floating in a slop of seawater. Still, a man could dream.

'You, fetch me some wine! And be quick about it!' he shouted at some imaginary servant who scurried away to do his bidding. He turned to the empty chair beside him. 'Indeed, *Vrouwe* Noorstrandt, I have witnessed many wonders in India and you should quake to see some of the things I have seen.'

He found a half-finished letter in the Commander*'s* meticulous handwriting. It was an inventory of purchases for the ship's provisions from their landing at Table Bay.

'Here, make a copy of this letter, Krueger!' he shouted. A roller crashed into the hull and the great ship shuddered under the impact. Then he remembered Krueger was gone, taken his chance with the others to try to swim to the islands.

He gritted his teeth and wrestled with his fear. I cannot die, he told himself. I cannot. The devil will look after his own.

CHAPTER 31

The low island

Cornelia lay under the canvas, too weak to move. Her throat was parched. Someone had upturned one of the water barrels, crawled inside, and was scraping the slimy bottom with a pannikin for the little moisture there. The sound was maddening.

Down at the water's edge, a child had drunk seawater and was rolling in the shallows, screaming. There was no one with strength enough to go down there and fetch him.

The pastor, unable even to rise to his knees, was gasping hoarse prayers for deliverance. One of his children was wailing. It was a wonder how he still had the strength to cry out.

A body lay bloated on the shore, stinking. The man had drowned trying to swim ashore from the wreck.

Cornelia and the other women had their own tent, if you could call it that; a few bits of canvas tied with rope to crossed spars from the wreck. There were a dozen of them sleeping under blankets on the hard ground. Not that any of them cared about that. The only thing that mattered was water.

A sea bird wheeled overhead, chasing rock crabs across the coral.

'*Vrouwe* Noorstrandt,' a voice said.

She thought she was back in Amsterdam, and her father was calling to her from down the stairs. She was late for her breakfast.

'*Vrouwe* Noorstrandt,' the voice said again. 'I've brought you some water.'

Someone raised her head. She felt a dribble of the precious liquid on her tongue. She sucked the last droplet of moisture from the pannikin, then stared at the face above her. She frowned, trying to remember a name.

'It's Michiel,' he said.

She smacked her lips, savoring the sweetness of water.

'Don't give up,' he said and laid her head back on the ground.

Somewhere off the Great Southland

A gale shrieked from the north-west, sending waves crashing over the bows of their tiny boat and soaking them all. The wind was too fierce for them to carry sail, so Schellinger had pointed her bow seawards, hoping to ride it out.

The sea and sky melded together, the color of lead.

Schellinger seemed unshaken by the ferocity of the storm. He sat at the tiller in the stern, like a marble statue. His face was intent on the waves and keeping their bow to the wind. There was no fear in him at all. Ambroise allowed himself a moment's admiration. He was a pig and a fool, but he had spirit. Even now, after he had run the Company's greatest ship onto a reef, his confidence appeared undiminished.

Some of the sailors started baling with cups and bowls, others with their bare hands. Ambroise joined them, scooping up the seawater with a pannikin. But he was trembling so violently with cold and with sheer terror that he spilled most of the water back into the boat.

There were too many of them in the yawl. No matter how frantically they baled, the bilge kept rising.

'The barrels!' Schellinger shouted over the wind.

'What?'

'We have to lighten the boat. The bread has to go, too. Everything over the side or we're finished!'

The men were too terrified to argue with him. Ambroise watched their precious water drift away on the angry sea.

And then it started to rain, sheets of it, drenching them all to the skin. God's little joke. Ambroise threw away the pannikin and slipped down into the bilges. I shall sleep, he thought, and dream of the drowning sea and wake in the morning to heaven or hell. Let Schellinger fight on if he must. I cannot fight any more.

Christiaan had retreated to the stowage under the bows. The wind hammered at the wreck like a rampaging mob, as breaker after breaker slammed into the hull. It was clear that Schellinger and the commander were not coming back for them. He didn't blame them. It was what he would have done in their position.

Most of his companions had abandoned the ship and struck out for the island. They had gone over the side in ones and twos, clinging to bits of timber and broken spars. Some had disappeared under the grey swell before they were even a musket shot distant. Joost was the last to go, hanging onto a piece of Baltic oak.

The storm outside howled like a coven of devils, ripping the tattered remnants of canvas. It can't end for me like this, Christiaan thought.

The low island

At first, Michiel did not know what it was, the wetness he suddenly felt on his face. He thought it must be sea spray. A larger droplet fell, and he opened his eyes and stared up at the leaden sky, hardly daring to hope. There were more drops. He sat up, cupping his hands and licking at the moisture in his palms. A chill rush of wind followed, and then it started to rain in earnest.

The downpour quickly formed into pools on the coral flagstones. Men and women cried out in amazement all around him. It reminded him of the pictures he had seen in his *kerke* of the Last Judgment, of dead souls rising from their graves. People who, a moment before, had lain motionless in the brush now scrambled to their knees and held their trembling hands to the sky.

He roused himself and started pulling his soldiers to their feet. He had to kick the slower ones into action, ordering them to rig up sail canvas to collect the drenching rain and funnel it into the barrels.

He saw Cornelia crawling through the brush on all fours, seeking out the water pools and lapping up the milky water. The pastor did the same thing. His wife took off her cap and rung it out, squeezing the rainwater into her mouth. Down by the shore, Little Bean stirred. He rolled over onto his back and opened his mouth, gasping at the rain like a beached fish.

CHAPTER 32

The rain had saved them. For now, there was plenty of water for all.

Michiel dispatched his soldiers to form work groups to set about the industry of survival. They built better shelters out of coral slate, brushwood and flotsam. He set the ship's carpenters to work on the beach, while the sailors poled flimsy rafts around the shallows salvaging barrels of salted pork and wine, and pieces of floating timber. They even foraged for pannikins and cook pots washed up in the sand.

Water was not enough; they needed food. The fish that darted through the shallows bit greedily at baited lines, but there was barely a mouthful in each of them.

Michiel sent the sailors out to fish in the deeper channel on their newly constructed rafts. A few hours with a heavy line delivered a huge bag of fish.

The next day, they crossed to a nearby island and bludgeoned some seals they found there. That night they ate well for the first time since they left the Cape of Good Hope.

Over the next few days they organized themselves as best they could. The only other inhabitants of the island were some strange black birds who made their roosts in the sand. They burned off their feathers in the coals of a fire and ate them half raw. They weren't much; just a couple of mouthfuls of stringy, fish-tasting meat, and usually some bits of hard charcoal from the fire stuck to the skin as seasoning, but they tasted like a prince's banquet when you were starving.

There was a kind of tern that nested in the thorn bushes. The meat was inedible but a handful of eggs, if you could get some, could make a breakfast.

How long before the island's population of birds was exhausted, Michiel could only guess. It was enough for now.

Cornelia joined the other women searching for food. She turned over rocks in the shallows, looking for crabs. Hendrika had her skirts up around her knees and was picking oysters off the rocks. Elisabeth found an apronful of tern eggs in an unguarded nest.

Meanwhile, the pastor had regained his strength and was wandering around the island exhorting them all to be steadfast and trust in God. He reminded them that fortitude and sacrifice were the keys to their survival; easy enough for him to say when he and his family had the best shelter on the island.

Day after day, dozens of survivors swam ashore from the wreck. Krueger and Ryckert washed up together, clinging to the same broken spar.

On the fourth day, Michiel saw Cornelia sitting alone under one of the makeshift shelters. She did not look like a fine lady anymore. Her hair was awry and her clothes were salt-stained and tattered. It was only her bearing that set her apart from the other women. He admired her. He supposed that any other woman would have been reduced by enduring such a hideous assault and then shipwreck, but she still carried herself as if she were on her way to a dinner at the Governor's mansion.

'Here, *vrouwe*,' he said, and held out a cup of water.

'What's this?' she said. He saw the other women look over at her, as if they thought she was getting preferential treatment.

'Since the storm we have enough for everyone to have three mugs of water a day,' he said. He turned to the women watching them. 'Go and see the provost if you're thirsty.'

The women jumped to their feet and ran out of the tent, pushing each other to be first.

Michiel shook his head. 'Why do they fight with each other? There's plenty of water now, even if it doesn't rain for weeks.'

'They think the men will steal it all again.'

'I have posted guards on the barrels, so anyone trying to steal water will get a musket ball for their trouble. The provost has a ration book. Everyone will get an equal share from now on.'

'What would we do without you?'

He was not a man accustomed to receiving compliments. 'I'm just doing what they trained me to do,' he said. 'Why weren't you sitting with the others when I came in?'

'Why do you think?'

'Because you live on Heerenstraat? At times like this, it shouldn't matter whether you're a lady or milkmaid. We're all in this together now.'

'Tell them that.'

He held out a handful of dry tack the sailors had salvaged from the ship's barrels. They were a hard biscuit, almost impossible to chew, but like honey cake when you were hungry.

'What do I do with this?' she said.

'Here, look.' He put the biscuit in the mug, tore off a twig from one of the saltbushes and stirred. 'You keep doing this until it dissolves. It will make a kind of thin gruel. It tastes even worse than the porridge the cook on the *Utrecht* served us for breakfast, but it will keep you alive.'

She took the twig from him and did as he had shown her.

'You can even warm it a little.' He found a flat piece of coral slate. 'When it's thickened up, put it on this and slip it into the fire. It's a little easier to get down that way.'

'Why do I get this special treatment?'

'The other women have each other. You don't have anyone.'

'Thank you, but you shouldn't pay me too much attention. People talk, even in this God forsaken place.'

'Well, if people gossip, it can't ever go further than this island,' he said and smiled.

There was a shout from the beach. He looked up. Someone else had made it to the shore from the *Utrecht*. Several of the soldiers splashed into the shallows to fish him out.

Michiel went down to see who it was. It was Stonecutter.

CHAPTER 33

The low island

The day after the wreck, great combers had rolled in from the ocean sending up seething towers of spray on the reef. Today there was just a lace of foam and barely a ruffle of wind. The *Utrecht* had all but disappeared under the water. Each morning there had been less of her above the surface, and today all that could be seen was the top of the stern castle.

Cornelia shivered in the early morning cool, and her nostrils twitched at the scent of smoke from a fire of green twigs. The *jonkers* – those that had survived the wreck - were cooking a tiny fish.

'*Vrouwe.*'

She looked over her shoulder. It was Joost. He did not look quite as grand now; there were salt stains on his coat, and his hair had been bleached by seawater and the sun. He had running blisters on his soft, pale skin.

'I see by your face, you thought I was dead,' he said.

'I am much relieved to find you safe and well.'

'As I you.' He gave her a look that unsettled her. He was not as deferential now they were no longer on the ship.

'Did you swim from the wreck?' she said.

'When she started to sink, I found a loose spar and clung to it, let the current do the rest.'

'God is merciful.'

Joost shrugged, unconvinced on that subject.

Cornelia noticed the coral cuts on his hands. She had thought him perhaps a little soft, like the rest of the boys, but the swim from the wreck would have taken great strength and more than a little resolve.

'I am glad to find you in good spirits,' he said.

'Well, we are alive at least. Some died of thirst. We thought we should all perish before the rain came. It was the Lord's miracle that saved us.'

'If the Lord had made it rain the day before, he could have saved everyone,' Joost said. 'Still, perhaps it was just the sinners that died.'

'The pastor believes it was through the power of prayer.'

'Of course he does.' He held out a small fish. 'This is for you.'

It was about the size of a bait fish and she supposed that once she would have considered a dozen of them adequate for a light breakfast. But now she could not have been more overwhelmed if he had given her a necklace of sapphires.

She stared at him, wondering if it was a trick. 'Why me?'

'Don't you want it?'

She took the small cold fish from his hands.

He looked around, his eyes unfocused. 'This is as desolate a spot as I could ever imagine.'

'The pastor says we must put our faith in God.'

'We have relied on His good graces enough, don't you think? It's probably up to us from now on.' He leaned towards her and gave her a leery smile. 'You're a pretty one and no mistake. Don't worry, I'll look out for you. Enjoy your fish.'

As he wandered back to his friends, his thumbs in his belt, she remembered how he had tormented the Groot girl during the voyage. Was his remarkable survival an act of God or was some other agency involved?

The Great Southland

As they came closer to the shore, Schellinger looked for a place to beach the yawl. Huge ochre-colored cliffs loomed behind a mist of spray, where the great combers smashed against the rocks. But the coast was guarded by honeycombs of reefs and there seemed to be no way through. Ambroise felt his frustration mounting. It was impossible to land here in such heavy surf. It seemed to him that God was laughing at their poor efforts once again.

The next day, the wind veered back to the north-west, and squalls howled in from the ocean. They captured what water they could in their pannikins as the rain dimpled the sea. The red cliffs appeared again briefly under the arc of a rainbow. Once more Schellinger tried for a landing, but could not find a beach, just rocks falling sheer to the waves.

At dusk he turned back out to sea, wary of the wind, keeping the lead swinging for soundings. A sail canvas had been stretched across the bows for shelter, and Sara and the sailors curled in the scuppers beneath it and slept there, exhausted. After a while Ambroise joined them, praying that the next day they would find a harbor and good water, and put an end to this torment.

The low island

The salvaging of the wine barrels from the lagoon had been a mixed blessing. Tonight, the sailors helped themselves to whatever they could find, and there was nothing Michiel or the provost could do about it.

Cornelia lay in her crude shelter, huddled in a threadbare blanket, as the wind whipped at the canvas over her head. The rough laughter of the men frightened her. Never trust a man with a bottle in his hand, she thought. Once he had a little grape in him, he believed he was God and wasn't likely to listen to a sergeant, a provost, or a pastor, not when the grim judges of Batavia were so far away.

A group of drinkers were huddled around a small fire not ten paces from where she lay. She could hear every foul word they said, though she tried to close her ears to it. Like animals, all they talked about was rutting and fighting.

And their stomachs, of course.

One of the men started sobbing. The wine had made him maudlin.

'So much for the great Jacob Schellinger. I will spit in his face if I ever see him again.'

'Shut up! You'd do the same thing in his position.'

'I was ready to swing for him. He said we were all in it together.'

'Keep your mouth shut.'

'Don't tell me to shut up, you're just a clerk. We were his companions to the death; that's what he said. Then he left us all here to rot and sailed away with that fancy commander; the one we were going to throw over the side! Feed him to the sharks, isn't that what the skipper told us? Now look, a bit of trouble and the officers all stick together, just like always.'

Cornelia hardly dared to breathe, straining to catch the words. She could not believe what she was hearing. But then, why should she think it so strange? Men who would do what they did to her would not stop at mutiny.

The speaker's companions were getting agitated, but he was too far gone with wine to be still. 'Fuck the lot of you!' he yelled. 'We're all going to die here. What do I care who knows about it now?'

'Take that fucking bottle out of his hand!' someone said.

'Get away from me, you bastard. You think I'm wrong?'

'The skipper's gone to get help. If anyone can do it, he can.'

'He's not coming back for us. He wouldn't dare go within a hundred miles of Jan Pieterszen Coen. He'll throw the commander over the side and then head for Melaka. I put my neck in the noose for him, and this is what I get. We're all going to die on this God-forsaken place.'

'Just shut up, Ryckert!'

'Fuck you,' Ryckert said and stumbled away.

Cornelia heard the sound of his water on the coral as he relieved himself.

His companions muttered among themselves, and then they moved off towards the beach, leaving Ryckert behind. A while later she heard snoring and decided that it must be Ryckert, fallen over dead drunk.

She lay rigid with fear. What had she heard? Was it just the raving of men with too much wine in their bellies?

If it was true, then they were all doomed. The Commander would not be coming back to save them. Nobody would.

She lay awake through the long night. Every small scuttling of a crab or cry of a bird made her heart leap.

Just before dawn she heard other noises. Something heavy was being dragged across the rocks. It splashed into the water, but she dared not leave the shelter to find out what was going on.

CHAPTER 34

The sea was blue and calm as a lake, lapping around the hull as if it had been drawn for a bath. Christiaan emerged from his sanctuary in the bow on all fours, drenched and shaking. The deck was littered with canvas and rope. The mizzen had snapped and one of the yards swung gently in the morning breeze.

A body had got tangled in her fallen lines. Bloated with gas, it floated alongside a cask of vinegar and a few broken timbers. Only the stern castle remained above the water and each breaker threatened to finally roll her into the deeps.

'Is anyone here?' he shouted. 'It is me, Christiaan! Am I alone?'

Clinging to the windward rail, he climbed along the canted deck as if he were scaling a cliff face. The money chests were still lashed to the mast, unclaimed, a ransom for the fishes.

There was rainwater pooled in a pillow of sail. He cautiously dipped one finger into it and put it to his lips. It was fresh, untainted by the sea. He lapped it up with his tongue. He looked towards the land. The low island looked impossibly far away.

A barrel floated from a gaping hole in the side of the ship and drifted with the current towards the islands. I should take my chances now, while the weather holds, he thought. If I cling to one of those barrels, I might yet save myself. He knew he was a dead man if he didn't.

The low island

Michiel stood outside Cornelia's shelter with a mutton bird in his hand. It was a desperate looking thing, blackened from the fire and with barely a mouthful of flesh on it, but the smell of the roasted meat made her stomach growl. She tried not to stare at it.

'I brought you something to eat,' he said.

She took it from him and started pulling at it with her teeth, sucking every last morsel of meat from the bones and licking the juices from her fingers. If anything, the taste of it only made the hunger worse. She had never known what it was to starve. It set you apart from yourself, made you forget about the way a Christian woman was supposed to behave.

'Thank you,' she said, suddenly ashamed.

He shrugged. 'They make a poor breakfast.' He looked around. 'Are you all right? The men aren't giving you trouble?'

She shook her head.

She was conscious of her appearance. Her dress was just a rag now; the velvet crackled with salt when she touched it. Her fingernails were broken and filthy, and her hair was as stiff as wool. She tried to smooth it down.

'Have you watched the herring gulls on this island?' she said.

He shook his head, puzzled.

'When they do their courting, they bring their lady bits of food. It's a very crude way of showing what a fine bird they are.'

'But of course there is a difference.'

'And what is that?'

'Herring gulls are all the same. They have the same feathers and the same nests. A bird can choose any other bird. Me? I'm a scrubby gull with bad manners and I know my place. Besides, you're a married woman.'

'Joost gave me a fish yesterday. But it was clear he wanted something in exchange for it.'

'Has he been bothering you?'

'Not yet.'

He shrugged and turned to go.

'I heard something last night,' she said. It came out in a rush.

He stopped.

'I heard men talking outside my tent. They did not know I was here, in the dark. They had been drinking and were a little too free with their talk. It sounded to me as if they had been planning a mutiny on the ship before we hit the reef.'

'Dear God. Did you recognize who it was?'

She nodded. 'One of the men was called Ryckert.'

'Yes, I know him. He's the master gunner, second in command on the gundeck. Anyone else?'

'One of them was David Krueger.'

'The clerk? He's just a milksop. Are you sure?'

'I know his voice. That was all I could make out. The wind was blowing.'

'I'd better tell the provost. We'll find Krueger and get the truth out of him.'

There was a shout from the beach.

They went down to the cay and watched three men wade in among the coral shallows towards what looked at first like another piece of flotsam from the wreck. They dragged it from the water and up onto the sand.

But it wasn't wreckage, it was a man. After so long, someone else had been saved. It was a miracle.

'It's the Undermerchant!' someone called out.

'God be praised!' the pastor shouted. 'A gentleman to guard our souls!'

Christiaan lay gasping on the clinker beach, choking water from his mouth and nostrils. His eyes had rolled back in his head, but one of the *jonkers* dribbled some water on his lips and he coughed and sat up.

The pastor raised his hands to heaven. '*Heer* van Sant lives! Everything will be well now, you will see. The good undermerchant has been saved from the wreck. God be thanked!'

That night, Michiel went out with Little Bean to catch mutton birds. It wasn't hard work at night; the light from the torches blinded them, and they fluttered around in panic, like chickens, and were easily caught. While Little Bean held up the lantern, Michiel grabbed them with his bare hands, throttled them, then threw them into a sack.

He took exaggerated care going after them. The ground was not always sure, and if you stumbled on a nest in the darkness you could fall in up to your knees and break your legs.

'So we have a new commander on the island,' Little Bean said. 'I liked it better when you were running things.'

'We are still in the employ of the Company and he is the senior officer. Once he has recovered from his tribulations, we shall have to do as he says.'

Little Bean's shoes crunched on the coral. 'What's he like?' he said.

Michiel shrugged. 'I don't know. There's something funny about him. But the Company doesn't employ fools as senior officers. I suppose he must know what he's doing. How's Stonecutter?'

'He wasn't too good when they pulled him out of the water, but he's still alive. Some men just won't die. God won't let him in heaven and the Devil doesn't want him in Hell.'

Michiel laughed at that. 'I was talking to the Noorstrandt woman this afternoon,' he said. 'She told me something interesting. She said she heard Ryckert and some others talking around the fire last night. Do you know him?'

Little Bean nodded. 'Gerrit's second in command. Face like a walnut.'

'She said he had too much to drink and started blathering over the fire, something about a mutiny.'

'Mutiny? He wouldn't dare. They'll break you on the wheel for that.'

'Only if they catch you.'

They heard a commotion ahead of them, a mutton bird floundering as it tried to escape, its wings caught up in the saltbush. Michiel grabbed it and threw it into the sack with the others.

'So what did Ryckert say?' Little Bean said. 'Did you ask him about it?'

'That's just it. I can't find him. Me and the provost, we searched the island and there was no sign of him.'

'That doesn't sound good.'

'No,' Michiel said. 'It doesn't.'

CHAPTER 35

The Great Southland

Ambroise dropped onto his knees in the sand. His uniform, soaked through in the storms, had dried in the wind and stiffened like tree bark. His mouth was gummy and his throat parched. What he wouldn't give for some of that putrid water from the ship's barrels now.

The vastness of the land chilled his soul. The coastline stretched away into the distance, with not a town, not a village, and not a person or animal to be seen. Schellinger said no white man had ever left his footprints in these sands, as if this was a matter for pride. The Great Southland, everyone said, was quite empty.

But it was not empty. It was full of flies. From the moment they reached the beach, hordes of them descended and would not be denied. They were not like the fat, lazy flies of Holland; they attacked with the gusto of bees, crawling into ears, eyes and noses. They even flew into their mouths, leaving them gagging.

And still there was not a drop of water to be found.

They climbed the sandhills, but all they saw were endless dry plains the color of rust. Dotted about these plains were what they first took to be huts belonging to the local natives, but when they came close up they found they were giant ant nests, hard as timber.

They returned to the beach and Schellinger ordered the sailors to dig holes in the sand. At the bottom of these pits the water was salt as well, and the men spat it out and cursed God.

Suddenly there was a shout from the foot of the limestone cliffs further down the beach. Decker and his men had discovered some pools of fresh water. Ambroise stumbled after the others as they ran down the strand. When he got there, he went at it shoulder to shoulder with the sailors. The water tasted so sweet and cool, he wondered why he had ever in his life thought to drink wine.

They collected eighty *kannen* of water from the pools. It was as much as they had when they left the Houtman Rocks just over a week before. It was not enough for salvation, but it gave them hope.

They sailed north. Once, they saw a party of natives as they came close to the coast. When they landed, they found the ashes of a campfire scattered with the bones of crabs. The ashes were still warm, and the sailors rekindled the fire and toasted the fish they had caught with lines off the reef. There was barely a morsel for each of them; only enough to set their stomachs growling again.

'There is more water somewhere in this vicinity,' Schellinger said. 'Another skipper called Remmessens mentions it in his log...'

'There is no water in this accursed place,' Sara said. 'You'd have more luck getting a fuck in a nunnery.'

The obscenity raised a laugh from the sailors.

My God, look at her, Schellinger thought. It would be embarrassing to show up in Batavia with her still clinging onto him. But as things stood, there was no good reason to go within a hundred miles of the fort. First, they had to make landfall in the Indies, and that was by no means certain. Do that and he reckoned he could navigate safely to Melaka. They would keep the commander alive for insurance, for the time being. Should they come across a Dutch warship and he wasn't with them, they would be hung as deserters.

'We have to find more water, or the people are doomed,' Ambroise said.

'You think there's a single one of that rabble still left alive?'
Schellinger said.

'After the storm they would have water enough to last them for
weeks. '

Schellinger scowled. 'If that's true, what do they need us for? We
should run for Batavia. By my reckoning we could be there in ten
days' sailing if the weather holds.'

'We have a duty to the Company's goods and the people.'

'Where's your sense, man? How should we get back there now? I
cannot sail into the teeth of this wind. We will have to wait here on the
beach for the weather to break and that could take days, perhaps
weeks. No, we head north while we still can.' Schellinger looked
around for support. To a man the others shouted their agreement.

Ambroise looked stricken.

It his conscience troubling him, nothing more, Schellinger thought.
He's glad I'm forcing him into it. He wants to save his own skin as
much as the rest of us.

The low island

Christiaan looked up from the fire, as two shadows emerged from the
darkness and sat down on either side of him; it was Joost and Krueger.
They had with them a bottle of Burgundy they had bullied from the
commander's butler. They passed it to him.

'We trust you are recovered from your ordeal,' Joost said.

Krueger nodded. 'We had quite given you up for dead.'

'I am well, thanks be to God. He would not suffer such an
ignominious end for me.'

'It would appear not,' Joost said.

'What truly grieves my heart is the silver lying out there at the bottom of that reef.'

'Is that why you did not want to leave it,' Krueger said.

'If it were not for Fortuna and that idiot Schellinger, we might be sailing off to a life of ease and riches by now.'

'Well, there are more serious matters to hand,' Joost said.

'You think our present predicament is not serious?'

Krueger stirred the coals of the fire with the tip of his knife. 'Our plans are no longer secret.'

Christiaan had feared this would happen, men being what they were. 'What has happened?'

'That fool Ryckert got himself very nicely drunk,' Krueger said. 'The next thing, he's going about the camp, the wind blowing his tongue about. Everyone knows of the conspiracy now.'

'Damn him to hell.'

'That part is done,' Krueger said. 'A pity we didn't send him there sooner.'

'What kind of special fool would speak of such things, even when they are drunk?'

'It forces our hand,' Krueger said. 'Joost and me, we reckon we should find out who stands with us and kill the rest.'

Christiaan threw back his head and laughed. What bloodthirsty ruffians the Honorable Company were appointing as clerks these days. A man might scarce dictate a letter for fear of being run through with pen and ink. But Krueger was serious. And there was never a doubt about Joost. He had picked him from the first as a sadistic little bastard and one well worth having around.

'What's so amusing?' Krueger said. 'Should we keep this rabble alive to eat our food and drink our water, so that they may betray us to the judges in Batavia one day?'

'I have no quarrel with your reasoning,' Christiaan said.

'The sooner we start culling,' Joost said, 'the longer the rations will last. Those not with us be against us, and they can taste my sword.'

'Except the women,' Krueger said. 'We can impale them on a different kind of weapon.' He laughed at his own joke.

'Let me think about this,' Christiaan said.

'What is there to think about?'

'Look around you, Krueger. There are enough soldiers and Company toadies on this island to defeat us twice over, no matter how much you wish things different.'

'There must be a way!' Krueger said.

Christiaan bade them to silence. Voices raised in the darkness were enough to give any soldier cause to move his hand to his sword. 'We must walk softly here, fellows. Leave it with me. I shall devise a strategy that will see us safe through this.'

Joost nodded. Krueger too, though he was slower to acquiesce.

'Keep your own counsel, both of you,' Christiaan said, 'and do nothing to arouse suspicion. Do you understand?'

'But let us not delay too long,' Krueger said. He took the bottle back from Christiaan and drained it.

'You boys do not seem to suffer overly much from the ration,' Christiaan said.

Joost laughed. He punched the clerk's arm, and they staggered away into the darkness to find their tents and sleep off the effects of their stolen wine.

Christiaan stayed by the fire, thinking. The Lord indeed moved in mysterious ways. He had thought to find the survivors in dire straits. Schellinger had reported to them, on that first day, that they had been beating each other with their fists in an effort to get to the water. But he had found the situation on the island not nearly as hellish as he had believed.

Michiel's soldiers had restored order. There was a guard, day and night, over their Spartan provisions, and the ship's council had even been reconvened to manage affairs. They had worked out a ration, which Salomon diligently recorded in a bound ledger like the good clerk he was.

There had been several rainstorms which had filled the water barrels. More casks of biscuit, wine and salted pork had washed up on the beach or been salvaged from the shallows by the flimsy rafts the carpenters had built from the flotsam.

By a further stroke of good fortune, the main mast had washed in on the same storm that broke the *Utrecht*'s back. It had provided enough canvas and timber for almost everyone to build lean-to tents and shelters.

There was yet a variety of natural food, though Christiaan reckoned it must soon run out. The mutton birds had at first provided a little meat, but these were all gone now. Some of the sailors caught lobster with their bare hands in the shallows, while others took oysters from the reef at low tide, or rigged lines. They pulled in fish from the channel. It was all delicious to eat, but not nearly enough for the two hundred mouths they had to feed.

Krueger was right. They needed to cull.

He made his calculations. He could count on twenty men of like mind; the *jonkers* were with him, according to Joost; and perhaps a handful of Stonecutter's soldiers. The sailors would do anything he wanted, if there was a drink or a woman at the end of it.

He held the passengers of no account. His *jonkers* were aristocrats and VOC officials, well-educated and from good families, while the majority of the passengers were tailors, coopers, carpenters and shopkeepers. They would defer to them as naturally as cattle followed a farmer to the abattoir.

Against this, he counted perhaps a hundred or so who might resist them, mostly armed soldiers still loyal to the Honorable Company. Many were veterans, English or French. They had set themselves apart from the rest. Their orderly tents, neat little fires, and weapons stacked pyramid-fashion were at odds with the amateur muddle of the civilians. They were professionals, accustomed to living rough and fighting hard; dangerous men who would trounce his following of disaffected nobles and malcontent Company timeservers, no matter what Krueger and Joost van der Linden thought.

He had to be rid of them, somehow.

Their task was easier now that the commander had disappeared with Schellinger, for it left him in charge of the council and the people, by rightful authority of the Honorable Company. Anyone who disobeyed him could be charged with mutiny.

Even if Schellinger never reached Batavia, the Governor would send ships to search for them sooner or later. The rich cargo of bullion now sitting at the bottom of the reef guaranteed that. When the rescue ship came, they would overcome it by stealth and take to the high seas.

He consoled himself with the thought that, although things had not turned out quite the way he had planned, they could still be kings one day. It was, in the end, God's will and a man should be humble before the greater design.

CHAPTER 36

The days settled into routine. The pastor preached each morning about good and evil, while the soldiers played *dobbelsteen*. The sound of the provost's voice calling the all's well at night was comforting. All anyone talked of was rescue, each calculating how many days it might take a ship to return for them.

Michiel had built a larger shelter for the women and placed a guard outside. Cornelia was accepted there, though grudgingly. Some resented her. Others felt intimidated by her presence among them.

Tonight, she sat in a corner and watched them huddled together around a dull lantern, speaking in whispers. Neeltje de Groot's baby was crying. The child had been born on the ship a few days out of the Cape, and he had not stopped fussing since his first breath. Neeltje fretted over him constantly. He would not thrive, and she feared aloud that she would lose him.

She offered the infant her breast, but he squirmed and would not settle. It had been going on all night and none of them had slept.

Finally, Cornelia went over. 'Perhaps I can help,' she said.

They all gave her a look.

'He has the colics,' one of them said.

'If Neeltje can't do anything, what makes you think you can?' another said. 'She's three of her own. How many children have you nursed?'

'I am not saying that I have any knowledge of these things,' Cornelia said. 'But the undermerchant may have a potion that will help. They say he was once an apothecary in Haarlem.'

'Apothecaries don't know how to help a woman with things like this,' Neeltje said.

'It wouldn't harm to ask him.'

Neeltje shrugged. 'All right, then. Like you say, what harm could it do?'

Cornelia gathered her skirts and ducked out of the door of the shelter.

Hendrika called after her and followed her outside. '*Vrouwe*,' she whispered. 'If you will speak with the undermerchant, perhaps you might also speak with him about the rumors.'

'What rumors?'

'About Ryckert.'

'What did you hear?'

'That there are *muyters* among us here on the island. A few of us are frightened something bad may happen to the undermerchant unless he is warned.'

'All right, I will speak to him.'

Hendrika gave her a wan smile. 'Thank you.'

Well, one of the women still trusted her, Cornelia thought. That was some consolation, at least.

Christiaan seemed to have regained his strength. The warmth of his smile when he saw her was a welcome surprise. He was a man of many moods and she had not known quite what to expect.

'Cornelia!'

'*Heer* Undermerchant.'

'I was so relieved to hear that you survived our disaster. You look radiant, despite our privations.'

'We all thank God that He has seen you safely delivered from the wreck. We thought you had perished.'

'It was incumbent on me to be the last to leave the vessel. I hoped somehow to protect the Company goods, but it was not to be.' He indicated the silver ewer set upon a driftwood table in the corner of his shelter. 'A glass of wine, perhaps?'

She shook her head. He poured himself a generous draught into a pewter cup. She frowned. Michiel had ordered that both wine and water be severely rationed.

'I need your help,' she said.

'I am at your service as always.'

'One of the women, Neeltje Groot, has an infant with her. He sickens. They say you were once an apothecary. I thought that perhaps you...'

'I regret that all my books and herbs are out there on the reef. I am sorry, *vrouwe*.'

She hesitated. 'There is something else I need to discuss with you. Something happened before you were saved from the wreck. Perhaps the provost has already told you of it.'

He frowned. 'You should tell me yourself.'

'It is to do with the gunner's mate, Ryckert. I heard him talking very loudly outside my shelter one night. He said that there was a plan to murder the commander before our ship was wrecked on the reef. The next day he disappeared.'

'A drunken fool. He most probably drowned.'

'Or perhaps what he said was true and he was murdered for it.'

'You think there may be *muyters* here on the island?'

'Of course.'

'I see.' He turned away and looked out to sea, thinking this over. 'Did he mention any names?'

'David Krueger.'

'Krueger? The clerk? Why would a clerk get involved in a mutiny? Did he intend to stab the commander with his quill?'

'I am only telling you what I heard. Ryckert also seemed convinced that we would not see Schellinger or Ambroise again.'

'Oh, I am sure they will be back.'

'How can you be sure? How can any of us?'

He turned around. 'I shall look into this, Cornelia. Trust me, while I live no harm will come to you.'

'That is not why I came here, *Heer* Undermerchant. If there are *muyters*, there could be danger to you.'

'To me?' He seemed surprised, but then he gave her a broad smile. 'Thank you for telling me all this. I shall take precautions.'

The Great Southland

Decker fingered the knife in his belt. Come on, you bastard, he thought. Once you sent me to Hell. Four days I rotted and screamed down in that box in the hold. Now it's your turn for Hell, and you'll be there for eternity.

Come on. Just go over that sandhill there, a little way from the others. I'll stick you with my knife, throw some sand over you and we'll be done with it. The skipper won't spend more than a few hours looking for you. They'll think you've wandered off looking for water and got lost and nothing to be done about it.

Ambroise stopped, hands on his hips, and looked around. Something had alarmed him. He turned around and headed back the other way.

Decker scowled. God's bones. He had been so close.

CHAPTER 37

It was excellent weather for plotters. The wind would carry away every word. The Beardman jug was passed around, hand to hand, as Christiaan and his chosen few sat around a fire of crackling brushwood. 'There are too many soldiers who stand against us,' he said. 'We have to get them off the island to change the odds back in our favor.'

Eyes glittered in the firelight.

'How do we do it?' Joost said.

Christiaan turned to Rees. 'You went over to the long island today?'

Rees nodded. 'We caught and skinned a seal. They're as trusting as lambs. It's as easy as clubbing your grandmother as she sits in her rocker.'

'What is it like over there?'

'A piece of rock with nothing on it but birds and bushes, just like here. You cut your feet to ribbons on the coral, and there's not a drop of moisture to be had but your own sweat and piss.'

'Good. What I propose is that you take some of Joost's fine boys and go back over there. I will tell everyone you are looking for water. When you return you announce that you found a soak with plenty for everyone. I will send the captain over there with all our empty barrels and tell them they have the task of filling them. I will keep behind Stonecutter and a few others he selects. Then we will leave them there and let nature do our culling for us.'

Joost nodded, impressed. The undermerchant knew what he was about, to be certain. 'So, once we are rid of the soldiers, no one can stand against us. We shall have the rule of law and the arms to enforce it.'

'Then we can set about ordering affairs more to our liking,' Christiaan said. 'Food for our bellies, water enough for everyone and women as you please.'

This last thought sent a thrill through all of them. They could finally stand as real men, do what they wished, do what they had always dreamed.

They would be kings!

Michiel found the provost on the beach supervising the loading of the empty water and wine barrels onto one of the rafts. 'What's going on?' he said.

'The undermerchant wants you to go over to the long island to collect water. He said some of the *jonkers* have scouted over there and say there's plenty for everyone. You're to take all these empty barrels and bring them back full.' The provost forced a tight smile. 'See if you can find some more wine while you're at it. I could do with a proper drink.'

'You're not coming with us?'

The provost rested a hand on the hilt of his sword. 'The undermerchant wants me and Stonecutter here to help him keep an eye on things.'

Michiel grunted. It sounded like hard work, but it was better than sitting around staring at the sea.

'The undermerchant says you can take your knives and some axes to chop wood but to leave all your muskets and swords here.'

Michiel shook his head. He didn't like the sound of that. 'I don't see why we have to leave our weapons behind. We're not soldiers without them.'

'The undermerchant's orders. Company rules, he says. You don't need them for collecting water, and he's worried the Englishers will start fighting with the Frenchies the minute you're out of his sight.'

'They got on well enough before. The three months they were on the ship, there was never any trouble.'

The provost shrugged. 'It's what he says. You can't go against the Company.'

'How many men should I take?'

'He wants Stonecutter to stay here with a dozen men, and you go over there with the rest.'

'Stonecutter! I wouldn't trust that bastard with the family cow! I want him with me where I can keep an eye on him.'

'That's the undermerchant's orders.'

Michiel turned and walked away.

Christiaan was in conference with the *jonkers* and didn't look pleased at being interrupted. He and Joost looked at Michiel like he was a stray dog who had wandered into their lean-to.

'Captain van Texel,' Christiaan said. 'What can we do for you?'

'The provost says you have ordered me to the long island,' Michiel said.

'Is there a problem?'

'Send Stonecutter in my place. I need to stay here and make sure there is order.'

'That is the provost's job. You are under my command, captain. It's Company rules.'

'Stonecutter is unreliable. It's not a good idea.'

'Are you questioning my orders?'

'I'm trying to save you trouble.'

'Do I smell mutiny here, captain?'

'I am telling you it is not wise, *Heer* Undermerchant.'

'You do know what the High and Mighty Seventeen in Amsterdam thinks of *muyters*, don't you? We may be far from Holland right now, but Dutch law still applies.'

Michiel looked into their faces and knew there was nothing he could do.

Cornelia saw him striding towards her along the beach. She had never seen him looking so angry. 'Is something wrong?' she said.

'I do not think I altogether trust our new commander.' As soon as he said it, he seemed to regret it. 'I am sorry, *vrouwe*. I should not say such things. He is a Company official and I'm just a captain.'

'Yet I felt safer when you were in charge of things. What is happening?'

'Joost says there is water on the long island. Me and my men are going over there to fill the barrels.'

'Don't be away too long.'

As he walked away, he stumbled on the shale. She had never seen him take a misstep before.

CHAPTER 38

The weather had turned foul again. They were back to grey skies and thunder. A huge surf was running out on the reef, and the high island to the west had disappeared behind a veil of mist.

Cornelia sat alone, staring at the march of wavelets on the clinker shore and the gulls with their heads turned towards the wind.

She was angry at Ambroise. How could he and Schellinger abandon them like this? Christiaan seemed to have no care for anyone but himself. He had the most elaborate of all the shelters on the island, built with a spar washed up from the wreck and an acre of canvas sheet. He had even requisitioned, for his own use, the great carpet that had once graced the floor of the Council Room.

Meanwhile, the sick and wounded lay in sparse shelters, open to the wind and the rain.

And he had still done nothing about David Krueger. Why did he hesitate?

Suddenly, she heard the sound of a child's laughter. She came out of her shelter and saw Maria Groot running among the bushes, picking the tiny white flowers that blossomed in this southern winter. They were strange blooms, for instead of petals they had long white threads like a tassel.

The only pretty thing that grows here, she thought. Children were so accepting of everything. Even stranded at the end of the earth, they could still find a game to play or something to interest them, like hunting for little crabs under the rocks or chasing the gulls on the clinker beach.

She saw Neeltje walking with Elisabeth Post. A group of *jonkers* were watching them. David Krueger was with them. Neeltje saw them and called Maria back to her. She took her hand and gripped it, tight.

As they went by, Joost snatched the flowers out of the little girl's hand. Maria turned around to retrieve them, but he hid them behind his back, grinning at her. Neeltje pulled her away.

Krueger called after them, 'How are these cold nights, Elisabeth? Shall I come and keep you warm tonight?'

Cornelia could not believe it. Was that really what he had said? Enough was enough. She had been an obedient daughter and a dutiful wife all her life, but what was taking place on the island was beyond all Christian behavior. It was time for someone to remind Christiaan van Sant of his duties and responsibilities.

When Cornelia walked in to Christiaan's shelter, the pastor was with him pontificating on how the godless behavior on the ship had brought this catastrophe upon them. Krueger and Stonecutter were there too, looking bored.

'I warned the Commander,' the pastor was saying, 'but he refused to listen to me. Now the Lord has shown his displeasure for the unholy ways some people lived their lives on the *Utrecht*.'

Christiaan looked irritated but his face brightened when he saw Cornelia. '*Vrouwe*,' he said. 'What a pleasant surprise. What can I do for you?'

'*Heer* Undermerchant, may I speak with you privately?'

He gave her a winning smile. 'You are among friends. I am sure these gentlemen should like to be privy to everything you say.'

Stonecutter leered at her.

'It is about the sick,' she said.

'What about them?'

'They need better care. Look at this shelter you have built yourself here. They should be housed here. It is certainly large enough. Do you not see the conditions they are left in, right there next to the beach?'

'I shall certainly pray for them,' he said, and smiled at the pastor.

'You would do better to bring them in here.'

'I am sure our undermerchant knows best how to manage our limited resources,' the pastor said.

She stared at him. 'They are in need of our help. Does not the Good Book say so?'

'Do not lecture me on the Book!'

'If you know it so well, then you should live by its words and not merely quote it to everyone for your own ends!'

There was an appalled silence.

'The lady has spirit,' Krueger said.

'The sick need more water,' she said.

Stonecutter shook his head. 'You might as well pour it in the sand as give it to a dying man.'

'I shall speak to the provost about it,' Christiaan said, easily. 'Now leave us. I have other business to attend to.'

'I insist you take proper care of them.'

'I insist you leave us now.' He advanced on her.

She stood her ground to show she was not afraid of him, but when she finally walked out she was shaking.

She went to the provost's tent to get her water ration from Salomon, who marked her name off in his ledger. She carried it down to the beach.

One of the soldiers, a man named Richard Merrell, lay untended under a sheet of torn canvas, a grubby bandage around his left arm.

His face was hot with fever. He had broken his arm on the night of the wreck, and now the open wound had become infected.

She held her water jug to his lips.

His eyes opened briefly and he smiled. 'Thank you,' he said. 'Will the captain be back soon?'

The long island

The beach was no wider than the gallery on the *Utrecht*. Beyond it, the island was just scrub. It was bigger than the low island, perhaps a mile long.

Michiel stumbled, cursing, through the shallows. They had been forced to leave on their buckled shoes, or the coral would have cut their feet to pieces.

He and the soldiers unloaded the empty barrels and stacked them on the beach.

Rees watched them. He had a feather in his hat now and was strutting around like he was a general.

'It doesn't look like much to me,' Michiel said, scanning the rocks.

'Not here,' Rees said, 'but the other end of the island is a water garden. You'll see.'

Michiel and Little Bean exchanged a look.

'There is a lake at the south end of the island,' Rees went on. 'You'll have to walk along the beach. There is no place to land down there.'

'It will be hard work with the barrels,' Michiel said.

'That's a soldier's life,' Rees said and laughed. 'When the barrels are all full, make a fire. When I see your smoke I'll come back and get you.'

'You're not staying with us?'

'The undermerchant ordered me to go back and fetch some of the others. He wants us to explore the other islands.'

Michiel frowned. Christiaan hadn't said anything to him about that. He didn't enjoy Rees's company overmuch, but he didn't like being stranded here, even for a few hours. Still, if those were their orders, there was nothing he could do about it.

Rees waded back through the shallows to the raft. 'See you in a few hours,' he said.

'What if they don't come back for us,' Little Bean said.

'Of course they'll come back for us,' Michiel said. 'They need the water.'

CHAPTER 39

The low island

On board the *Utrecht*, the ship's affairs had been decided by the ship's council; Ambroise and Schellinger headed it, assisted by Christiaan, Decker, the provost and the pastor. At Christiaan's request, the provost had reconvened the council, replacing Schellinger and Decker with the two VOC clerks, Krueger and Salomon. Christiaan had assumed his place at the head of the council.

It was not one of the grand affairs that had taken place in the state room of the *Utrecht*, with its great mahogany table laden with silver ewers of wine. Today the five men had to squat in the sand outside Christiaan's tent. The people were allowed to listen to their deliberations, but none had a voice save the councilors themselves.

The pastor arrived for the meeting in his long black coat, with his Bible in his right hand. Christiaan imagined a gaggle of men just like him sitting in judgment on Torrentius and ordering him to be put to the question. Their little minds were shut off to the higher ideals of God. They claimed to do the works of the Lord, but they were better suited to clerking.

Smiling, he called the council to order and got straight down to business. The island, he said, was too crowded for them all to survive together in harmony. He had decided it was time to spread their community among the islands.

He waited as they muttered to each other like fishwives on the wharf. Some of the people wouldn't like it, he knew that. They had already fallen into a routine and were comfortable even with their spartan accommodations and scant provisions.

'Is this necessary?' the provost asked.

'Hygiene is bad here,' Christiaan said. 'We have to fetch food and firewood from the other islands. It makes good sense to separate our communities in order to better husband our resources.'

'What do you intend?' the pastor said.

'The provost here will take the rest of the crew to the seal island and take care of them there.'

'But that is more than sixty men,' the provost said.

'The seal island is a bigger island and it has more food.'

The pastor nodded. 'I think it's a good plan,' he said, with an oily smile in Christiaan's direction. 'It has my full support.'

Christiaan returned the smile.

Only the provost seemed unconvinced. But what can he do, Christiaan thought. He cannot go against my authority. 'Furthermore,' he said, 'I have heard reports of bloodshed before I came to the island.' There was a deadly silence. He looked around the group. 'Is this true?'

'There was indeed some lawlessness,' the pastor agreed.

'I have therefore decided that all weapons are to be surrendered and lodged with me, in the chest in my tent. That way there can be no repeat of unchristian behavior.'

A few of those soldiers who had not gone with the captain to the long island glanced nervously at each other. Even the pastor looked shaken at such a radical step.

'Does the council agree?'

There was almost a full show of hands. Christiaan stared at the provost and finally his hand went up as well.

'Good. We shall institute these changes immediately. Be assured, that when the commander returns he shall find us hearty and hale. He shall scarce believe his eyes when he sees us established here as if we are back in Amsterdam. Now, let us ask the pastor to lead us in prayer.'

North of the Southland

Men lay in the bottom of the yawl, sprawled across each other like corpses on a battlefield. Some were delirious, with festering salt sores on their legs. One of the sailors had gone mad after drinking a cupful of seawater. They had been forced to bind him and throw him in the bilge, where he lay raving and frothing at the mouth.

Ambroise made an effort to maintain the dignity afforded him by his office. He had somehow contrived to retain his black felt commander's hat, even through the wild gales they had encountered after leaving the islands. Though his lace edged collar was crusted with salt and grey with wear, it set him apart from the common sailors.

Decker stirred, his eyes bleary with exhaustion. 'Where are we, skipper?'

Schellinger sat at the tiller, his features set like rock against the spray and wind. It seemed to Ambroise that he was almost inhuman in what he could endure. 'We'll sight land soon,' he grunted.

'You said that yesterday,' someone grumbled, 'and the day before.'

Schellinger snorted in derision to show what he thought of a common sailor's opinions.

'It's a week since we left the Southland,' someone else said.

'You don't know where we are, do you?' It was Messeker, one of the understeersmen.

'I shit on your head,' Schellinger said.

'If you hadn't been so busy covering that little tart,' Messeker said, nodding at Sara, who was snoring like a pig at the skipper's knees, 'we'd still be on the *Utrecht*.'

She didn't look like a girl worth risking so much for now, Ambroise thought, slumped in bilge like an old saddlebag from a horse.

Schellinger's cheeks flushed scarlet.

'Can't say you weren't warned,' Messeker said. 'You wouldn't listen.'

Schellinger drew his knife. 'Maybe the fish will listen to you, idiot.'

'We should let the skipper do his job,' Ambroise said evenly, and all eyes turned to him. He looked around. 'Can anyone else here find our way safely to Batavia?'

That quietened them. Messeker grumbled, but he shut up. There was a mumbled acknowledgment from everyone else that the skipper was, indeed, their only hope on this vast empty sea. The dangerous moment passed.

Schellinger put the knife back into his belt.

Ambroise caught his eye and received an almost imperceptible nod of the head in acknowledgment; all he would ever get by way of thanks from a man like him. But for the first time in nine months of voyage, perhaps they were on the same side.

The long island

The wind rushed over the surface of the lagoon, raising ripples on the water. A seagull, its feathers ruffled by the southerly wind, strutted along the shore, leaving arrowhead prints in the salt crust. Twenty paces distant, a seal lay in the long grass watching Michiel with a velvet eye.

So this was Rees's water garden; one salt depression of stagnant water fringed with moss and reeds.

They had searched for two days. At first Michiel thought that if a pair of idiots like Rees and van der Linden had found water, then it must be running in streams a mile wide. But there was nothing. They had covered every inch of the island and found no wells and no soaks. It was no more than a spit of sand, coral and stunted bushes, a mile long and a cannonball's shot wide at its widest part. It was as dry and barren as the cay from where they had come.

He joined the others on the beach and threw himself down, exhausted and thirsty.

'That fucking *jonker* never found any water,' Little Bean said. 'What was he playing at?'

'Never trust a Dutchman,' one of the Frenchies said and spat in the sand.

'I wouldn't do that,' Little Bean said. 'You might need that spit later.'

'The undermerchant said we're running out of water over there,' one of the Englishers said. 'If we go back empty handed we've got some real problems. What's going on?'

Michiel said nothing, though he suspected he knew very well what was going on. He felt an oily stirring of fear in his belly. 'We better light a fire and get those bastards back here to get us,' he said. 'We stay here much longer, we're going to die of thirst ourselves.'

He watched them light their fire but he didn't want to tell them that it was useless. Rees wasn't coming back for them. He stared across the channel towards the Houtman Rocks. After all the things he had seen men do in war, he still found it hard to credit what they would do in peace.

The low island

Christiaan stared at the skein of smoke above the long island. He put down his eyeglass and smiled. So, they were panicking already. Tonight, over the fire, he would raise a toast to those brave boys, with their blackened tongues and parched throats, who gave their lives so others might live. It was a heroic achievement.

He and Rees would drink to that.

The strips of bandage Arentson had put on Richard Merrell's arm were stinking. A jagged end of bone had broken the skin. The surgeon had tried to reset it, but the limb was still crooked. Merrell's face was flushed with fever, his eyes unnaturally bright.

Cornelia and Hendrika had made new bandages from strips of cloth they had plundered from Company goods. Cornelia washed away the sticky yellow fluid oozing from the purple swelling and wrapped the arm as best she could, while Hendrika dipped a rag in a bowl of cool seawater and tried to cool Merrell's forehead.

It stank in the sick tent. Well, if you could call it a tent, Cornelia thought. It was just a piece of canvas, open on two sides to the weather, roughly supported with broken spars and timber. A dozen or so men lay inside on thin blankets, with flies crawling over them. Some of them were sick with the flux, others still had injuries from the night of the wreck. Arentson had done what he could, but he had lost his instruments and his medicines to the sea. Even if he still had them, Cornelia supposed there wasn't much he could do.

Merrell opened his eyes. 'Thank you,' he whispered. 'Thank you both.'

'Are you in much pain?' Hendrika said.

He shook his head, but Cornelia knew it was a lie.

'Is the captain still not returned?' he said.

After a while, he started raving in his Englander language. There was little more they could do for him. They left him to go and nurse the others. There was a little boy whose leg had shattered when he fell into the yawl the night they abandoned the ship; and a sailor whose foot had become infected from a coral cut. It had swollen to the size of a cannonball.

'Perhaps Joost will help us,' Hendrika said.

'Really?'

'He likes me.'

Cornelia wondered at her innocence.

'We should go to him and ask him to give us bandages and water. He is friendly with the undermerchant. He may persuade him to be more open-hearted with the sick.'

'I suppose we can try,' Cornelia said.

They found Joost dicing and drinking on the beach, even though it was still morning. He was with his usual crowd of toadies. Stonecutter and Rees were there as well. He looked up as they approached,

'May we talk with you?' Hendrika said.

He got to his feet and made an elaborate bow with a sweep of his hat, for the benefit of his friends. 'At your service,' he said.

'We need your help.'

'Of course, anything for such beautiful ladies. What is it you want?'

'*Maistre* Arentson needs more bandages for the sick.'

'What for? They're all going to die anyway.'

'A few strips of cloth is all I need.'

'You wish me to steal from the Company? *Heer* Undermerchant would not like that.'

'The undermerchant has acres of cloth in the chests in his tent,' Cornelia said.

'How do you know that?'

'I saw it with my own eyes.'

Joost looked at his fellows and made a face. They laughed along with him. 'Some silk to wrap the pus in? Is that what you want?'

'Please,' Hendrika said. 'And brandy.'

'What?'

'Just a little. To help them sleep and clean the wounds.'

Joost gave an astonished laugh. 'I might have to take it out of my own ration.'

'You'll just have to drink more wine!' Stonecutter said and the others roared again.

Joost stretched out a hand and stroked her hair. It did not seem like affection to Cornelia, but rather a statement of ownership. 'I'll see what I can do for you, pretty one.'

'Thank you,' Hendrika said, with as much dignity as she could muster, and she and Cornelia went back to the sick tent.

Sara sat in the stern of the yawl, leaning against Schellinger. He had one hand on the tiller, the other arm around her shoulders. He was like a mountain, she thought. The rest of them lay around the boat, their lips bleeding and their skin burned and peeling, looking half dead. Not her man.

'What happens when we get to Batavia?' she said.

'What do you mean, what happens?'

'To me.'

'I'll look after you don't worry. You won't go short.'

'I don't want money. I want to be married.'

'I can't marry you. I told you, I have a wife.'

'I'm going to have a baby.

He didn't even draw breath. 'Get rid of it,' he said. 'I have enough brats at home. The harbor in Batavia is deep and wide. There's a whole orphanage at the bottom of it.'

She sat up. She couldn't believe what she was hearing. 'Forget about your wife. You've got me now.'

He glanced down at her. 'Look at you. You wouldn't get a jump in a whorehouse looking like that. Who do you think you are?'

He said it so casually, she thought her ears were playing tricks. 'But you said-'

'A man says a lot of things when he has some gin inside him. You shouldn't pay so much attention.'

She sat back and stared at him. So this was how it was going to be. Well she had a few cards up her sleeve, too. 'You should be careful how you talk to me. I know a lot about you and your friends that you wouldn't want the Governor to know.'

'What are you talking about?'

'You know what I'm saying.'

'You tell the Governor what you did, you'll hang with the rest of us.'

'Oh, they won't hang you Jacob. Not for rape and mutiny. That would be a kindness. You know what they'll do to you.' The look on his face frightened her, but she wasn't about to back down, not now.

'You betray me,' he said, 'and you betray yourself.'

She opened her eyes wide. 'But Governor, the skipper came to me and said he wanted to talk to my mistress, so I called to her in her cabin. I didn't know those men were hiding there. The skipper didn't tell me what they were planning.'

'You wouldn't dare.'

'I was shocked, I was, Governor.'

He looked frightened. She didn't think she would ever see the day when Jacob Schellinger looked scared of anything. 'I want five hundred guilders.'

'Five hundred guilders. Are you mad?'

'I'll need that money for me and the baby if I don't have a good husband to take care of me.'

He looked away and sighed. 'I'll see what I can do. Coen will have to put me in charge of the ship that searches for the *Utrecht,* and there'll be reward money. I'll take care of you.'

'Good,' she said.

CHAPTER 40

Ambroise woke, dreaming of water. He had lost all track of time. How long had they been at sea, he wondered, days, weeks? Or was it months?

The crew hardly moved from their positions now. Only Schellinger was up to the task. He sat there at the stern, one hand on the tiller, never seeming to sleep or despair.

Ambroise saw something lying in the bilge and picked it up. It was a necklace, made with cheap and gaudy glass beads. He looked at Schellinger. 'Where's the maid?' he said.

'You're awake, are you commander? You missed all the fun.'

He couldn't see the skipper's face. The sun was rising over the ocean behind his shoulder, and he had to shield his eyes. 'Fun?'

'She was trying to drink the sea water and she fell in.'

Ambroise was thirsty and exhausted, and he couldn't seem to think straight. 'Where is she?'

'I told you, she's gone. Happened last night. I tried to grab her, but she went in and the currents here are too strong. She was a fathom distant before I knew it.'

'I heard nothing,' Ambroise said.

'Well, it all happened so fast. Sad. But once you start drinking seawater it's the end anyway. Probably for the best.'

'I thought you were enamored of her. You do not seem in the slightest affected.'

'Enamored? That's a grand word, commander. Fond is a better one. But not so fond as I would have jumped in after her.'

Ambroise looked around. The rest of the men were asleep, or pretending to be. He knew he should protest. But what good would that do? There was a more pressing question. Would he be next?

Christiaan had called an emergency meeting of the new island council. Cornelia was among the spectators. She had heard the women talking about it. They all said there was going to be trouble.

The night before, one of Stonecutter's soldiers, who had been assigned to guard the wine barrels, had himself tapped off some wine and then given some to his fellow guard. The idiots had drunk themselves into a stupor and passed out on the spot. They were discovered snoring like lords the next morning.

Christiaan kept the council waiting in the sun for almost an hour before he finally appeared. He had on a fresh lace collar, pilfered from the private clothes chest that the commander had sent ashore. He also wore a white felt hat with a gold chain around its brim; another trophy from the commander's personal possessions. Beside the rest of them, in their salt-stiff clothes, he looked utterly ridiculous. Cornelia would have laughed if the look on his face had not so disturbed her.

She had rarely seen him without his empty, benign smile, but this morning he looked agitated. His eyes were unnaturally bright and his expression was quite at odds with his dandy clothes.

He did not sit down, but paced the sand outside his shelter, hands on hips, glaring at them all. Only Krueger did not seem perturbed by his manner.

'Well,' he said at last. 'You all know why I have called the council together.'

'*Heer* Undermerchant,' the provost said, with an ingratiating smile, 'please, take your ease and we will discuss the matter.'

Christiaan ignored him. 'These two men have flagrantly defied the laws which I have set for our own survival here. They are worthy of death without grace and without delay.'

The councilors stared at each other, horrified. The onlookers fell to frozen silence.

The provost shook his head. 'I agree that the soldier Jean Monfort has indeed violated the law and should be punished. But the other, Abraham of Delft, is clearly simple in the head and was led into it by his fellow. It was only a little wine.'

'I will not be defied in this!' Christiaan shouted.

There was an appalled silence.

The provost tried again. 'We do not defy you, *Heer* Undermerchant. But a decision such as this is surely the responsibility of the whole council. You are talking of two men's lives.'

'If you allow these fellows to steal our rations without punishment, what hope have we to survive until rescue comes?'

'Just a flogging perhaps,' the provost said. 'No more than that.'

'You will vote that they both be put to death!' Christiaan's face was set like stone.

Salomon and the pastor murmured to each other, clearly panicked by what was happening. Krueger did not join in their deliberations. He sat back, his mind on the matter apparently made up.

'I demand the punishment of death for Abraham of Delft and Jean Monfort, soldiers in the employ of the Company,' Christiaan said. 'What say you?'

Only Krueger raised his hand.

'How can you let this happen?' Christiaan shouted at the other three men. 'Well, soon enough, you will have cause to regret it!'

He stormed off. Krueger jumped to his feet and hurried after him. Everyone else sat in stunned silence as a sense of foreboding settled over them.

Later that day, Cornelia found Salomon slumped on the beach. He was alone and his long face seemed more troubled than usual. His fingers coiled and uncoiled around each other like bloodless worms.

He got to his feet when he saw her and bowed. '*Vrouwe*,' he said.

'What's going on, Salomon?'

'The council has been dismissed. *Heer* Undermerchant has replaced me with Joost van der Linden and the provost's place has gone to Stonecutter.'

'That clod? On the council?'

He nodded.

'The provost has allowed this?'

He shrugged. 'What can he do? Captain van Texel and his soldiers aren't here. There's nothing he can do about this until they get back.'

'They should have been back days ago. Michiel said it would take them just a few hours to fill the wine barrels. Where is the provost now?'

'He has taken those the undermerchant selected over to the seal island. I think even he's scared.'

She sat down. He squatted down beside her, at a respectful distance.

'It was only a matter of time, anyway,' he said.

'What do you mean by that?'

'There are things going on here most of the people don't know.'

'What things?'

Salomon picked up a piece of coral and tossed it into the shallows. 'Do you know how much wine we have, *vrouwe*, how much water?'

She shook her head.

'Neither does anyone else, except for the undermerchant. But I can tell you this: we have more than he says.'

'He is lying to us?'

'It was his wine the soldiers stole.'

'So that was why he was so angry?'

'I don't know. Perhaps he was just pretending.'

'But why?' she said.

Have you been to his tent these last days?'

She shook her head.

'Only a favored few are allowed entrance. He does not want anyone to see how he lives. He has claimed the commander's great carved chair, which they salvaged from the wreck, together with one of his Persian carpets. He also has the commander's silver candlesticks and his ink pots. Anything of value goes to him now.'

'Well I suppose he is our most senior official.'

'But why should he need such luxuries here?'

'Have you spoken to anyone about this?'

'Just the pastor. When he confronted the undermerchant about it, he went into a rage.'

A shadow fell along the beach. Christiaan was watching them. 'Salomon,' he called out. 'Shouldn't you be helping Krueger with his work?'

Salomon jumped to his feet.

Cornelia looked at Christiaan. He had his back to the sun and she had to shield her eyes against the glare. He was smiling. He looked so different from the man that morning at the Council.

'All these clerks want to do is sit around all day doing nothing,' he said. 'Idle hands make mischief, do they not?'

South west of Banten, Java

The sky was the color of pewter and the sea flat as oil. It was Schellinger who saw it first. There was *steenkros* floating in the water - seaweed torn from the rocks.

'You see, man?' he jeered at Messeker. 'Eight days since we left the Southland coast. What did I tell you?'

Their first glimpse of land was a mountain that at first they mistook for cloud. Slowly, a green cape came into view behind a veil of drifting rain. In front of it lay an island, guarded by a reef. They saw a village but kept sailing, not trusting that the inhabitants would be docile. It might be within the kingdom of the Matarams, with whom the VOC were at war.

They anchored off the coast, under a quarter moon, sweltering and gasping for water. The gales and freezing winds of the Houtman Rocks were a distant memory now. Two men lay unmoving in the bilge, black tongues protruding from their mouths. The madman had died during the night and had been pitched over the side for the shark fish.

Schellinger sat by the tiller next to Ambroise, sipping his meagre ration of water. It was too hot to sleep.

Ambroise listened to the slap of gentle waves against the hull and the snores of the sailors. Schellinger leaned over to him and put his lips close to his ear. 'What happens when we get to Batavia?'

'We must find a ship that can take us back to the site of the wreck as soon as it is possible to sail.'

'I mean between you and me.'

'What are you saying?'

'What will you say to the Governor about what happened on the *Utrecht*?'

Ambroise took his time. He knew his life depended on his answer. 'I would have to tell him how you saved all our lives and somehow navigated this skiff to the Indies, against all odds.'

'Will you tell him it was my fault she came upon the rocks?'

'You will have to answer to Coen about the wrecking of the *Utrecht*. I know nothing of nautical matters so that is beyond my judgment.'

'What about Table Bay?'

'I find my memory is short these days. I can remember no further than this past week. It must be due to the privations I have suffered.'

'And Jan?'

'You mean the attack on *Vrouwe* Noorstrandt? That is not so easily forgotten. Your bosun will have to answer for what he did.'

'Because, you know, I think he will try and say that I was somehow involved in it. That I knew. He has threatened me so.'

'Why would he say that?'

'To bring me down with him. Out of spite.'

'Have you anything to answer for? Because there is nothing I can do if you are guilty of such a terrible crime.'

'I swear to God and on my immortal soul, I am innocent of any wrongdoing.'

Ambroise thought it through. As much as he hated Schellinger, he needed him to back up his version of events when they came face to face with Coen. Besides, no other skipper in the Indies would be able to find the way back to the wreck, and if he didn't salvage the Company's silver his career would be over.

'Let me tell you something, man to man,' Ambroise said. 'We are both in a situation here. You have lost the ship and I have responsibility for the treasure on it, so the Governor will be asking us both some hard questions. We could help each other out.'

'That is what I think also.'

'I have to admit it, Jacob, for all our differences in the past, you have proved yourself to me these last days. I cannot think of any other man who I would trust to find the *Utrecht* and rescue the silver.'

It was the first time Ambroise had called him by his first name and Schellinger smiled. 'I'm glad you see it that way.'

Ambroise smiled back and bundled his jacket against the thwart so that he could rest his head there. In moments he was asleep.

Schellinger watched him sleep. He was relieved they had reached an understanding. It seemed that, after all that happened, the wind still blew fair for Jacob Schellinger. If the weather came from the south in the morning, he would sail to Melaka, as they had planned that night in the steerage. When they got there, he would let Decker do for this doughy bag of wind, with his blade.

But if the wind came from the north, or they came upon a Company ship in the straits, he would accept the Commander's plaudits in front of Governor Coen and then go back for the *Utrecht* and rescue the people from the Houtman Rocks.

He stared at Decker, asleep under the canvas by the prow. He was like an old dog; faithful in his way, but when he got past his years of usefulness you had to remember he was only a dog.

The warm offshore breeze carried with it the smell of overripe fruit and corruption. He waited on the weather to decide all their fates.

CHAPTER 41

The low island

Christiaan appeared, unannounced, in the women's tent. The shelter had been set aside from the others, as was proper, but he walked straight in as if he had right of entry.

Cornelia wondered what their Commander would say if he saw Christiaan now, strutting around like a peacock in Ambroise's own crimson braided jacket and ruffed white shirt. And the gold medallion; where had that come from?

'My lady,' he said to her and gave her a look, head to foot, as if she was a dock front whore and he was inspecting his purchase. 'You have everything you need here?'

'Everything,' she said. 'Sand flies, constant thirst, not a moment's privacy. What else should we ask for?'

'I am endeavoring to put such hardships behind you. Just a little patience and I am sure I can vouchsafe your future comforts. I wish you to know that I have placed you under my personal protection.'

'From what?'

He ignored the question. 'It is cramped,' he said, looking around as if the tent was lodgings in a tavern, and he was about to demand of the landlord a better room.

'I should prefer a bed with down pillows and a fire in the hearth.'

'You should not be sleeping with these other women.'

'Surely you would not have me sleeping with the soldiers?'

'I shall try to improve on these arrangements.'

'We all suffer, *Heer* Undermerchant. I count myself lucky to be alive.'

'You can trust me,' he said. He turned to go.

'What has happened to Captain van Texel and his men?' she said.

He looked back. 'Is that your concern?'

'It is all of our concern, is it not? They went to the long island to find water for us.'

'They are still looking, I suppose.'

'We have all seen the fires they have lit.'

'To keep themselves warm at night.'

'The provost told me they were signal fires; that they wished to return.'

'The provost isn't here,' he said and went out.

After he had gone, she saw the other women looking at her.

'So you are to get favored treatment again,' one of them said.

Neeltje was nursing her baby. She shook her head. 'I don't think what the undermerchant has in mind is the sort of favorable treatment any of us would want. I'm sorry to say it to you, *vrouwe*, but it's true.'

Banten, Java

They stumbled through the shallows and fell on their knees, kissing the black sand as if it were the wife they had left behind in Holland. Those who had been to the Indies, and knew its secrets, attacked fallen coconuts with their knives, tipping back their heads and gulping the sweet juice down their parched throats.

Ambroise heard Schellinger shouting. He had found a waterfall. They all ran like children into the jungle after him, tearing off their clothes and throwing themselves into the cold, clean water. They drank until their bellies were distended.

Ambroise lay on his back in the shade of the ferns. He heard the other men around him. Some were weeping, others were praying.

'A good northerly breeze has brought us home,' Schellinger shouted and they all cheered.

Ambroise laughed along with the rest, then he helped them fill their water casks and drag them back to the boat. He went back into the undergrowth and unhitched his breeches for the simple pleasure of answering nature's call, for the first time in a month without other men watching.

Decker watched Ambroise head down the jungle path. He had not believed that a soft bastard like him would survive in the boat so long. He was such a sickly little man with his fevers and his pale skin. Just goes to show, he thought. The skipper said he was a weakling, but the skipper wasn't right about everything. If he was, they wouldn't have all ended up here. But now he had saved them, it was time for a man to think about his own skin.

He had kept his eyes on the commander all through that morning, waiting for this chance. He drew his knife and followed him into the forest.

He looked over his shoulder. There was no one watching. The undergrowth was green and clicking with insects. A man just had to take a few strides and he became invisible, with only the distant shimmer of the water to show the way back to the beach.

And there it was, through the leaves, the Commander's lily-white backside. Drinking all that water had given him the squirts, him and a few others by the sounds of it.

Suddenly, Decker felt a hand go across his mouth and his arm was twisted up behind him. The knife dropped with a soft thud onto the damp earth.

Ambroise stumbled to his feet, his face pale with shock.

Schellinger grinned at him over Decker's shoulder. 'Now didn't I tell you to watch yourself when you were away from our little ship, Commander?'

They sailed past Prinsen Island and saw the glow of the Krakatoa volcano, to the north, turning the sky orange over an oily dusk. As soon as they entered the Sunda strait, the wind eased off, and for two days they drifted with the current.

At *Dwers in den Wegh* they found a breeze that took them past endless beaches and palm trees. It dropped away at sunset and the tide took them back the way they had come. Schellinger ordered them all to the oars and they fought the sea by the light of a half moon.

The next day, they dropped anchor by the Topper's Hat. The men slumped over their oars, exhausted, their backs roasting in the fierce sun, while they prayed for a breeze.

It was sunset when they saw sails astern, the topmasts just visible behind the palm trees. Schellinger dropped a kedge anchor in the lee of the island to wait for the ship to come up.

'We're saved,' Ambroise said.

'Maybe,' Schellinger said.

'What do you mean?'

'Could be pirates, which will be bad luck for us, because then we're all dead men.'

'After we have survived so much? God could not be so cruel.'

'Couldn't he? Then you've got a different god to mine,' Schellinger said and laughed.

CHAPTER 42

The low island

Ever since the soldiers had left, a stillness had settled over their little colony. The weapons the soldiers had surrendered before their departure had not been placed under guard, as Christiaan had promised, but had instead been redistributed among the *jonkers* and Stonecutter's favorites.

The two men who had been found guilty of stealing the wine had mysteriously vanished, like Ryckert. No one knew what had happened to them. People had started talking in nervous whispers and they all started at the cries of gulls.

With half the people now on the seal island, the cay seemed almost deserted. Every day Cornelia saw a skein of smoke rise into the air from the long island, but no one set out on the rafts to fetch Michiel and his men. Instead, the *jonkers* and Stonecutter's bully boys practiced on the beach with their new weapons, and drank wine from Christiaan's private barrels.

Cornelia spent more and more time with Hendrika, helping Arentson in the sick tent. One evening, right on dusk, she went down to the beach to fetch another bowl of seawater for the fever rags. When she looked up, she was surprised to see no one else in view. It was a rare thing to find yourself alone for even a moment, and she stood there with the wind on her face and closed her eyes.

She heard the crunch of boots on the rocks. She took a deep breath, ready to scream.

'Don't be alarmed,' Salomon said, speaking so low she could hardly hear him over the wind. 'I don't want any of those *jonkers* and their bumflies to see me over here.'

She stared at him, wondering what to make of this. He looked grim and nervous. He produced a knife from under his cloak.

'One more step and I'll scream for the soldiers,' she said.

'No, it's for you,' he said.

'What do you mean?'

'There's things going on here you don't know about.'

'What things?'

Some men appeared further down the beach. It was Stonecutter and Rees.

Salomon laid the knife among the rocks. 'Take it,' he said. 'Don't let them see it.' Then he turned and walked away without another word.

The sun dipped below a grey sea. The wind was colder tonight and from somewhere she heard a piper scream plaintively in the shallows.

The Sunda Strait

The ship arrowed towards them from the lee of the island. They jumped to their feet, waving desperately, almost overturning the yawl in their excitement.

Ambroise spared a glance at Decker, trussed like a hog in the bow. He had never seen such hate in a man's eyes. But that was the way of it, he told himself. If it weren't for Schellinger, he'd be lying in some shallow grave in the jungle with his throat cut.

The ship had the Company flag at its masthead. It was the *Zandaam*, by God. What about that for fortune? Schellinger had promised him they would come up with the rest of the fleet in more northerly latitudes. He couldn't have ever imagined the circumstances in which they would do it.

Sailors lined the deck of the *Zandaam*, staring down at them in astonishment. Ambroise was welcomed aboard by the ship's commander and hustled swiftly below. Cryn Raemburch was a Councilor of India, of the same rank as Ambroise, yet Ambroise felt like a beggar being presented to a lord.

Raemburch was wearing a starched ruff, and his hair and beard were neatly trimmed. He had a gold medallion gleaming at his breast. Ambroise's hair was stiff with salt, and the stitching was rotting away on his clothes. He was wasted almost to a skeleton and he stank. The felt hat he had so carefully preserved through his month's ordeal seemed only to add to his dejection.

'What has happened to you?' Raemburch said when they were alone in his cabin.

Ambroise looked around. The *Zandaam* was not as grand as the ship he had lost, but the cabin was not unlike. There was a Bible on the table, a linen towel draped across the bunk, and Raemburch's oak chests were stowed in the corner; the symbols of his rank.

A butler placed a glass of Burgundy before him.

He started to tell his story. It was the same tale he had rehearsed in his head so many times for Governor Coen: *I did my duty by the people and the Company goods in the only way possible. I never once thought of my own personal salvation.*

But he was unable to finish. He choked on the words and started to shake.

CHAPTER 43

The low island

Elisabeth Post was shivering in the corner of the women's tent, her knees hugged to her chest. One of the other women had her arms around her, trying to comfort her. Neeltje Groot was rocking her baby, who was still fussing, perhaps sensing his mother's agitation. A single guttering candle was the only light.

'What was that noise?' someone said.

They listened.

'I didn't hear anything,' Cornelia whispered.

'Maybe just a gull or a mutton bird,' Neeltje said.

'There it is again!'

They all heard it this time; a human cry quickly carried away on the wind. It had come from the other side of the island. They fell silent, but the only sound was the rush of the wind and the whipping of loose canvas.

The pastor was again on his knees, asking the Lord to intercede. Cornelia wished that he would take the authority the Lord had given him and make something of it here on the island, instead of waiting for God to do everything Himself.

She stood by, until he had finished his prayers and was dusting the grey sand from his breeches.

'What is it, *vrouwe*?' he said.

'Did you sleep well?'

She knew from the moment's hesitation that he knew what she was talking about.

'As a man does when he is blessed in the Lord.'

'You did not hear the scream then?'

'What scream?' he said but would not meet her eyes. 'You heard a gull perhaps.'

'It wasn't a gull, father.'

'A bad dream.'

'All of us women heard it.'

'You were mistaken. Now please, I have things to do.' He walked away.

Cornelia tallied the faces that morning with the list of survivors that she kept in her head; Salomon was there, and the cabin boy, Strootman. But where was the surgeon? He should have been in the sick tent. She asked for him among the soldiers, but her questions were met with indifference or with hard, cold stares.

He was not with the carpenters working on the beach, or the men fishing in the shallows. She even looked in on Christiaan and his council, smoking their clay pipes and passing around the wine bottle inside Joost's tent.

She walked to the far end of the island. She saw something on the coral and bent down to examine it. It was blood, thick gobs of it, congealed like rich brown pudding on the stone. There were fresh marks in the scrub, as if something had been dragged through the bushes to the water.

If it was a mutton bird they had heard, then it was the biggest one God had ever made.

A shadow fell across the sun. She looked around. It was Rees. She shuddered.

'What are you doing here, *vrouwe*?'

'I was looking for *maistre* Arentson.'

'What do you want with him? He's gone over to the seal island with the provost and the rest.'

'Why would he do that? He's needed here with the sick.'

Rees took a step closer. 'You shouldn't be out here on your own, this far from the women's tent, not a lady in your position.'

'What have you done with Arentson?'

'Go on, get away from here.'

She turned and walked away. Who could she tell about this? Not the pastor, who had his head in the sand or in the Bible. Michiel was not here and the provost was on the other side of the channel.

There was only one man who could keep the rule of law.

It was the first time Cornelia had stepped inside Christiaan's tent since she had come to warn him about Ryckert. She saw for herself that the rumors she had heard were true; Christiaan fancied himself as a lord among them now. Compared to their sad colony of hovels, his quarters were as grand as a palace. There was a Persian rug on the ground under her feet. It was stiff with salt, but as arresting here as if it were in a Mogul's seraglio. There were silver candlesticks on the driftwood table, which was laid with a cloth of Italian lace, and pewter dishes filled with painted lobster. One of the commander's fine tapestries kept out the winds.

Christiaan's bed was covered with purple brocade.

He seemed delighted to see her, as if this were an unexpected social call from an old friend. He sent Krueger scurrying outside and invited her to sit on the stool the carpenters had made for him. It was covered with red velvet.

'Some wine,' he said taking a silver ewer from the table.

She shook her head.

He looked disappointed but poured a cup for himself. She noticed there was a new ruby ring sparkling on his finger where before there had been garnet. Shipwreck suited him well.

'What is wrong, *vrouwe*? You look pale. You are not sick?'

She shook her head.

'You slept well?'

'What is going on, *Heer* Undermerchant?'

He seemed puzzled.

'What happened to *maistre* Arentson?'

'Who?'

'Our surgeon.'

'Ah, that one.' His face took on a pained expression. 'Such unpleasantness. I am sorry you had to learn of it. I don't know why men behave the way they do.'

She waited for his explanation, one without all the beard tugging and sorry looks.

'What happened to him?' she repeated.

'I am sorry to inform you that we discovered that he was a thief. He has been stealing Company goods. As commander here, I was forced to deal with him for the safety of all. Don't worry,' he added and put his hand on her shoulder. 'I won't let anything happen to you.'

She jerked away.

'I was forced to discipline him. I had no choice in the matter.'

'You murdered him?'

'It would not be murder, should I order it. You forget, I am the Company's senior representative here on this island, and I have the power to punish men with their lives should it be necessary. But to answer your question, Arentson is yet alive.'

'I found blood on the rocks.'

'I sent Joost and Krueger to search his possessions and retrieve what he had stolen. He resisted.' He took a sip of wine and studied her over the rim of the pewter cup. 'After he was subdued, I sent him to the seal island to the care of the provost.'

'Why were we not told of this?'

He stopped smiling. 'I did not know there was a woman on the Council. When did you need to be informed of these affairs?'

'I am not speaking of myself. The pastor also knows nothing of it.'

'I am commander here, not the pastor, nor any of those other shopkeepers.' The smile insinuated itself once more on his face. 'It is for the best of all,' he said.

'Did Stonecutter murder him?'

'Stonecutter is a soldier in the employ of the Honorable Company,' he said evenly. 'I told you what happened. The surgeon is on the seal island, where the provost can keep an eye on him.'

He could be persuasive, and for a moment she imagined her terrible allegation might actually be unfounded. Perhaps she was going mad. Since that night on the *Utrecht,* she could not trust her own thoughts anymore. She imagined violators everywhere. But the blood on the coral was real enough.

'There is no need to be afraid,' Christiaan said. 'You can trust me, Cornelia. No one will harm you.'

He knelt down beside her and put his hand on her knee.

Krueger was waiting for her outside. He leered when he saw her. 'He has his eyes on you, that one,' he said.

'I am a married woman.'

'In Batavia you are. But Batavia's a long way away.'

'Remember your place!'

Krueger thrust his face close to hers. He had breath like a bear, and the smell of him was more intimidating even than his physical size. 'None of us has a place anymore. We are all just sand birds now.'

She found Salomon and asked him who had been sent to the seal island. The provost and his family, he told her, just as the undermerchant had said. He had been told to keep order there. The rest were mainly crew, though Christiaan had kept the coopers and carpenters here with him. If the surgeon had been sent over there, it was the first Salomon had heard of it.

Later that day, all of Cornelia's possessions were brought from the women's tent, without her knowledge or consent, and carried to what had previously been the provost's private shelter. When she saw what was happening and protested, she was pushed aside and told it was the undermerchant's orders.

She looked around her new quarters in bewilderment. There was a driftwood table and a bed of salvaged timber, made by the carpenters on the beach. The bed was adorned with fine silks and velvet cushions, plundered from Company goods. Christiaan had even had one of the tailors make her a new dress; royal blue velvet bordered with gold *passementerie*. It was laid out on the bed, ready for her to put on, as if she were going to attend a dinner at the royal palace in Amsterdam. There was a silver ewer filled with fresh water. It would have been commonplace in Leleistraat, but here on this parched little island, it might as well have been the Holy Grail.

'Do you approve?'

She turned around. Christiaan was standing in the doorway, smiling at her with great satisfaction.

'What is this?' she said.

'You are a fine lady, accustomed to the finer things. I don't want to see you suffer. Those other women, what would they know?'

'Why are you doing this?'

'For your own protection. Did I not tell you so? You are a beautiful woman, alone among all these rough types, sailors and such. I would be failing in my duty if I did not do all I could to ensure your safety.'

She closed her eyes, remembering that night on the ship. She could still smell those men and feel the calloused hand clamped around her mouth, choking her. She hadn't been safe then, how could she be any safer here?

'I liked it well enough with the other women,' she said.

'You deserve better company than them,' he said. 'I'll give you time to settle in. Don't worry, I shall be back to check on you as often as I can.' He gave her an unctuous smile.

After he had gone, she felt for the knife hidden in the folds of her dress. The point pierced her finger and the sharp pain reassured her. She wondered if she would be able to use it.

It seemed unthinkable.

CHAPTER 44

Batavia Fort

Ambroise stood on the poop of the *Zandaam,* staring at the green slopes of Gunung Gedeh. He felt his gorge rise and swallowed back the acid taste of his own fear. When he saw the grim walls of Batavia's fortress, he had to lean on the rail to keep his legs from collapsing under him.

They were met in the harbor by a painter from the shore, and he scrambled down the cleats to board her. *Heer* Raemburch and his officers followed. Brown-backed natives bent to the oars and rowed them past the other Indiamen in the harbor towards the forbidding walls of the castle.

The cannons on the battlements were pointed away from the sea, towards the thick green jungle. The castle was under siege by the Sultan of Mataram. The soldiers they had left on the reef had been headed here to help fight this war. Another Company asset richly squandered; he knew that's what Governor Coen would say.

They passed through the entrance to the *Waterpoort,* gliding along the canal that divided the fortress from the town. They sailed by a guardhouse and merchant's houses with white Dutch gables and tree shaded courtyards. He picked out the godowns, the arsenal, the armory and the *kerke,* as he remembered them from his previous visits. They reached the landing steps just on sunset.

Darkness fell quickly, as it did in the tropics.

Native slaves led the way inside with torches. He saw several corpses swinging from the gibbets, and the stink of them stayed in his nostrils long after he entered the castle.

The low island

'Salomon,' Christiaan said. 'We need to talk.' He enjoyed the look of terror on the younger man's face. He watched the blood drain from his cheeks. The little Jew could not keep a secret if his life depended on it - which in many ways, it did.

He sat down on the stool Salomon had fashioned for himself outside his lean-to. It was a piece of driftwood balanced on two thick coral slabs.

'Sit down,' he said.

Salomon hesitated, then dropped obediently onto his haunches on the hard ground.

Christiaan stared at him, and was gratified by the effect his silence had on the poor boy. His hands started to shake. He looked as if he were about to cry.

'Give it to me,' Christiaan said.

Salomon contrived to look puzzled, but did a poor job of it. 'What is it you want, *Heer* Undermerchant?'

'You know what I want.'

'But I don't.'

'Do you want me to ask David Krueger and Stonecutter to get it from you? They will not ask you quite so courteously. Krueger has never liked you. You know that.'

'The commander said that...'

'The commander is not here. I am the senior VOC man now and I am responsible for all Company goods. Should anything befall them, I will be the one they blame, not you, so I think it is better that you hand the casket over to me for my safekeeping.'

Salomon got to his feet, but he was so frightened, he could barely stand. He went inside his lean-to and came out a few moments later holding a carved wooden casket. He handed it to Christiaan.

'The key,' Christiaan said and held out his hand.

Salomon reached into his coat and gave it to him. Christiaan put it into his pocket.

'There is something else. Don't play games with me, Salomon.'

Salomon hesitated then went back inside a second time and reappeared holding a small wooden crate, no larger than a wine flagon.

Christiaan took it from him and stood up. He shook his head as if he had just received bad news. 'I don't know,' he said.

'*Heer* Undermerchant?'

'I don't know if I can use you or not. You are not trustworthy.' Appearing fretful, he walked away, leaving Salomon to sleepless nights and troubled, fearful days.

Batavia Fort

Ambroise sat at the window of the Governor's apartments, with Raemburch beside him, holding a glass of fine French brandy. He watched the lighters scurry like water beetles between the shore and the Indiamen anchored in the gage roads. The unfinished gateway of the castle lay directly below, a painful reminder of his failure. Much of the great portal that the Amsterdam stonemasons had fashioned for that gate now lay under the waves beating around the Houtman Rocks.

Gossip about the disaster had travelled quickly around the tiny colony. Old friends, who had welcomed him with elaborate sympathy that first night, now treated him with a great deal more circumspection. They did not snub him, exactly, but he understood they were waiting to see what Governor Coen would make of his actions, before they declared themselves his friends.

He spent every hour of this waiting in an agony of self-examination. He still had fever, and this had now been compounded by the flux. He could not digest the rich foods and wines they offered him, after so many weeks living on plain water and hard biscuit. His cheeks were hollow, his vitality gone. He looked in a mirror and saw a yellowish skeleton, grotesque in its borrowed finery.

He did not want others to know how sick he really was. Although he dreaded the prospect of another long sea voyage, his abiding fear was that Coen would not grant him command of the rescue ship that would return for the *Utrecht*.

He had to get back to the Houtman Rocks. Every night since their rescue by the *Zandaam*, he had lain sleepless in his bed, asking himself the same question over and over: *Could I have done things differently?*

'By the way, Ambroise,' Raemburch said, breaking the silence. 'I believe there was a certain lady named Cornelia Noorstrandt among the passengers on the *Utrecht*.'

Ambroise felt a dull ache in his chest at the mention of her name. 'Indeed.'

'Did she survive the wreck?'

'I saw her myself onto the lifeboat,' he said. That was not strictly true, he supposed. He tried not to let Raemburch see how his enquiry had disturbed him. There was not a moment he did not think about her, or any of the passengers, without suffocating guilt. 'She was on her way here to join her husband,' he added.

'Such irony.'

'I beg your pardon?'

'He's dead. I made enquiries for you. He died of the fevers, two months back, while you were on the way from Table Bay.'

CHAPTER 45

Governor Jan Pieterszen Coen regarded Ambroise from an immense carved chair. He was grim and straight backed, as if posing for an official portrait. He looked resplendent in his ceremonial ruff, and a thick chain of gold nestled against a doublet of black velvet. A dark tapestry hung on the wall behind him.

Coen was a legend in the Company. A man of pious disposition and rigid discipline, he had a reputation as a ruthless administrator. His dark eyes examined Ambroise with an unbending gaze.

'So,' he said, 'you have lost the ship and left the people.'

Ambroise couldn't breathe. The blistering judgment had been delivered before he had been allowed to utter a word in his own defense. 'The wrecking of the ship was by no account a fault of mine,' he stammered.

'You took a sighting from instruments?'

'Indeed, Governor, on the island where we...'

'What was it?'

'The last position, the day before the disaster, was at thirty degrees on a heading north by east.'

'The Houtman Rocks are at twenty-eight and a third degrees, of which all skippers were warned in the directive you received from me before you left Amsterdam. Is that not correct?'

'I warned the skipper.'

'Warned him?'

'I took issue with him. He was of a mind that we were still six hundred miles from the Great Southland. I had been sick and...'

Coen dismissed this quibbling with a wave of his hand. 'We have established that the *Utrecht* is lost to us. What of the other Company goods, with which you were entrusted?'

'I was unable to salvage the chests. They are still on board the ship.'

'You left the ship without first salvaging the money?'

'I meant only to restore order among the passengers on the land. But then the wind came up and I was unable to...'

'And the jewels?'

'Those are in the care of my assistant, Salomon du Chesne.'

Coen toyed with the heavy ruby ring on his first finger. His face might have been carved out of granite. 'I see.'

'By your leave, I beg that I be given a fast yacht so that I can return as soon as possible to the wreck... to the people stranded there, so that I...'

'Ah, yes, the people.'

'I fear for those left there.'

'As you should.'

Ambroise wanted to say, but how you describe it is not at all how it happened. I had my reasons for doing as I did. But Coen's gaze stilled him.

'You know that your first duty was to secure the Company goods?'

'It was not my intention to leave them. And afterwards I made every attempt to retrieve them.'

'What possessed you to abandon the people without government?'

'After the wrecking of the ship I did not trust the skipper, Jacob Schellinger, to return as he promised, so I...'

'You trusted him to navigate you onto the Houtman Rocks.'

Ambroise gripped the edge of the great desk. The dark tapestries and the candles in their silver holders seemed to spin around him. Exhaustion, sleeplessness, fever and flux had wasted him. He felt as if he was coming apart. He took a moment to compose himself.

'There is the matter of the attack on the woman,' Ambroise said.

'Ah yes, *that*. You had many untoward adventures on the *Utrecht*, didn't you, Commander?'

'None of my doing.'

'So you say.' Coen examined the documents in front of him. 'Your high boatswain, Jan Decker, shall be put to the question. We shall discover the truth of your allegation against him. Are you all right, Commander?'

'By your leave, I feel unwell.'

'I dare say your adventures have exhausted you. They would have exhausted anyone. Let us hope they do not also bankrupt the Company. We shall enquire more thoroughly into this matter. In the meantime, we shall do our best to make you as comfortable as possible. You should get some rest.'

Ambroise was escorted out of the room.

The long island

It had rained twice while Michiel and his men were on the long island, but the fall was only enough to put a few inches in the bottom of the water barrels. Their situation was desperate. They had given up trying to get the attention of Rees and the others on the low island. It was clear no one was coming for them.

Little Bean wondered if a pestilence had broken out among them. Michiel said perhaps, but privately he knew what Christiaan and the rest of those bastards had done. We shall have to look to our own salvation now, he thought. An island this size, there must be water somewhere.

He watched the sun sink low over the ocean. The colors on the shoreline faded to grey and the dead coral on the beach looked like piles of small bones. The mutton birds headed back with the sunset, circling overhead and making their strange moaning cry, like lost souls.

Birds have to drink, he thought, same as a man does. Where do they get their water?

One of them swooped down and disappeared into a hole at the rim of the limestone ledge. He stood up and went after it. He noticed a gap in the rock, not much bigger than a man's fist.

He scrabbled at it with his fingers, pushing away the crumbling coral slabs, and finally made a gap large enough to put his arm through. The bird came screeching out, and as it did he heard the soft plop of a loose rock dropping into water.

A mutton bird had just saved their lives.

Batavia Fort

Schellinger looks so sure of himself, Ambroise thought, striding in here in his sea boots and clean white linen shirt. He was a colossus of a man. The way he towered over Governor Coen seemed almost disrespectful.

Coen's cold and deep-set eyes studied Schellinger warily, like a man weighing the prospects of taming a large and unfriendly dog.

Schellinger nodded and winked at Ambroise, who was seated just behind Coen, at last relieved of the Governor's forbidding gaze.

Coen came directly to the point. 'My preliminary investigations into the wrecking of the *Utrecht* are complete,' he said. 'I have recommended to the Council that your conduct and seamanship should be more thoroughly investigated.'

A muscle rippled in Schellinger's jaw.

'Do you realize the size of the loss the Company has taken due to your negligence?'

'When we return, we will salvage the Company's goods. You have my word on it.'

'You will not be part of the salvage mission. Commander van Himst is returning on the *Zandaam*, and that ship already has a skipper.'

Schellinger stared at Coen in astonishment. 'That mongrel couldn't find the way to his own privy in broad daylight!' he shouted.

For a moment, Ambroise thought he was about to slam his fist on the Governor's desk. But then he thought better of it.

'I'm the only skipper in the whole Company who could find that wreck again. You ask the commander about my powers of navigation.' He looked up, waiting for Ambroise to repeat the promise of full support he had made in the yawl.

'I have already questioned Commander van Himst at some length about your conduct on the voyage from Holland. He has given me a full report on a certain incident that occurred in Table Bay, and this has been corroborated by the skipper of the *Zandaam*. The Commander has also given me a full account of how you corrupted the morals of the ship with your relationship with *Vrouwe* Noorstrandt's maid.'

Ambroise was glad he was seated behind the Governor, and there were soldiers at hand around the room armed with cutlasses and pikes.

The look on Schellinger's face was terrifying. If they were anywhere else, the skipper would have gone for his throat. Schellinger's hands bunched into fists at his side and a vein bulged at his temple.

Did he really believe me to be such a fool? Ambroise thought. Did he think that I rose to this high office by being utterly without guile? I know what he planned for me after the wreck. It is a miracle I am still alive.

My miracle and his ill fortune.

'We have put the high boatswain to the question,' the Governor went on. 'He has confessed to us that he, Stephanus Ryckert and a soldier he knows only as Stonecutter perpetrated the ungodly attack on *Vrouwe* Noorstrandt. But he says her maid was involved in the outrage, at your suggestion.'

Ambroise watched the angry look on Schellinger's face dissolve into one of sheer terror.

'Of course the bastard's going to blame me!' Schellinger said.

Coen said nothing for a long time, weighing him in his gaze. Finally he said, 'You forget who you are talking to.'

Schellinger's Adam's apple bobbed in his throat like a cork. 'You want your treasures back, you have to send me on the *Zandaam*.' He pointed a finger at Ambroise. 'You don't think he can find it, do you?'

'He will find it. He has no other choice.'

Coen sat back, the interview over. Three guards stepped out of the shadows at the back of the room and surrounded Schellinger.

'Captain Jacob Schellinger,' Coen said. 'I am arresting you on charges of gross negligence in relation to the sinking of the *retourschip Utrecht*. Take him away.'

Schellinger lurched forward but did not get very far. The guards held him and dragged him, struggling and roaring, out of the office.

CHAPTER 46

The low island

The culling was under way.

They started with any soldiers whose loyalty Stonecutter questioned, and a handful of other sailors and gunners who could not be relied on. A few were killed secretly at night, their throats cut as they stumbled out of their lean-tos to relieve themselves in the bushes. Their bodies were dragged out into the shallows for the shark fish to find. Others met with accidents on expeditions to the smaller islands.

Only a handful got away. They left at night, suspecting they would be next, taking their chances with the currents to try to swim to the provost on the seal island.

Well, much good it would do them, even if they made it, Christiaan thought.

Trails of smoke hung in the sky above the long island, where they had left the captain and his soldiers. Their water should have run out by now. How were they still alive?

'You don't think they actually did find water, do you?' Joost said.

'We should have dealt with them when we had the chance,' Krueger muttered.

Well, that is bold, Christiaan thought. Now he believes himself so hardened with bad deeds he can criticize me. He looked over his shoulder. Some of the women were watching them, wondering about this secret gathering on the beach and their lowered voices. He motioned for them to move further away.

'We can hunt them down like mutton birds, any time we like,' he said. 'For now we have more important business.'

'The provost and those others on seal island?' Stonecutter said.

Christiaan nodded. 'Sooner or later we will have to make an accounting with them. One day, if a rescue ship comes, we can have no one alive to get warning to it.'

'Let's make it sooner,' Krueger said.

Krueger, Stonecutter and the *jonkers* set off later that afternoon, telling everyone they were going hunting. Cornelia watched them go. It was no surprise to her when they returned later that night without any meat at all. Yet they all had the look of men coming out of a whorehouse; sated and furtive. It was clear to her what had happened. You didn't need a pike, a sword and a morning star club to kill a few seals.

When she got back to her shelter, Hendrika was waiting for her. 'Come quick,' she said.

Cornelia followed her to the women's tent. Neeltje Groot was huddled in the corner sobbing, her baby still mewling on her chest. Maria had gone missing. Some of the women thought she must have drowned, but no one had seen or heard anything.

They spread out across the island and walked from one end to the other, calling the little girl's name. Suddenly Elisabeth Post gave a squeal of horror and pointed.

At first, Cornelia thought it was a piece of driftwood come away from the wreck. It was floating on the current, fat as a maggot and bloated with seawater. She grabbed it as it went past.

It was the provost. His eyes were gone, eaten away by the crabs and the sea lice, together with most of his ears and lips. His intestines floated beside him, grey green, like some awful gunny sack. Cornelia did not recognize his face, or what was left of it, but she knew him by his uniform and the tattoo on his forearm. His wrists had been fastened behind his back with rope.

She let go.

The body drifted away. They all watched it bob on the sea-bright water, the current dragging it towards the channel where it would make a fine meal for the shark fish

That night Cornelia decided to sleep in the women's tent for safety. As she made her way through the dark, she heard men's voices gathered around the fire. They carried clearly to her on the wind. She recognized Joost van der Linden and Stonecutter and, of course, Krueger. He sounded as excited as a child with a new toy.

'You should have heard him!' he was saying. 'He was crying like a little girl. Every time I went to strike him, he crawled on his knees begging me not to do it.'

'What did you expect?' Joost said. 'He was only a shopkeeper.'

'He should have more self-respect,' Stonecutter said, 'and learn to die like a man.'

'The knife went through him just like butter. I never dreamed it would be so easy.'

'My one,' Joost said, 'I beat in his head with my morning star, and I saw his brains on the point right there but he was still screaming.' His voice was hushed in wonderment. 'I never would have believed it. I had to hit him three more times before he was still.'

Just then they saw her, silhouetted against the moon. They all fell silent. Joost got up and strode towards her. She gave no thought to running. She wondered if he would kill her too, but instead he dragged her back to her tent and had a guard placed outside it.

Later, Christiaan came and told her she was forbidden to speak to anyone on the island without his express permission.

She lay in her bed, rigid with horror, hearing their voices over and over in her head. In the middle of the night she heard screams coming from the women's tent.

Perhaps they're going to murder all of us too, she thought.

The long island

Michiel woke suddenly. He thought he had heard a scream. He got up and went down to the beach. The guards rounded on him, hearing his footfall. A good sign. They were awake and alert.

A full moon rode high in the sky, and the swell was running hard against the reef. He looked across the silver lagoon. Christiaan has miscalculated, he thought. He supposed he was leaving us here to die, but this is a paradise compared to what they have over there.

They collected water by crawling into the mutton bird holes and scooping it up in the shells of the giant balers they found on the beach. It was good water, fresh and clean, enough to support them for as long as they were stranded there.

Food was plentiful. They had birds, eggs, even strange little hopping cats with big hind legs who carried their babies in pouches under their bellies. A man could easily run them down and catch them. When they were cooked over roasted coals they tasted like chicken. The low tide exposed countless shellfish on the rocks, and there were colonies of grey-whiskered seals, trusting as lambs, that lay dozing in the sunshine every day and were easily killed with pikes and clubs. Just two of them made dinner for the whole camp.

But he was troubled. He had told his men that Christiaan had decided to sacrifice them to save the rest. They didn't like it, but they understood that kind of thinking. It was what any ruthless general would do. But the more he thought about all that had happened, the less he believed it was simple expediency.

He looked over at the Houtman Rocks. There was not a light anywhere. Birds wheeled like ghosts in the moonlight and their harsh cries made the sentries jump. The moon dipped behind the clouds and shadows moved on the beach.

CHAPTER 47

The low island

Cornelia crept down to the water's edge to wash. The other women gathered in a miserable huddle a little further along the beach. Neeltje was sitting on a flat rock with her head bowed. She looked like all the juice had been squeezed out of her.

'Did you find Maria?' Cornelia called out, but Neeltje looked right through her.

Elisabeth Post was crouched in the shallows, trying to wash the blood out of her skirts. Alida was on the beach, her eyes red-rimmed from crying. She was staring vacantly into the water. She had a plum-colored bruise on her cheek and a swollen, bloodied lip.

Cornelia stared at them in horror. 'What did they do?'

'You don't want to know,' Elisabeth said.

The pastor paced the shore, pale and trembling. 'It is an abomination before God. Christiaan and his so-called council behave like savages. Their treatment of the people is a reproach to all civilized and God-fearing men!'

His family were gathered outside his tent, watching him. Hendrika had her arms around the younger children. His wife stood apart from all of them, terrified.

'You have to do something,' Cornelia said.

'No, come away,' his wife said. 'It is nothing to do with us.'

He stared at her, his eyes bright with messianic rage. 'Satan is walking among us. I must face him!'

'Perhaps we should pray instead.'

'Have we not prayed constantly since the wrecking of the ship? God is testing our resolve. We must stand fast against Satan just as we would in Holland.'

'You are the only law they may yet listen to,' Cornelia said.

He started down the beach towards Christiaan's grand tent, his long black coat flapping in the wind. Christiaan's bully boys watched him come. They started to laugh and called out to Christiaan that he had a visitor.

He appeared, hands on hips. 'Well, well,' he said. 'The Lord has sent a messenger. What is the word of God this morning, old man?'

The pastor stopped to catch his breath, holding out the Bible in his right fist. 'Know you not this Book?'

Christiaan snatched it from him. He flicked through it as if he had not seen it before then, with one sudden movement, he tore out a handful of pages and let the wind scatter them.

The pastor gasped and tried to take it back, but Christiaan would not release it. The others howled with laughter at this sport.

'God will strike you down for that!'

Christiaan looked up at the sky in a dumb show of bewilderment. 'When?' he said.

'The Lord himself has said...'

Krueger grabbed him and threw him onto the ground.

Hendrika ran forward. She turned to Joost. 'Do something! Help him.' Joost shrugged, helplessly.

Christiaan tossed the Bible aside and it landed with a splash in the shallows. 'There will be no more talk of your 'Lord'. We have been wrecked here so that the true word can pass among men, and I am the instrument of it. There will be no more preaching from you, pastor. From this time, you shall come to me to know God's law.'

The pastor scrambled to his feet and fled, stumbling on the stones. Gulls rose from the beach in front of him, screeching like the devil's battalions as they flew into the sky.

CHAPTER 48

Batavia Fort

Ambroise endured the long and terrible silence in an agony of apprehension, as Governor Coen reviewed the transcripts of his reports. Finally he laid them aside. 'I have read your account of the unfortunate events on the *Utrecht*, and I have to tell you, I am not as impressed with your abilities as they are in Amsterdam. Your actions will be examined more fully at a later date.'

Damning judgment, Ambroise thought, but not official and permanent, not yet. He still had time to redeem himself.

'The most important thing, for now, is that you go back to the wreck to salvage the Company's goods and treasure, and rescue any of the people as still survive. You will take the *Zandaam* and return there with the upper steersman from the *Utrecht*. Together you are charged with the task of locating the reef where she foundered.'

Coen drummed his fingers on his desk. 'You shall set sail tomorrow in the name of God and shall hasten your journey with all possible diligence. Go.'

Ambroise nodded and took his orders, leaving without another word.

The *Zandaam* cleared port and sailed west once again, bound for the Sunda Straits and the mysterious Southland. Ambroise stared out to sea, his eyes sunken and yellow with fever. He looked like a skeleton in ruff and cloak. His mind was a chaos of self-recrimination and outrage. One moment he castigated himself for those things he had done; the next he was consumed with anger at the injustices done to him.

If anything at all gave him cause for satisfaction, it was seeing Jan Decker's corpse blackening in its chains outside the castle. The bosun had finally paid for what he had done to Cornelia Noorstrandt.

Schellinger had been put to the question also. Even a man like that, he thought, will break eventually. Well, he couldn't feel sorry for him. He'd brought it all on himself.

He was the only one who could hold his head up. When the truth finally came out, people would see that.

The low island

Christiaan strutted around the island like a prince, his entourage following. There were the fancy boys out front - Joost van der Linden and David Krueger - with the hard men prowling behind them. They made their way towards the pastor's tent.

The pastor stood outside watching them. He cut a lonely figure. His wife huddled behind him. Their young daughters clung to Hendrika's skirts.

Cornelia went down the beach to stand with him. 'We have to get away from this island,' she said. 'Your family is in terrible danger. We all are.'

'There is no way we can escape.'

'We have to steal a raft.'

He was not listening.

'Pastor!' Christiaan called. 'The very man I wanted to see. It seems there has been a misunderstanding between us.'

Cornelia watched the pastor's demeanor change. 'A misunderstanding, *Heer* Undermerchant?'

'I have treated you harshly. Perhaps the strain of looking after so many people has affected me. I have come to make amends.'

'I am much relieved to hear you speak this way. I should like the opportunity to speak again to the people and reassure them that we are not lost to God's laws. I fear that, due to our privations, we are not all behaving as God-fearing men.'

Christiaan smiled. 'God-fearing? I do not fear him, for God has saved me from all manner of disasters. Indeed, he plucked me from the wreck and put me here on the island to act as shepherd to you all. He has protected me, while others around me have met with diverse misfortunes.'

'We should thank God for it.'

Christiaan put a hand on his shoulder. 'Indeed you should.'

'Don't toady to him,' Hendrika said. 'Can't you see what he's doing?'

Christiaan glared at her and, for a moment, Cornelia thought he would strike her. Then he threw back his head and laughed. 'You have chosen a spirited little filly,' he said to Joost. 'You should sleep with a dagger under your pillow.'

'Chosen?' the pastor said.

'What say you, Hendrika? This fine young fellow here wants you for his wife.'

'What?' The pastor sounded surprised.

'Of course. We are not animals. Everything must be done properly. What do you say?'

'No,' Hendrika said, behind him.

The pastor waved her to silence. He saw opportunity here. 'As long as it is all done in accordance with the law.'

Cornelia heard Hendrika catch her breath.

'I am glad you see the sense in it,' Christiaan said. He put an arm around the pastor's shoulders. 'I hope we may become firm friends. There has been needless dissension between us. Do you not think so?'

'Reconciliation is the warmest wish of my heart.'

'We should certainly consider restoring you to our council.'

'I should be honored.'

'I shall have to think on it.'

'Much depends on your daughter,' Joost said.

'I am sure you will find her dutiful.'

'Good,' Christiaan said and smiled at Joost. Then he turned back to the pastor: 'Come to dinner tonight in my tent. Bring Hendrika. Cornelia, you will come too. We will have a feast to celebrate. Good day to you.' He went back down the beach to his tent, his thumbs in his belt. The others followed.

'Well, I think everything is going to be all right now,' the pastor said.

Cornelia shook her head. 'How can it be all right? You just sold him your daughter.'

'Let us trust in the Lord.'

'Are you mad?'

'They are not such bad fellows. They had to be firm with the thieves to keep order. If we are going to survive, we need such discipline.'

'They went to the women's tent last night and raped them. Maria is still missing. Everyone believes they have murdered her. Do you not understand?'

He looked at her blankly.

'They are monsters, every one of them.'

He closed his eyes. 'The Lord will protect us. You'll see.' He hurried Hendrika and the rest of his family inside their tent.

Cornelia looked across to the long island. Smoke from a dozen cookfires smudged the cold, blue sky. Michiel was still alive. It yet gave her hope.

That night a cold southerly hurled itself at the beach. Sparks from the campfires carried on the wind. There were snatches of laughter from Stonecutter's soldiers and their *jonker* friends, and the chink of pewter as they drank endless jugs of wine from the barrels outside Christiaan's tent.

The pastor made his way through the scrub. He had the much-worn Bible he had salvaged from the shallows tucked under one arm. Cornelia followed behind with Hendrika.

'We shall bring them to repentance,' he said to Cornelia. 'Trust that I know what I'm doing.'

'We both know now what Christiaan wants, and it isn't to repent,' she said.

'We will observe the proper forms. Joost van der Linden comes from a fine and God-fearing family. He will remember himself.'

'You cannot let them do this.'

'No, it will be all right. You will see.'

Joost stood outside his tent, golden hair streaming in the wind. His cloak, Cornelia noticed, had been embroidered with *passementerie*; Christiaan's pet tailor must have been at work again.

He ushered them inside. Silk hangings, plundered from a Company chest, shimmered in the light of the gimbal lamps that hung from the cross spars. Lobster tails, roasted mutton birds and oysters were artfully arranged on the driftwood table.

'Eat as much as you like,' he said.

Christiaan entered, glorious in a red surcoat of *laken*. He had his golden medallion about his neck. Joost bowed to him, and addressed him as Captain-General, a title that Cornelia had never heard before.

They sat down and Ambroise's former cabin boy, Strootman, waited table. He brought wine, freshly roasted fish, and gobbets of toasted Gouda cheese. Cornelia gaped at it all. Everyone else on the island was starving, reduced to sucking the marrow out of mutton bird bones.

Joost did not take his eyes off Hendrika. A smile played about his lips. 'You're a pretty little thing, aren't you?' he said and reached out to touch her cheek.

She recoiled.

The pastor paid no attention to her. He gulped down oysters and lobster tails, while listening to Christiaan's plans to divide the people further in order to preserve the food and water and prevent lawlessness. He put up a hand. 'But we must ensure that we maintain a good and virtuous community while we await our rescue,' he said.

Joost poured some wine into a pewter cup and handed it to Hendrika. She took it, and at his urging she swallowed a mouthful, but her hands were shaking so badly she spilled most of it on her dress.

'Goodness and virtue,' Christiaan said, amused. 'I think all men would lead good and virtuous lives, provided they do not have the chance to do otherwise.'

'Surely we must all guard against sin,' the pastor said.

'It is easy to guard against sin when it is difficult to achieve, pastor. Don't you think so? A blameless life is something most men have by virtue of laziness or lack of opportunity. Most of your congregation in Holland were only assured of heaven through complacency and the living of a dull life.'

'You are wrong. The Devil places temptations everywhere.'

'And you think that if a man resists it, then he is to be commended? For myself I think it is only when a man submits to temptation that he truly becomes interesting. What happens if we dazzle him with the promise of gold and there is no one to prevent him from slipping it into his pocket? Or if we leave him alone with a beautiful woman. What will he do then?'

'Such things are the Devil's work. We must resist.'

'The Devil's work!' Christiaan crowed. 'I have heard men say: 'The Devil made me do this, the Devil made me do that.' But I ask you, pastor, if it was the Devil doing it all, then why have a day of Judgment, for the Devil surely then is guilty of everything?'

'The Devil exists to lay the path to sin. This is why we pray, 'lead us not into temptation.''

'But what if there is no such thing as the Devil? Perhaps he is just an invention by you preachers to keep brave men enslaved. I say that all things come from God, so if God puts desire in a man's heart, how can that desire be bad?'

Cornelia recognized this philosophy. It was a creed espoused by the heretic Torrentius. So, the rumors were all true. 'You said you wished to restrict lawlessness,' she said to him.

'I do. Stealing other men's food and wine, yes, this is lawless. There are immutable rules for the survival of all. But other laws are the result of men's petty fears of their own nature. For instance, I believe women should be the common property of all. A man's lust is natural and comes from God. Do you not agree?'

She felt the color rise to her cheeks. 'I think a good man honors a woman and protects her.'

'There are many ways to honor a woman's beauty.'

Cornelia waited for the pastor to rebuke him. But he kept his silence. Perhaps because his mouth was full of lobster.

Christiaan clapped him on the back. 'Come, no more talk of religion. Your daughter is to be married tomorrow. This is a time for rejoicing. Strootman, bring us more wine!'

'This is not such a bad thing for us,' the pastor said as they made their way back across the bleached coral flags from Christiaan's tent. The flaming torch he held in his hand sent long shadows dancing over the scrub.

Cornelia gripped Hendrika's hand tight in hers and felt the answering pressure.

'I don't know how you can say that,' Cornelia said. 'He is a libertine and perhaps a murderer as well.'

'He has kept us from becoming lawless. The execution of thieves is sanctioned by the laws of the Honorable Company.'

'And the rapes? Were they sanctioned also?'

'They cry rape afterwards. Who knows what they said and did at the time? You know that some of the women had been trading sexual favors for food?'

'They are starving them deliberately. This is Christiaan's doing.'

'He requires instruction, that is all. When I am restored to the council, I shall be able to influence affairs better.'

'He is a heretic!' Hendrika said.

'Heretic? What do you know of such things?' His voice dropped, as if in conspiracy. 'It will do us no good to challenge these people head on. It requires a subtle hand. You are too young to understand.'

'It is your wish that I marry Joost?'

'It is better that you are kept legally by one man than misused by the many. It will all be done within the tenets of the law. Besides, you were making eyes at him every time he walked past you on the ship. I had to constantly upbraid you for it.'

'That was before I knew what kind of man he was.'

'Enough,' the pastor said.

Cornelia was buffeted by another blast of wind. It almost knocked her off her feet. 'I never thought you would behave so meekly in front of them,' she said.

'Do not be fooled. They think they have me duped, but they shall see that I can be clever also.'

He threw open the flap of their tent. It was empty. The gimbal lamp that had hung from the spar was shattered, and there were slash marks in the timber struts, as if made by a cutlass or axe. Everything was upturned. The meagre chest they had salvaged for a bed and the driftwood table made for them by the carpenters lay in splinters about the floor. There were thick gobs of blood everywhere. The ground was slippery with it.

Cornelia could see where they had dragged the bodies of the pastor's wife and children over the coral flags to the water.

The pastor dropped to his knees and screamed.

CHAPTER 49

A windswept morning. Flurries of rain were driven by the ceaseless wind. The pastor stood swaying on the beach, with a missal open in his hand, and read the wedding ceremony to the gaily dressed wedding party. Hendrika's face was pale as a corpse. Beside her, Christiaan was resplendent in his fine red surcoat and abundant necklets of gold. His lieutenants, Stonecutter, Krueger and Rees were arrayed behind him. The groom boasted a new feather in his tall black hat, and the silver buckles on his shoes had been polished by one of his lackeys until they shone.

Stonecutter placed a fat emerald ring on the missal book. Cornelia shuddered. He had not even bothered to wash the blood from under his fingernails. Christiaan whispered to her that the stone had once been in the possession of a Roman Emperor.

The pastor read the words to the ceremony, his voice reedy and thin. The tenets of law having been completed to the satisfaction of the bride's father, Hendrika became the wife of Joost van der Linden, newly named the Lieutenant of the Kingdom of the Southland Isles.

Life on the island took on a ghastly routine. The new aristocracy was firmly in place, distinguished from their subjects not only by their manner of dress but also in the way they passed their days. Their servants did their fishing and collected their oysters, crabs and eggs, passing every moment in fear of their lives.

Meanwhile Christiaan and his lieutenants paraded before their *bijwijven* - pleasure women - each day dressed in a new red coat and silk stockings, their boots well-polished with seal oil.

By night they relaxed with red wine glinting in their beards, terrified women under their arms. They sang foul songs and supped at fish soup, lobster and precious Gouda cheese. It was the diamond life they had always dreamed of, and here, at the cost of a few worthless sailors and tailors and their brats, they had established the kingdom of their dreams.

The pastor sat on a rock, his lips moving silently as he read his torn and salt-stained Bible. His black coat was just a rag now, his polished and buckled shoes rotted with seawater, stiff as iron on his feet. His beard had grown. Even the fat belly had withered, and his breeches were held up with rope.

Cornelia saw Joost promenading along the beach with Hendrika. He was dressed in all his purloined finery, as if he were a burgher with his wife on the Heerenstraat. Hendrika wore the dress Joost had ordered one of the tailors to make for her from Company silk.

When Joost saw the pastor, his spirits seemed to lift. She knew what he was thinking; now here was a game.

He stopped in front of him and nudged him with his boot. 'Is that what you do when a gentleman and his lady pass?' he said. 'Get up and bow.'

The pastor did as he was told. He kept his head lowered, like a dog waiting for his master's boot.

'A fine match you have made for me, Father,' Hendrika said. 'I am a gentleman's lady now. Are you not proud?'

'Could you ask them to give me some food?'

'Are you hungry, churchman? That's because you never learned to fish. Doesn't it have something in the Good Book about fishing?' Joost knocked the Bible from his hand.

Rees and Krueger came loping down the beach to join in the fun. 'Is this man bothering you, lieutenant?' Rees said. 'You want me to get rid of him?' His hand went to the sword at his belt.

'Well, what good is he?' Joost said.

'We could at least use him for sword practice,' Rees said. 'Pretend he's van Texel.'

Joost considered this.

'Shall I get some rope to tie him up?' Krueger said.

The pastor's knees gave way and he dropped onto the sand. He looked up at his daughter, his face melting to tears. 'Hendrika, love,' he said. 'Help me.'

'Let him be,' Hendrika said. 'Who else will pull your rafts out for you when you want to go fishing?'

Joost sighed. 'She has a point.'

'Though he's not very good at heavy work anymore,' Rees said. 'He's getting slower.'

'Let's give him another day,' Joost said, 'see how he turns out.'

Rees and Krueger grinned at each other and walked away. It was a bit of sport, that was all. No one was murdered on the island without Christiaan's authority, and they all knew their Captain-General wanted the pastor alive a while longer yet.

'Come, Hendrika.' Joost held out his arm for her and they walked on, as if skirting an importunate beggar.

That night, Cornelia huddled in her shelter listening to the men drinking by the fire. She knew all their voices by now. 'Loves it, that Elisabeth,' she heard Rees saying. 'She can't get enough of it.'

'That's not the way I remember it,' Krueger said.

'That's because she likes me better than you,' Rees said and they all laughed.

'I've had all of them,' Stonecutter said. 'I say Alida is the best. I'm going to have her again tonight.'

'Maybe I'll have Elisabeth,' someone else said. 'I'll find some place no one here's been.' It was the cabin boy, Strootman. Scarcely a man, with not even a beard on his chin, and fouler than any of them. On the ship he had barely spoken a word.

She heard them get out the dice to play for first turn.

'What about Miss High and Mighty?' Krueger said.

'She's off limits,' Stonecutter said. 'Christiaan is saving that one for himself.'

'It's a pity,' Krueger said. 'I'll bet I could show that one a few tricks.'

'He'll get tired of her one day,' Strootman said. 'Then I'll add her to my collection.'

Cornelia covered her ears. She could not stand to listen anymore. When she unblocked them again, it was quiet.

Then she heard boots crunching on the coral outside her shelter. The flap was pushed aside and she saw Stonecutter's ugly face peering in. 'The Captain-General wants you,' he said. 'Now, will you come agreeably or do I have to persuade you?'

It was a wild night. It seemed that the wind was about to uproot even Christiaan's sturdy shelter. Flurries of rain threw themselves against the canvas walls like handfuls of grit. The cold was biting.

Christiaan did not seem to notice. He recited poetry to her from a book as she sat huddled on a wooden stool, shivering inside her cloak.

She did not know if the poem was his own composition or he had copied it from somewhere.

Lovely eyes, then the beauties have bound them,
And scattered their shadows around them;
Stars, in whose twinklings the virtues and graces,
Sweetness and meekness, all hold their high places:
But the brightest of stars is but twilight,
Compared with that beautiful eye light.

So this was how he intended to seduce her. With poetry. Stonecutter used his fists and threats. She was not sure which was more frightening.

She tried to remember that she had once been the owner of a house on the Leleistraat, her life circumscribed by the gold ring on her finger and the expensive velvet gowns she wore to dinner. The reef had stripped all that away, and she no longer knew this woman with whom she had shared a lifetime. Was she that woman, or the coward who had stayed in her tent listening to the screams the night they attacked the women? All her moral certainties were gone.

Christiaan's voice droned on.

O, how blest, how divine the employment!
How heavenly, how high the enjoyment!
Delicate lips, and soft, amorous glances,
Kindling, and quenching, and fanning sweet fancies,
Now, now to my heart's center rushing,
And now through my veins they are gushing.

'What was that?'

Christiaan stopped and put down the book. He seemed disappointed at the interruption. 'Have you not been listening?' he said.

'There was a scream.'

'Just the wind. Let me continue. Lose yourself in my words.'

'Someone was calling for help.'

'A bird perhaps.'

There it was again. She jumped to her feet and before he could stop her she had run outside the tent and into the teeth of a blinding gale.

Outside, the moon hurtled across the sky, racing storm clouds as black as ink. She saw shadows on the beach, before the moon was blotted out again by the clouds.

'Cornelia!' Christiaan grabbed her by the shoulders, and tried to drag her back inside. She broke away.

There were needles of rain in her face as she ran. She fell, her ankle twisted in a mutton bird hole. She dragged herself to her knees, and for a moment the moon reappeared, illuminating the beach.

She saw a group of men splashing into the shallows and heard shouts and another scream. She recognized Krueger's voice down there, and Strootman's. Then the moon disappeared again behind the gathering stormcast, and rain exploded over their heads. It was like being pelted with small stones.

CHAPTER 50

'Now Salomon,' Christiaan said, 'how long have you been a clerk?'

Salomon stammered something, but could not meet his eyes.

'Isn't it time you became one of the Devil's Own?'

'Of the what?'

Christiaan spread his arms to include everyone in the tent; the jonkers, Stonecutter, Krueger and the rest. 'Are you afraid of the Devil, Salomon? There is no need to be. The Devil is your freedom. It is only the pastor and his religion that keeps you in chains.'

'Yes, Captain-General.'

'Can I rely on you?'

'Of course, Captain-General. I won't let you down.'

'It is not enough just to say the words. Anyone can say words. A man must be tested.'

He leaned closer and lowered his voice. 'I can be the harbinger of your dreams, Salomon. If you would only let me. What is it you want?' He picked up a heavy *rix-dollar* from the table and let the candlelight reflect on the engraved head on the reverse. 'Become one of us, and there is more money than you ever dreamed.'

He tossed it to him. 'Here, take it, I have chests filled with them. No? Perhaps you wish to visit the women's tent tonight with Krueger and Stonecutter. Who would be your fancy, do you think? Little Alida Post is skinny but sweet, they say. Or beautiful Elisabeth with her blonde curls? Who would you choose?'

'Don't kill me,' Salomon said.

He spoke the words so softly Christiaan could not hear him, and he made him repeat them. 'Is that all, Salomon. Such a humble ambition to hold.' He looked around at the others, inviting him into their conspiracy. 'Yet you may achieve it. First, you must pass the test.'

The gulls dived, screeching for tidbits in the channel as the mackerel chopped through a school of smaller fish. There was the promise of a storm on the rain-scented wind. Crabs scuttled on the clinker beach.

Cornelia washed the bandages in the shallows, as best she could, then headed back up the shore to the sick tent. She saw Krueger and Stonecutter outside. The little monster Strootman was with them. Since her sham of a marriage to Joost, Hendrika was not able to help her. Elisabeth Post had volunteered to help in her place.

She saw Krueger saying something to Elisabeth. By the look on his face she knew something terrible was going to happen. Elisabeth seemed resigned to it. She shrugged and walked away.

'Elisabeth!'

She looked over her shoulder and shook her head.

'Get along now,' Stonecutter said to her.

'Get out of my way. There are sick in there I need to attend to.'

She heard a shout. Christiaan was heading along the beach. He had Salomon with him, his arm around his shoulders like they were old friends out for a walk.

They stopped outside the ragged shelter and Christiaan made much play of sniffing the air. 'I smell death,' he said. 'Who do you have in there.'

'One of the soldiers, Richard Merrell,' she said. 'Simon Oddyck, the bosun's mate, has flux. Hollert and a couple of other sailors have fallen ill lately.'

'You think they will recover?'

'That is up to God.'

'That is where I disagree.' He turned to Salomon. 'Now boy, have you killed anyone yet?'

Salomon jerked, as if someone had jabbed him with a knife. 'Captain-General?'

'You're no good among the Devil's Own if you've no sin on your soul. Ask anyone. Ask the preacher.'

Salomon stared at Cornelia in dumb appeal.

'Please, let him go,' Cornelia said. 'Dear God, no more blood.'

Christiaan shrugged, as if the matter were out of his hands.

'Do it for me,' she said.

He smiled, delighted. 'For you, my love?' He told Strootman to fetch him a cup of wine. They waited for him to run back to the tent and return with a brimming silver goblet.

Christiaan handed it to Salomon. 'Drink it. Come on, boy. You heard what I said! It will give you courage.'

'Courage for what?'

'For life, of course.'

Salomon drank it down. Red wine leaked down the corners of his mouth. Then Christiaan took the jeweled dagger from his belt and handed it to him. 'Now then, do what must be done. See if you truly are one of us.'

'What do you want me to do?'

Krueger laughed.

'These sickly people in there are a drain on us. It is the law of survival, Salomon. The strong must go on and the weak must die. It is God's law.'

'Don't do it, Salomon,' Cornelia said.

Christiaan bent down and peered into the lean-to, where the sick lay half conscious and covered with filthy blankets. 'It is unfortunate. But, you see, most of the people here on the island will die anyway. Why waste any more of our precious food and water? They are suffering and we have no medicine. I tell you, it is almost a kindness.'

'You mustn't do it,' Cornelia repeated.

Christiaan smiled, apparently pleased with how things were turning out.

'No,' Cornelia said.

'Only the strong survive,' Christiaan said to him. 'The weak have to die. Are you strong or are you weak?'

Salomon brushed past her. She grabbed his arm and tried to wrestle the knife away from him. Krueger threw himself between them and easily pushed her aside. She fought him and he hit her once around the head with his closed fist. The blow stunned her and knocked all the fight out of her. Her legs gave way and she stumbled to her knees.

The *jonkers* laughed about it among themselves.

'You're nothing better than animals,' she screamed at them.

Salomon ran out of the tent, dropped the bloody knife on the ground, and stumbled down to the water's edge. He retched into the shallows.

Krueger and Stonecutter cheered.

'Let's call him 'Cannonball,' from now on,' Strootman said. 'He can kill five men at once.'

Christiaan nodded to Krueger. He picked up the knife and cleaned it, with a clerk's precision, in the seawater before handing it back to Christiaan. Salomon, meanwhile, was scrubbing at the bloodstains on his hands, arms and face. The seawater around him was already stained pink.

Strootman and Stonecutter went off, laughing, to dig graves among the mutton bird nests.

CHAPTER 51

That night, Cornelia heard scratching outside her tent and drew back the canvas. It was Salomon, lying on his belly, half concealed in the brush. He had crawled up to her tent through the saltbushes hoping none of the Devil's Own would see him. His face was grey as a corpse.

'What are you doing here?' Cornelia said. 'They'll kill you if they see you.'

'I have to talk to you,' he said.

She let him inside. She remembered him from before, at the dinner table on the *Utrecht;* a pale boy with fair hair and studious ways. Now look at him. What had these monsters done to him?

'You shouldn't be here,' she said.

He started to cry with his head on his knees.

She put out a hand to touch his shoulder, but he shrank away from her. 'You don't want to touch me,' he said. He shook his head, violently. 'I'm sorry. They made me do it!'

She spared an anxious glance for the doorway.

'It's all right if someone makes you do something, isn't it? They made you be Christiaan's whore, right?'

'I'll never give in to him,' she said.

Suddenly there was fear in his eyes. That wasn't what he had wanted to hear. 'They were sick,' he said. 'They were going to die anyway. Christiaan said.' He looked up at her, his eyes pleading his case. 'You would have done the same.'

She did not answer him.

'Say something,' he said.

'They were helpless, Salomon.'

'I had to do it,' he said.

Christiaan came to her tent unannounced, with merry eyes, a winning smile, and sporting a new mutton bird feather in his hat.

'All alone?' he asked her.

'As you wished it to be.'

'Not even Salomon du Chesne to keep you company?'

So, he knew.

'Are you going to murder him, too?' she said, surprised to hear the exhaustion in her own voice.

'I have to. It is for your own protection.'

'From Salomon?'

'He's unhinged. You saw it for yourself. He murders sick people.'

'Then I'm in no danger from him. I am not sick.'

'A man like that, he wouldn't discriminate.' He reached out and touched her face, tender as a lover. 'I would not have anyone hurt you.'

'Let him be. Please.'

'I shall certainly not touch a hair on his head,' he said, 'if that be your wish.'

And he went out, shouting to Krueger to have his court attend him.

That night Christiaan and Stonecutter found Salomon in his shelter, curled miserably on the hard ground. He started shaking as soon as he saw them.

'What's the matter, Salomon,' Christiaan said. 'You look like you've seen the devil.' He held up the torch. The clerk's face shone with sweat. He stared up at them with such exquisite fear on his face. He looked around for escape. There was nowhere to run, of course, but that hadn't stopped some of them from trying.

'Can we trust you, Salomon?' Christiaan whispered. 'You know, some of the *jonkers*, they say you can never trust a Jew boy. I told them they're wrong about you.'

'I've done what you said. I murdered all those people.'

'It wasn't murder, it was mercy killing. I told you that. They were suffering.' Salomon flinched as Christiaan crouched down and put an arm about him. 'That's what I told them. I said you were loyal. To the death.'

'Please don't hurt me,' Salomon said. He looked as if he were about to cry.

Stonecutter started laughing.

'Do you hear that noise?' Christiaan said. They all listened. It was Neeltje Groot's infant, howling in the darkness. The mite wasn't getting enough water, she had told Rees.

'Can you stop the baby crying for us, Salomon?'

'Please,' he said. 'I did everything you said. Now let me be.'

'You said you were loyal,' Christiaan said, stroking his arm. He turned to Stonecutter. 'Isn't that what he said?'

'That's what he said.'

'But it's only a baby!'

'Exactly.'

Christiaan stood up and waited to see what Salomon would do. He thought of it as a divine experiment, an exquisite exploration of that diffuse substance that made up the human soul. Through the ages, men had pondered what might be done to make base metal into gold. But what of turning gold into dross? The process could be no less fascinating.

Some called it alchemy. That's what he was. An alchemist.

It was like watching a play, or some fine entertainment in the street. You stood there, one hand upon the hip, and a glass of wine in the other, and watched. The human soul was endless entertainment.

He could hear Neeltje's baby still wailing in the women's tent. The case was cut and dried.

Salomon du Chesne had been charged and convicted in absentia with disobeying an order, and there was a surfeit of willing executioners to be had. Stonecutter led them along the beach. Krueger followed with Strootman. They looked like children playing in the sun, splashing happily through the shallows, intent on their prize.

The accused had seen them coming and was trying to escape. Where did he hope to run to on such a small island? He slipped on the coral flags and twisted his ankle. Now he was reduced to crawling. They caught him in the shallows, the three of them. There was nothing dainty about it. They stood over him, their swords out, waiting for Christiaan's orders.

He had Joost fetch him another goblet of wine and then walked down the sand to administer justice. Justice and order; they were of supreme importance to any society of men. Without it, there was chaos.

Salomon lay in the shallows, sobbing.

No use crying now, Christiaan thought. I gave you your chance. You should have taken it.

'Please don't hurt me,' Salomon said.

'We're not going to hurt you,' Christiaan said.

'I'll do anything you say.'

'Ah, we have caught you in another lie.' Christiaan crouched down beside him. 'You disobeyed an order.'

'I couldn't. Not a baby.'

'Stop whimpering, boy. It's just a game.'

'What game?'

'I'll explain everything in a moment,' Christiaan tossed Strootman his sword. 'I have a job for you.'

Strootman acted like he had been thrown a bag of silver *rix-dollars*. He couldn't wait to get to it.

Krueger shook his head. 'That boy couldn't cut butter with an axe in both hands. Let me do it.' He grabbed the sword hilt and tried to wrestle it away. But Strootman hung on, imploring Christiaan to make good with his promise.

Stonecutter wanted them to get on with it. He clubbed Strootman behind the ear and sent him sprawling.

A fine thing, Christiaan decided, two young men fighting over which of them would remove a man's head. He would never tire of his new friends.

'Let's have a blindfold on him,' Krueger said.

'Please don't,' Salomon said.

Christiaan took a good silk kerchief from his pocket and tied it around Salomon's eyes.

'What are you doing?' Salomon sobbed.

'If we tolerate disobedience, what will become of us?' Christiaan said and nodded to Krueger.

'I want to take this off,' Salomon wailed and reached up for the blindfold.

Krueger brought down the sword. Christiaan felt a draught of air as he swung. It was done in just one stroke with a skill worthy of a professional executioner. The body keeled over onto the stones, blood gouting from the neck. It spurted once, twice, three times before the heart stopped.

Stonecutter applauded and Krueger grinned and bowed.

'I could have done that!' Strootman shouted.

Christiaan looked up the beach. Cornelia had been watching. Look at that face. If only the girl had a sense of fun, she would be perfect.

He had perfume in his beard, a new dagger at his belt and a silver medal on his black felt hat. He paused to admire himself in the gilt mirror he had sent to her shelter. He examined his reflection this way and that.

Finally, he turned around and gave her a broad smile, as if noticing for the first time that she was there. He sat down on her bed. 'Come,' he said, patting the coverlet, 'sit here beside me.'

He poured wine from the ewer into a pewter cup.

She did not move.

'My dear Cornelia. What is wrong? Such a long face. Are you not comfortable here?'

'Do you think I did not see what happened today to Salomon du Chesne?'

He threw the cup across the tent. The red wine sprayed across the canvas. He stared at the mess he had made and then frowned and turned away from it, as if it were someone else's mistake. 'You do not understand,' he said. 'I am the one trying to keep order here as best I can. The judges in Batavia sentence men to the ultimate penalty all the time. Might I not do the same, when my resources are thinner and the lawlessness far more prevalent?'

'You are a monster.'

'It may seem that way to those who do not understand me. Do you not understand how hard this is for me? I walk a tightrope. Have you seen how Krueger has changed since the wreck?'

'Krueger does your bidding.'

'You're wrong. They would have done to you what they did to the rest of the women if it were not for me. They are evil men. Only I can keep you from this madness.' He offered her the cup again. 'Come, life is too short to be miserable.'

She turned away.

'Have you ever seen me lay a hand on anyone? Well?'

She didn't answer.

'You do not think I could stop what is happening here on my own?' When she still did not answer him, he picked up his hat from the bed. 'Well, I am insulted. I see that you must think me the very devil.'

But whatever offence she had given him quickly passed, and he lay down again on her narrow bed, his gold medallion gleaming in the folds of the commander's ruffed shirt. 'Come here, lay by me, Cornelia.'

She turned to stare at him. 'I am a married woman.'

'Marriage. It is a form of enslavement! Do you want to be a slave? It is ungodly for a woman to belong to one man. It is by no means a natural state. All men still desire her, and the desire was put there by God. We meddle with God's natural laws.'

'That is just words.'

'Not at all. Men will always lust after women, and it is only a commonality of women that can make for an orderly and peaceful society. The want of women makes men go to battle.

'You say it is ungodly for a woman to belong to one man, yet you do not allow others to come near me.'

'I am the most powerful man on this entire island,' he said, speaking of their barren plot of rock and bushes as if it were Spain. 'Does that power not excite you?'

'I do not understand why you think I want you to court me. I would rather contemplate sharing the society of a cockroach.'

He controlled himself, but with difficulty.

She knew she was treading a fine line with him. But somehow she no longer cared what he did to her.

'I do not know what I have done to deserve your distaste,' he said, finally. 'I hope that in time God opens your eyes to the truth of all this.' He stood up, paused for a moment at the opening to her shelter, but then changed his mind and went out.

CHAPTER 52

Rees and Krueger were setting out for the channel to fish. Strootman and Stonecutter were about to join them. They called for the pastor to drag a raft through the shallows for them. Cornelia found it hard not to feel sorry for him, as he stumbled on the razor-edged coral and fell headlong into the water. The two men on the raft hooted with laughter, and their jeers were echoed from the beach.

'He's useless,' Strootman said. 'Why don't we just carry him out to the deeps and drown him?'

'Let Krueger have him,' Rees shouted. 'He's looking to try out his new sword.'

The pastor stood in the shallows, dripping wet, his mouth hanging open like a dumb animal, as he waited for them to pass sentence.

'Let him catch us a fish for supper,' Stonecutter said.

Rees and Krueger leaped off their raft after him. The pastor tried to stumble away but they caught him easily. They made him stand in the sea up to his waist, fumbling with the baited line they gave him.

'Look at Welten,' Strootman said. 'What's he doing?'

Welten was one of the carpenters from the ship, who had been pressed into service making beds and chairs for Christiaan. Cornelia watched him splash through the water towards the raft, which was now drifting unattended a few feet from the shore.

Stonecutter shouted a warning to Rees, but he and Krueger were having too much of a good time humiliating the pastor to see what was happening.

He's going to escape, Cornelia thought. He's seen his chance. She silently willed him on.

She saw another man, Pieter Robben, down at the beach baiting lines. He was the tailor who had stitched all the *passementerie* onto the jonkers' coats. He saw that Welten had almost made it to the raft. He dropped the fishing line and set off after him.

'Welten, wait for me!' he yelled.

Strootman and Stonecutter ran back to their tents and reappeared with their swords and bucklers. Cornelia grabbed at Stonecutter's arm as he ran past. He threw her off and she went down hard, hitting her head on a rock. She blacked out.

By the time she came around, Welten had already poled the raft away from the beach and Robben was fighting with Strootman in the shallows. Strootman slashed at him with his sword. Robben ducked his head and pushed Strootman in the chest, and he fell back into the water.

Stonecutter lunged at him and hit him a glancing blow on the back, but Robben, instead of flinching away, went at him with his fists. He was almost half the big sergeant's size so it was something to see. He yelled and swung at Stonecutter who wasn't ready for the fight in him. He took a step back and went tumbling over Strootman.

Then Robben swam after Welten and the raft.

Rees and Krueger came splashing back up the beach but they were too far away. By the time they got there, Robben had reached the deeper channel. Stonecutter tried to go after him but fell over again and came up screaming, cutting himself to ribbons on the coral.

Robben had almost reached Welten.

'Get after him!' Krueger shouted from the beach.

Strootman struggled back to the shore. 'I can't swim!'

Cornelia saw Welten haul Robben onto the raft. He was covered in blood, but he was alive. Welten steered them out towards the middle channel. The tide and the current were with them and in no time they were a dot on the horizon.

They had escaped, with one of only three serviceable rafts the *muyters* had, and were headed straight for the long island.

The long island

Michiel and his soldiers gathered around Welten and Robben, as they sat exhausted on the beach. The raft had been hauled up onto the clinkers after them. Welten's face was ashen as he told his story. It defied all belief. Michiel could not credit that among Christian men and women such things could take place.

'The undermerchant rules the island as if it were his own personal kingdom,' Welten said. 'Some madness has overtaken him and all those with him.'

'What about the provost?' Michiel said. 'What has he done about it?'

'The undermerchant sent him and most of the crew to the seal island. He said the cay was too small for everyone.'

'Do they survive?'

Welten shook his head. 'Stonecutter and some others went over early one morning on their rafts with swords and cutlasses and murdered them all. I heard Krueger boasting about how it was as easy as killing mutton birds.'

'David Krueger, the clerk?'

'It's Lieutenant Krueger, according to him. He's as bloodthirsty as the rest of them now.'

'What about the women?'

'They've put them all in one tent and the undermerchant and his followers use them for their personal pleasure. They forced the pastor's daughter to become Joost van der Linden's wife.'

'What about *Vrouwe* Noorstrandt?'

'They say Christiaan is saving her for himself.'

Both men were shaking with fright and with cold. Robben had a sword slash to his back; the muscle had been sliced clean through to the bone. He was lucky to be alive. Blood had soaked his shirt and still ran in rivulets down his spine.

They helped them off the beach to a makeshift shelter they had built.

Michiel told his men to find them blankets and to bandage their wounds as best they could. 'Drag the raft up the beach,' he said to Little Bean. 'Hurry now. It will be dark soon.'

'What do you make of it?' Little Bean said.

'There is only one thing to make of it.'

'But the undermerchant is a Company man.'

'Not anymore.'

Michiel stared across the channel. Now they had a raft, it would only be a matter of time before that murderous bunch of clerks and fancy boys came after them as well. They would have to make provision. Weapons or not, they were in for a fight.

The low island

Christiaan ranted, pacing back and forth, a froth of spittle in his beard. 'How could you allow them to steal one of our rafts?'

'It was those two,' Strootman said, pointing to Krueger and Rees. 'They shouldn't have got off the raft.'

Krueger kept his head lowered and scuffed the sand with his buckled shoes.

'Well?' Christiaan said.

Krueger refused to answer.

Rees looked at Stonecutter. 'If you had got on the other raft instead of trying to swim after them, they wouldn't have got away.'

Christiaan turned away from them, disgusted. 'Do we know who it was?'

'Welten, the carpenter.'

'The other one was Robben, the tailor,' Stonecutter said. 'I cut him with my sword. Strootman tripped me up or I would have finished him.' He held up his arm to show the deep gouges in his arm from the coral cuts.

'I didn't trip him, Robben pushed him over.'

Christiaan would have slit their throats, but they were his most trusted men. How could they have been so careless? It had been so easy until now, but this complicated their plans. If Robben and Welten had reached the long island, it would change everything.

We must get that raft back, he said.

None of them liked that idea. Facing van Texel's soldiers would not be as easy as running down a few frightened boys on the seal island.

Christiaan turned to face them. 'They are unarmed. It doesn't matter how many of them there are. Besides, thanks to your stupidity, we have no choice.'

CHAPTER 53

The long island

Among Michiel's soldiers were two Englishmen who had served apprenticeship as coopers before they joined the Company. Michiel had put them to work, breaking up some of their water barrels to fashion a new arsenal. Hardened hoop iron made enough spearheads for several pikes, which were then sharpened and bound to pieces of driftwood. Other men made morning star clubs from flotsam timber washed up from the wreck and spiked with nails. They built up cairns of coral slabs to use as missiles.

In a fair fight, Michiel knew they would chase off the fancy boy bunch of cadets and clerks in a few minutes, and then skewer Stonecutter and the handful of men he had with him. After all, they were professional soldiers, hardened in real wars against the Spanish and the Matarams. But this wouldn't be a fair fight. Christiaan and his men were armed with the muskets and steel swords he had forced them to give up.

At least they weren't totally defenseless anymore.

Every day Michiel drilled them, turning them back into soldiers again after their long months of inactivity.

He scouted the island thoroughly, to satisfy himself that there were no other places on the island that Christiaan and his murderous dogs could land. He decided they must attack the beach where Welten and Robben had landed. There was no other way across. They would run their rafts with the current, straight across the shallow mud flats from the lagoon on the low island.

He posted sentries all along the island anyway, and set up a twenty-four-hour guard. They must not be caught by surprise. Once the *muyters* were off the rafts and on dry land, they would have the advantage. It was while they were still in the shallows, scrambling to get ashore, that his soldiers had their best chance of beating them off.

Every day that Christiaan hesitated allowed them time to prepare themselves a little more. Armed with the few poor weapons they had fashioned for themselves, they would not die as easily as the tailors and shopkeepers left behind on the island.

Christiaan gathered the Devil's Own in his tent and sat them down. He took out the commander's casket, that Salomon had surrendered, and unlocked it to show them the treasure trove of chains, medallions, bracelets and rings, snug in their trays of red velvet. None of them dared breathe, in awe of such riches.

With a theatrical gesture, he lifted the tray and produced a second key to unlock another box beneath. There was a gasp as he produced the great cameo of Constantine in its frame of silver gilt. It was large enough to fit into both his outstretched hands. He held it up for them to see.

'This likeness is of the Emperor Constantine, one of the great Roman kings of ancient times. He is depicted on his chariot, and the two centaurs in the traces are trampling his fallen enemies. This very piece was presented to the Roman king himself thirteen hundred years ago. It found its way into the hands of the painter, Rubens, who handed it to our commander to be traded privately in the East. It was lately intended for the Indian emperor, Jahangir, himself. It is worth at least ten thousand guilders!'

The men whistled and shook their heads.

Next he reached for the small wooden box beside the casket. 'Then there's this. Even the Company directors do not know of its existence.'

He held it up for them. It was a vase, scarcely seven inches high. It was cut from a single piece of agate, and the color of it changed from honey to milk white further up towards the neck. It had a design of grapes and vine leaves, that had been so finely worked that in places it appeared almost translucent. On the handles were carved two faces of the lecherous woodland god, Pan.

He returned it to the casket. 'Such an impossible treasure, and all of it in two small caskets. Just think how many more treasures we might plunder when we leave these islands in our own great ship.'

'But how may do we do this?' Krueger said.

Christiaan sipped brandy from a silver cup. His lips shone in the glow of the oil lamp. 'When the rescue yacht arrives, the officers will certainly come ashore first. We shall laugh, drink and celebrate our rescue together. And when it is night, and they are all drunk, and we have shown them the treasure we have safely kept for the Company, we will cut their throats for them.'

Stonecutter chuckled deep in his chest.

'Then, under cover of darkness, we will row back to the yacht and overpower what is left of her crew. If Schellinger is with her, it will be even easier, for he will surely assist us. Then we will use the ship to plunder the Honorable Company and the Specks, whoever we find, before we retire as rich gentlemen to Barbary.'

'My Lord Krueger,' Joost said and nudged the big clerk's shoulder, eliciting a boyish grin. He liked the sound of that.

They drank a toast to their future success. Never was the world warmer than on that bleak night in those lonely islands, for they had all they could wish for; *wijnte en trijntje* - women and drink - and the promise of more riches and ease to come. It was a beautiful night to be alive, with a sword in your belt and brandy in your belly.

Cornelia started awake. Christiaan stood in the doorway of her shelter. She hadn't heard him approach.

She sat up, feeling for the knife in her gown.

He knelt down in front of her. 'I have here something you might like to see,' he said. He had a casket in one hand and a key in the other. He turned the key in the lock with almost mocking deliberation. 'Would you care for a glimpse?'

'What game are you playing now?'.

'Come now, a lady like yourself could never resist a fine jewel.'

'What do you want from me?'

'It doesn't hurt to look,' he said. He opened the lip of the casket and pretended to suppress a theatrical gasp.

'Do you think to seduce me this way?'

His eyebrows rose in great twin arches. 'The Commander told me of this piece during the voyage. It was unwise of him, in the circumstances, don't you think so?'

'What piece?'

'It is a cameo from the treasure house of the Roman Emperor, Constantine. Imagine. Thirteen hundred years old!'

'I don't believe you,' she said.

'It belongs to Rubens, that overpaid portrait painter.' He leaned towards her and she felt his hot breath on her cheek. 'A kiss, *schaapjes*,' he breathed.

She recoiled.

'A prince would pay ten thousand guilders for such a gem. All I ask is a kiss and it is yours.'

'I don't want it and it is not yours to give.'

'No? I have it here in my hand. I am the power and the life here. Anything you wish, I can grant you.'

'Then take me to Batavia so that I can be with my husband.'

His voice grew soft. 'Do you really yearn for this Boudewyn? Does he make you feel that every day is a joy and a wonder? Was it him you dreamed of as we crossed the swelling oceans from Amsterdam?'

She edged away.

He reached out and stroked her hair. 'Such a pretty lady. You were made for jewels. Your husband can only polish them for others to wear. You want a man who will make you a great lady, a queen.' His fingers touched her cheek.

'Don't touch me,' she said. She felt for Salomon's knife hidden under her skirts. I should stick him now and be done with it, she thought. Straight into his belly and twist. Or open up his neck in a bloody gash.

But it was not an easy thing to kill in cold blood. She had her fingers around the hilt and still could not find it in herself to pull it free of its leather scabbard and do what needed to be done.

'Just one kiss, *schaapjes*, and everything in this casket is yours.'

'Get away from me.' She pushed him so hard that he fell sideways onto the ground. His face contorted in rage and she waited for his assault. Instead he got up and went out of the tent.

Later, she lay awake, waiting for him to come back, starting at every footfall in the darkness. Just before dawn she fell into a troubled sleep. A wind from the south brought a flurry of sleet. She jerked awake at the sound of a cry in the darkness.

They were killing again.

CHAPTER 54

Christiaan heard the angry shriek of gulls overhead. He looked up and saw a flock of them as they drifted on the wind, scrapping and freewheeling. Those accursed birds were getting on his nerves. He wished he could take a musket to the lot of them.

Strootman went down to the beach with Krueger to bait the pastor as he sat in misery, eating grass stalks to still his hunger.

'Is there anyone around here that needs their ears boxing?' Strootman said. 'I'll do it, for a tot of gin.'

'Come now, you devils with all your sacraments,' Krueger shouted up at the sky. 'Here I am, ready for you. I wish now I saw a devil, don't you, Strootman?'

'Indeed, I do.' He grabbed the pastor by the hair.

Krueger pulled out his knife. 'Who would like to be stabbed to death? I can do that, you know, and very beautifully.'

Hendrika ran down the beach and shouted at them to leave him alone. They saw Joost with her and went off, laughing.

Christiaan knew he would have to do something. There was barely anyone left to kill, so now his fine lads played at dice and cheated each other for a handful of silver cash they would never spend.

He looked across the bay at the grey silhouette of the long island. Until now, the weather and seas had been against them. The skies were finally clearing. They would have to get that raft back.

Stonecutter came to stand beside him. 'We should do something about the Noorstrandt woman. You're too soft on her.'

'No.'

'What's the use of her? Let's put her with the others, or else give her to the fishes.'

'I said, no. She just needs a little persuasion.'

Stonecutter grimaced, as if he'd just bitten down on something foul. 'If it's persuasion she needs, leave it to me.'

Christiaan thought about it, battling with himself. 'All right. Do as you see fit.'

Stonecutter stood in the doorway of her tent. He looked her up and down with as much insolence as any man could muster. 'Pretty Cornelia,' he said. He grabbed her wrist and yanked her towards him. He held her face in one great fist and seemed pleased when she cried out.

'You think you are such a big man when there are only women and children to bully,' she said.

He pushed her down onto the narrow bed and smiled with mossy teeth. 'I've been hearing things about you, Miss High and Mighty. Complaints.'

'What complaints?'

Stonecutter took out his knife. 'A strange fellow, our undermerchant. A romantic.'

'What do you want of me?'

'I don't want anything of you. It's the Captain-General who wants you. If it was me, I'd have you bent over that table right now, and I'd take what I wanted whether you wished it or not.' He put his face close to hers. 'Just like I did that night on the ship.'

She tried to twist away from him but he held her tight. So it was him. He laughed at her struggles to get free.

'But see here, Christiaan is a gentleman. He's not rough like the rest of us. He has a delicate way about him. If it wasn't for him, you'd be doing general service like the others. The way you are, you'd end up food for the crabs and the fish, like as not.'

He let her go. She straightened her skirts and stared at him. Don't show him you're afraid, she thought, even if you are.

She went to walk past him but his hand shot out, quick as a snake, and grabbed her by the hair. His knife was at her throat. 'Christiaan has had enough of your little games. He wants you to know he's withdrawing his protection. Be nice to him tonight or tomorrow you go to the women's tent.' He leaned closer, his foul breath in her face. 'I'd like that. I wouldn't mind another dip in the honeypot. Then it will be Krueger's turn. I think you'll find us less delicate in our ways than the undermerchant. Remember that.'

The *Zandaam*

An albatross soared from the bow of the *Zandaam*, circling on the warm spring currents. It watched the cross trees of the ship dip in the swell, the bow throwing up spray as she beat into the waves. In the distance, its small bright eyes could make out the ruffle of foam around the Houtman Rocks.

But these were sharper eyes, and better placed, than those of the sailors on the *Zandaam* below. The ship headed away from the reef towards the south east, making slow progress against unfavorable winds.

Ambroise scanned the empty horizon in an agony of frustration. Thirty-seven days under sail already; it had taken them less time to reach Batavia on a yawl barely larger than a fishing boat. They should have sighted the islands long ago.

The people must all be dead by now, he thought. They had been almost two months with scarce enough food to eat or water to sustain them. It would be a miracle if any had survived. An ugly thought occurred to him. Did he really want to find anyone alive when they would surely point their accusing fingers at him?

But such speculation was unworthy.

He searched the horizon again with the eyeglass and prayed that, when they finally arrived at that accursed reef, there would somehow be a moment of redemption for Ambroise van Himst.

Barefoot in the shallows, Cornelia turned her face towards the reef. Is there another way out, she thought. The pastor said souls would burn in hell for self-harm, but it was hard to imagine any hell worse than this.

She started to wade out towards the deeps.

The mud was slippery underfoot, and she gasped as she stepped on a piece of sharp coral. Her heavy velvet dress, soaked with seawater, dragged at her legs. It was not easy to die, even when you had nothing to live for.

The water was cold when it reached her waist and she caught her breath. It was such a beautiful morning. The sea was glittering and still.

She closed her eyes in resolve and waded out further.

She heard someone splashing into the sea after her. She tried to get to the deeper water but trod on another wadcutter. It pierced the sole of her shoe and she cried out and went under. Someone pulled her to the surface, and she did not have strength enough to stop them. Her spirit turned traitor and clung to life.

She heard Christiaan shouting for assistance as he dragged her back to the shore. By the time they reached the beach, his arms and legs were bleeding from coral cuts.

She lay on the sand, coughing water from her mouth and nose.

Christiaan stood over her, eyes red-rimmed. 'Why did you do that?' he said.

She choked up more seawater.

'Haven't I protected you and honored you? I would have given you everything you wanted.'

She lay with her cheek on the hard coral, tears running down her face. 'Just let us go,' she sobbed.

CHAPTER 55

The long island

Michiel sat with his men by a crackling fire of brushwood. There was no warmth in it and precious little light. They all shivered in the cold. They had found some small creatures that looked like cats and trapped a few. They had dried the skins and tied them around their calves as leggings, for none of them were large enough to make a proper cloak.

'Now we have the raft,' Michiel said, 'I say we go over there and rescue the women.'

'We don't even know if there's any of them left alive,' Little Bean said.

'Oh, they're alive,' Welten said. 'The soldiers made it plain what they wanted them kept alive for.'

'So why risk it?' one of the Englishers said. 'We lose good men for nothing. And we risk the raft, too. This is our only chance of warning the rescue ship. I say we bide our time and leave the women.'

Michiel looked around the group. Many of them wouldn't meet his eyes. They agreed with the Englisher.

Michiel shook his head. 'I'll not do it,' he said. 'If they send a ship for us, and they ask us what we did while the women were being used like this, what will we say to them? Before, we had no choice. We had no way of getting to them. Now we do.'

'He's right,' Gabriel, one of the Frenchies, said.

'So it must be done in darkness, and we will have to pole hard against the current. But it will be easier coming back.'

'It's a big risk you're taking,' Little Bean said.

'I know that. I'll not force any of you to do it. I want two volunteers to come with me.'

'Just three men against so many?'

'We are not going there to do battle. If we get to the island, and if we can find the women in the darkness, we must leave enough room on the raft to bring them all back.'

There was silence.

'Like I said, I won't order any of you to go.'

Every one of them put up their hand.

He chose two men, Gabriel and Fontaine. He would leave Little Bean in charge in case he did not come back.

'Then we're decided,' he said. 'We will leave after the moon has set. We will take them by surprise and get away again before they know what has happened.'

There was a long silence.

'God's death, it's cold,' Little Bean murmured.

CHAPTER 56

The low island

Cornelia jerked awake. Something moved outside her shelter. A boot crunched on a piece of loose coral and she heard a man breathing hard. She peered out. She saw a cluster of stars but no moon. It must be late. All the men would be drunk and snoring by now.

He would be out there somewhere, Christiaan. Getting up the courage. Fine at persuading other men to butchery but all thumbs with a woman.

She felt under the silk pillow and found Salomon's knife. This time she would not hesitate. She held her breath and waited. The intruder crawled right to the entrance of her shelter.

'Cornelia?'

The whisper was so soft she could hardly make it out.

'Michiel?'

'Shh.' His hand reached inside for hers and slid down the edge of the knife. 'God's breath!'

She quickly put the knife back into its scabbard and grabbed his arm with her other hand. He pulled her outside.

'You came back.'

'I said I would,' he whispered. 'My God, I'm bleeding everywhere.'

'I'm sorry, I thought you were one of them.' He smelled of woodsmoke, salt and sweat.

'It doesn't matter,' he whispered. 'Just stay by me. Keep quiet.'

She saw shadows moving in the dark; other women scrambling down the rocks to the beach. She dared a glance over her shoulder at the *muyter's* tents. One of them was snoring like a pig. They drank hard every night after they'd been to the women's tent.

She stumbled on a piece of loose coral and snagged her dress in the saltbush. But she kept a tight grip on his arm until they were in the shallows. She saw a raft with a single mast silhouetted against the lagoon. Her dress was soon soaked. She could barely move in it.

She heard the other women wading in. One of them took a tumble and went splashing headlong into the water. Could they make any more noise? She waited for Christiaan or Joost to come roaring down the beach.

Michiel helped her onto the raft, then went back to help the others. She felt it rock every time he lifted one of the women aboard. Neeltje's baby started crying. Gabriel hissed at her to keep him quiet. She fussed over him and tried to get him to nurse, but the little boy was having none of it. His cries grew louder.

There were shouts from the shore.

'For God's sake hurry!' Michiel said.

She saw a bright flash and the crack of a musket shot.

'Lie flat!' Michiel shouted. 'Don't give them a target!' He told his comrades to start poling.

Alida was last aboard. She tried to pull herself up but fell back in. The raft rocked alarmingly as Michiel lifted her up a second time. There was another musket flash and someone gasped in pain.

'Gabriel's been shot,' Fontaine said.

There were lamps bobbing all along the shore. The *muyters* came splashing into the shallows after them.

'What about Hendrika?' someone said.

'Why isn't she with you?' Michiel said.

'She's married to Joost now,' Cornelia said. 'She's in his tent.'

'There's nothing I can do about that,' he said. 'We have to get away from here now.'

He hauled himself onto the raft. The current carried them swiftly away from the rocks and out into the lagoon. The outgoing tide would sweep them most of them way back.

CHAPTER 57

The sun was inching above the horizon as their raft drifted towards the long island. Cornelia woke, stiff with cold, and sat up. Michiel's soldiers stood along the shore watching them float in with the current.

Fontaine poled them into the shallows and the soldiers waded out to meet them. Gabriel was lifted off first, then Michiel and Fontaine slid into the water to help the women off. Other soldiers dragged the raft in.

Cornelia stood on the narrow beach, wind-battered and cold. For the first time in months she was not afraid.

Michiel called for Little Bean. 'Mount a guard on the women day and night. Our men haven't seen a skirt in a while. I won't give any of these women reason to fear anything from us after all they've been through.'

'Sir.'

Cornelia went to the water's edge. 'How's your wounded man?' she said.

'It looks bad,' Little Bean said. 'It's a lung shot and we have no doctor.'

'Is he going to die?'

'Looks like it,' he said and went back up the beach to organize the men.

Cornelia looked at Michiel. There was blood dripping from his fingers. 'Look at your hand. We should bind it up.'

'Where did you get the knife?'

She showed it to him, in its weathered leather scabbard. 'Salomon gave it to me.'

'He's alive?'

'No, they murdered him in the end. Krueger did it.'

'What about Richard Merrell?'

She shook her head.

'I should have taken him with me.'

'He had a broken arm. You had no choice.' She felt the strength go out of her and she fell to her knees. 'Thank God it's over,' she said.

'It's not over,' he said. 'They'll come for us now. But we're ready for them.'

The low island

Christiaan sat in his tent drinking brandy and listening to the Devil's Own squabbling with each other on the beach. He picked up the Constantine cameo and tossed it in fury across his tent. One of the jewels in the frame sprang from its casing and landed in the sand.

How could this happen?

'So much for telling us there was no water on the long island,' he heard Krueger say to Rees.

'There isn't any.'

'Then how is it they're still alive?'

'We should have killed them while we had the chance,' Joost said.

'It was Christiaan who said we should send them over there,' Stonecutter said. ' *Let them rot in the sun,* ' wasn't that his words?'

'We wouldn't have to worry about them if you hadn't lost the raft,' Strootman said to Krueger.

'It would have been all right if you knew how to use a sword,' Rees shot back.

'Never mind blaming the cabin boy,' Stonecutter said. 'The raft was Krueger's responsibility. But no, you had to play your stupid game with the pastor and you left it unguarded.'

'Who knew that bastard would think of doing something like that?'

'My brother had a cow once with more brains than you. She was more use too. At least he could milk the fucking thing.'

Christiaan had heard enough. As he stepped outside he saw a knife blade flash in the sun. Joost grabbed Krueger by the arms and held him. Stonecutter was on his feet too, reaching for his own knife.

'Stop!' Christiaan stepped between them. 'What's going on here?'

'Stonecutter called Krueger stupid.'

Christiaan smiled. 'There is argument about that?'

They all laughed, except Krueger; it was nervous laughter, certainly, but it broke the tension. Stonecutter sat back down. Joost and Rees relaxed.

'You forget why we are here,' Christiaan said to them. 'Look at you all, some little thing goes wrong and you are at each other's throats.' He took a silver *thaler* from his pocket. 'Look.' He held the coin up to the light. 'There are whole chests of silver bullion for each one of you if you have the courage for it. Or do you want to fight with each other, instead of fighting the men who stand in your way?'

He turned on Stonecutter. 'It's just a few women we've lost. We'll go and get them back. Or are you all scared? Easy to kill other men when they don't have weapons but it's different against real soldiers, isn't it?' He shook his head, like a schoolmaster with unruly pupils. 'I can give you whatever you want. All you have to do is trust me. One little setback is not going to stand between us and our destiny.' He looked round at them. 'Well, do you trust me?'

One by one they nodded their heads.

'How do we do it then,' Krueger said. 'How do we get our women back?'

'It's not about the women,' Stonecutter said. 'The raft is more important.'

Christiaan nodded, trying to make them understand. 'Yes, yes! Don't you see? Now they have a raft, they will be able to alert the rescue ship when it comes. If that happens, it is all over for us. We have to get that raft back. To do that we have to kill them, all of them.'

'How much time do you think we have?' Krueger said.

'It could be months,' someone said, one of the sailors. 'Maybe years.'

'What are we waiting for?' Strootman said. 'Let's do it! Look at the fun we had on the seal island. The provost thought he was a hard man and he died as easy as the rest.'

'You are talking about soldiers like me,' Stonecutter growled at him. 'You wouldn't kill me as easy as you killed a few tailors.'

'But they don't have weapons.'

'I know van Texel. He will have thought of something. And believe me, if you came at him with a sword, he'd take it off a little runt like you with one hand and break your neck with the other.'

'We should use the muskets,' Rees said. 'We'll make short work of them then.'

They all looked at Christiaan for his agreement.

'How many musket balls will it take to subdue them all?' he said. 'We must husband our powder and shot, for we may need it to overcome the rescue ship.'

Krueger looked at Stonecutter. 'You have half a dozen men, all armed with swords,' he said. 'You'll make short work of them.'

'Maybe we don't want to kill all of them,' Christiaan said, 'If we are to go pirating, we need all the men we can get.'

Stonecutter thought about that.

'Well?' Joost said. 'You think we might yet turn some of them to our side?'

'Maybe some of the Frenchies,' Stonecutter said. 'They've been living like dogs over there for weeks. They may be ripe for persuasion.'

'How do we do it?' Joost said.

'We will take the preacher with us,' Christiaan said. 'He will sweet talk the Englishers, promise them blankets and food and perhaps even some weapons if they give us back the raft.'

'They won't fall for that.'

'It doesn't matter. We just need to split them into two groups. Meanwhile Stonecutter talks to the Frenchies, gets some of them onto our side. Any that don't turn we put to the sword.'

'I still say we take the muskets,' Rees said.

Christiaan looked at Stonecutter, who shook his head. 'We don't need muskets.'

'That's settled then,' Christiaan said. 'Tomorrow we will go over to the long island, recruit some more men and finish the rest. Then we take our raft and our women back. This time Miss High and Mighty goes to the women's tent!'

They all cheered.

The *Zandaam*

Lying awake in his bunk, Ambroise heard the drum roll of breakers on the reef. They were in calm seas, and every day they saw the gentle ruffle of foam on uncharted reefs, but there was still no sign of the wreck or the people. It was impossible to sleep, even though his body screamed with exhaustion. He dressed and went back on deck.

The only other member of the *Utrecht* he had brought with him was Arie Barents, the understeersman.

Barents said that the ship had foundered at thirty minutes of latitude, but Ambroise suspected that he had lied deliberately to avoid blame. When they hit the rocks, they were at twenty-eight degrees, at either fifteen or twenty minutes – the latitude Governor Coen had warned them to avoid. Barents' dissembling had cost them weeks of fruitless searching.

It was only yesterday Ambroise had finally persuaded Evarts, the *Zandaam's* skipper, to search further south.

He patrolled the deck and fretted. He was afraid that when they found the islands they would find only skeletons picked clean by the birds and crabs.

The dark and whispering sea seemed to mock him.

CHAPTER 58

The long island

The wind whistled and moaned through the saltbush, lifting a fine mist of grit across the island. Michiel's men lay huddled for warmth in little depressions in the sand, watching the sea and waiting. Their clothes were rotting on their bodies, and the tattered cats' hides they wore were poor protection against the biting cold of the Southland winter.

'We should not lie here so close like this,' Michiel said, turning to Cornelia. 'You're a married woman. It's not right.'

It was a poor bed. The hard ground might be a nest to a mutton bird, but there was no way to get comfortable on it.

'I confess I don't know what's right and what's wrong anymore,' she said. 'Nothing is as it seems. Our ship's captain turned out to be a lecher and a drunk, our undermerchant a monster and our commander a coward.'

'Don't be too hard on Ambroise. None of us knows how we will behave until we are tested in the fire ourselves.'

'Perhaps. But cowardice is one thing. Evil is another.'

'You are surprised at villainy?'

'In men I thought I could trust, yes. You are not?'

'I have lived a different life to you. People think to find monsters as they would recognize madness - by the blood between the teeth, a crazed look in the eye. But a real villain will smile at you, make you laugh and put you at your ease before he cuts your throat or forces you onto a bed.'

'Like Christiaan.'

'The world is full of men like him. They only need a shipwreck to reveal them for what they are. Villains will work at ledgers in warehouses or lounge in the salons of fine houses. They might be spoiled young men with dainty manners and soft hands, or wait on your table with their eyes lowered, while their minds run to razors and rape. All villains are the masters of disguise.'

'I can understand lust. But not murder. They went at killing like it was a joy.'

'In a war, there are two kinds of soldier. Some kill because they have to, but they never get a taste for it. But there are others – and Stonecutter is one - they can't ever get enough of it.'

'Why did you become a soldier?'

'I'm like Joost. My family had influence enough to get me a commission in the Company, but not enough money to live.'

She laid her head against his chest. 'I can hear your heart beating.'

'You should not be doing this.'

'Are you really this noble?'

'I am trying to be.'

'One day soon, Christiaan and his *muyters* will come and we will all be dead. It is only wrong if God is watching. After all that has happened, I am convinced he has turned the other way.'

He kissed her.

The wind howled over the island. She sheltered from the gale under his body.

Her wedding bed in the Leleistraat had feather down and four posts; her husband had worn a nightshirt and she a linen gown trimmed with lace. But she knew that should she ever get away from these islands, she would think of love as a small depression in the shale, cold and blasted with sand, and a man and woman fumbling with salt crusted clothes.

The low island

The pastor shivered. His feet were bare, his coat in tatters. At some point he had even lost his Bible. Lost or cast aside, Christiaan wondered. Now that would be interesting to know.

Christiaan sat in the Great Chair, which had been placed outside his tent so that he could hold audience. He let the pastor stand there in the wind for as long as it pleased him. Finally he said, 'We need you to act as emissary for us.'

He detected a flicker of hope on the old man's face.

'I have decided these islands are too poor to sustain us. Although I have done my utmost, by the strength of God Almighty, to preserve the peace here among the fractious survivors of the wreck, we require more food and water than I am able to provide. I therefore intend for us all to sail to the high island you see in the distance. But to do that we need the raft the soldiers have stolen from us.'

The pastor nodded, as if he understood.

'I want you to act as our intermediary. Tell them we will exchange the raft for cloth, wine and blankets. When it is done, we will leave them in peace and may God have mercy on their souls.'

'If I do it, will you let me go?'

'Let you go? You sound as if you are my prisoner.'

'Surely I am a burden to you?'

'You want to stay on the island with the soldiers?'

The pastor looked like a cornered animal.

'What about Hendrika? Could you really stand to be parted from her and your new son-in-law.' He turned to Joost. 'What do you think? Will your wife agree to this, do you think?'

'She would be most heartsore. But if that is what the pastor wants, then I shall console her as best I can.'

'I'll tell you what. Do this for me, and I'll let you have a place back on the Council. I'll even give you a bigger shelter. I have always treated you well, haven't I?'

The pastor nodded.

Christiaan smiled. It just showed; you could beat a dog all you liked, but bring him one bone and he was still yours to command.

The *Zandaam*

They came upon the reefs on the forty-seventh day of sailing. Ambroise saw the white sprouting of reefs ahead of them.

It seemed impossible that it had taken so long, and he wondered again if Schellinger had been right when he told Coen he was the only one that could find the wreck.

Evarts saw them too. He gave orders to bring the ship around.

'You cannot turn back!' Ambroise shouted at him. 'We must find a way through the reef!'

'It's too dangerous,' Evarts said. The look on his face was plain: *You've supervised the destruction of one ship. You're not going to watch over the destruction of mine.*

Ambroise turned away in frustration. He was sure that the islands they could make out in the distance were the same ones where he had landed the people after the wreck.

The *Zandaam* headed back out to sea.

CHAPTER 59

The long island

Michiel watched the pastor wade ashore, clutching a pole with a strip of white linen tied to it. A flag of truce, he thought. Well, this should be interesting. He looked thin. Michiel supposed he wasn't getting his full ration from Christiaan.

'What are they up to?' Little Bean said.

'We'd better find out,' Michiel said and made his way down to the beach.

Two rafts stood off in the shallows. He and Little Bean were within range of their muskets, but they appeared to have left them behind. He could see no burning powder. They were overconfident, he supposed. That was good. Besides, Stonecutter would be the only one out of this shower who knew which end of a gun to hold.

'Pastor,' he called out.

The pastor looked pleased to see him. His face split into a smile of pathetic gratitude. 'Praise be to God,' he gushed, 'the *muyters* want to help you!'

Michiel kept his eye on the men in the rafts. Now there's a sight a man doesn't see every day of his life, he thought. The way they were dressed, in scarlet coats and with thick gold chains around their necks, they looked like they were freshly returned from a beggar's costume party. Christiaan looked the dandiest of them all.

The pastor had tears on his face.

'What's the matter?' Michiel said.

'You don't know how I have suffered.'

'Well, this has not been an easy time for anyone.'

'You don't understand. They have slaughtered my family. I have been reduced to eating grass. You must help me, sir.'

Michiel had no time for this whining. He again looked beyond the churchman's shoulder to the boats. Christiaan and his band were poling their raft further down the beach. Stonecutter was with them.

Do they know we have weapons, he wondered. No, that's impossible. So why haven't they come ashore and tried to slaughter us? It's what I would have done. It's what I have been counting on.

'What is it they want?' he said.

'They have commissioned me to tell you that they intend to sail to the distant high island, as we are low on food and water where we are and cannot survive there much longer. If you will but give the raft back to them, they have promised to leave you in peace. In exchange they will give you a cask of good wine and two chests of cloth and blankets, so that you may make new clothes.'

'Those I stand in have served me well enough.'

'Let them have the raft, sir, so that this nightmare can be over.'

Michiel turned to Little Bean. 'Would you trust Christiaan van Sant at his word, corporal?'

'If he were tightly trussed and gagged and his balls were in my sea chest.'

Michiel looked down the beach. Christiaan's raft had drawn closer into the shallows, and Stonecutter was calling out to one of the Frenchies on the shore. He couldn't make out what he was saying.

He turned back to the pastor. 'What if we don't want to trade?'

The pastor stepped closer. 'I beg you sir, don't send me back. In the name of the Lord, I cannot stand another moment as their prisoner.

Their treatment of me has been abominable. You cannot know how I have suffered.'

And he began to weep again.

Christiaan stood on the beach, one hand on his hip, with Stonecutter and Joost either side of him. Several of the French mercenaries had gathered around, eager to hear what they had to say.

'How are things with you boys?' Stonecutter said. 'We have been worried about you.'

'Liar,' one of the Frenchies said. 'You left us here to rot.'

Christiaan contrived to look remorseful. 'It is true that Rees tricked you into believing there was plentiful water here. He tricked all of us. I knew nothing of this until it was too late. He did it because he wished there to be more food and water for the rest of us.'

His hair was carefully brushed and his gold medallion nestled in the ruff of his collar. He knew he made for a breath-taking vision on this drab morning. These poor fools looked as stunned as chickens goggling at the butcher's knife.

'Then why didn't you come back for us?'

'I had some trouble to attend to first. There was mutiny on our island and I had to suppress it for the good of all.' He spared a glance down the beach. Michiel was still talking to the pastor. This was going to be easy.

'That's not what Welten and the women say,' the Frenchman said.

Christiaan made a face, to show what he thought of listening to women. Somebody laughed. Christiaan warmed to his task. 'You know what women are like. They all have many words and few thoughts. As for Welten, he is a carpenter. Do I need say more?'

He looked at Stonecutter and Joost. They had their hands on their swords, eager to be at their former comrades. He shook his head. He just needed a little more time to work on the soldiers. Soon he'd have them eating out of his hand. Then they could deal with van Texel and the rest and get their women back.

'Now look here,' Stonecutter said, sweetly reasonable. 'You all know me. I was a hard sergeant, yes, but I was always fair, wasn't I? What the Captain-General here says is the truth.'

'He's not a Captain-General. He's the undermerchant,' the Frenchman said.

Christiaan sighed. 'Look, let's get this straight. That drunkard skipper is not coming back for us, or the commander. The Houtman Rocks is too miserable to sustain us further, and Krueger and the *jonkers* want us to try our luck on the high island you see over there. Why don't you come with us? We have wine and plentiful food and blankets, that you might keep yourselves warm through these cold nights.'

'The cloth belongs to the Company.'

'I think, in the circumstances, the Company will not mind. They can have your old breeches in exchange.'

Even some of the Frenchies laughed at that. Christiaan was delighted to have an appreciative audience. He was enjoying himself now.

He turned to Joost, who unwrapped the blanket he had brought with him from the raft. Inside was a roundel of Gouda cheese. He tossed it to one of the soldiers, who caught it with a look of stunned surprise. Then he held up the blanket for them all to see. They stared at it as if it were woven silk and not poor-quality wool.

'Join us,' Joost said. 'Fill your bellies and get warm. Now that everything is in order again, it is safe for you to come back.' He jerked a thumb over his shoulder at van Texel and the Flemish and English mercenaries further up the beach. 'Forget about them. You signed on to the Company for one reason, right?'

The men looked at each other.

Christiaan reached into his pocket and pulled out a handful of silver *rix dollars*. 'There's plenty of these for everyone who comes over to us.'

'How are we going to spend it? Do we give it to the mutton birds for a good time?'

Christiaan laughed along with them. But when he spoke again, his voice was sharp. 'So none of you wants to be rich?'

'What are you talking about?'

'When the Company sends their rescue ship – and they will - we will be taken aboard and no one will suspect that poor starving wretches as ourselves have teeth. When we are safely on the ship, she will be ours.' He looked from face to face.

'That's mutiny,' one of them said.

'I call it opportunity,' Christiaan said. 'How much will the Company reward you for your loyalty here - for starving and freezing your balls off on this God forsaken island, month after month? Come with us and you won't ever have to take the Company's pittance again. You can make your own fortunes and be your own men! We will be the new East India company!'

He held one of the silver dollars in front of their eyes. The bright metal caught the sun, mesmerizing them. Christiaan had never felt so eloquent, so masterful, or so much in control. He jingled his purse.

'Our silver is better than theirs and you'll have a lot more of it. Let us be friends again.'

He saw by their faces that he had them. Damned garlic eaters, they'd sell their own mothers if there was profit in it. You'd never find anyone in the world as amoral as a Frenchman, he thought. Not even a Spaniard.

'Here,' he said, throwing more coins at their feet. They went tinkling among the rocks. 'Take the money. It's yours.'

'We'll have to talk about this,' one of the Frenchies said, and they went back to the rock ledge and started whispering among themselves.

Christiaan turned around. 'You see?' he said to Stonecutter. 'A good silver coin speaks any language.'

Stonecutter drew his sword.

Christiaan span around. The Frenchies came at the charge. Where had they got those weapons from? They must have hidden them among the rocks. He turned and ran back through the shallows to the raft. He'd let Stonecutter do the fighting; that was his profession, after all.

He was their leader and too important to lose.

The rest of the soldiers came rushing down the beach, armed with pikes. Even those men who had at first stood their ground were falling back now. The soldiers pursued them into the shallows, jeering at them as they ran.

Stonecutter stumbled in the mud and went under. When he came up, there was a gash running from his temple to his ear and watery blood was streaming out of it.

Christiaan could not credit their perfidy. He had come under a white flag. Had these men no honor? He heard Strootman screaming. He and several others were being cut to pieces.

Stonecutter launched himself onto Christiaan's raft and lay there, his hair matted with blood. A stream of gore dripped steadily from his nose onto the wet timber. He had lost his fine hat in the commotion.

Both rafts rocked dangerously as the other *muyters* scrambled aboard, while van Texel's soldiers mocked them from the beach. Christiaan ordered them to turn the rafts around and let the current drag them back into the lagoon.

CHAPTER 60

The *Zandaam*

Barents was grey from the long watches; Evart's face was haggard beneath his beard. The sailors were all bone-tired and freezing from struggling with lines and rigging, from furling and unfurling the canvas, and from searching the same stretch of ocean over and over again. Ambroise himself was on the point of collapse. It was only his will that kept him standing; his will and the ghosts of the people he had left behind.

He had not had a good night's sleep since the voyage had begun, and the sleeplessness grew worse the closer they came. They had been fifty-six days at sea, and still they could find no way through the reefs.

What could I have done differently, he asked himself. The fevers robbed me of my powers of reason when I needed them most. It was my want of revenge that now has the skipper in irons. Should I have laid aside my personal enmity and given him a chance for his own redemption as well?

They ran into another squall. He paced the quarterdeck, shivering in his wet clothes. His body was racked with chills again.

He turned to Barents. 'Why are we not seeing the islands?'

'The wind is against us here.'

For weeks now it had been the same story. Barents blamed unfavorable currents or contrary breezes. Every morning the wind blew from the south east, so they carried the mainsail at half, losing latitude as they crept towards the Southland. Then at evening they would head back out to sea, for fear of striking the reef, and in the morning the quest would begin again. They were always either too far south or too far to the west. They had sailed backwards and forwards for weeks now through this same latitude, looking for passage.

'This is ridiculous. We reached Batavia in a tiny yawl in just thirty days. Yet here we are, in one of the finest yachts in the Company's fleet, and we have been more than fifty days up and down the Southland coast and not found the wreck or the people.'

'That is no fault of mine,' Evarts protested. 'It is notorious that the *Utrecht* was lost through her skipper's carelessness, but it cannot be allowed that the *Zandaam* founders through negligence as well. As for the bearings we have followed, well it is hardly surprising to me that they are at fault, since it was bad navigation that lost the *Utrecht* in the first place.'

Barents rounded on him in a fine temper. 'It was no fault of the steersmen that the *Utrecht* foundered, God's death!'

There was a long pacing silence on the deck as they tried to regain their composure.

'You should go below, sir,' Evarts said to Ambroise. 'You seem unwell.'

Ambroise shook his head. 'I am well enough.' He looked down into the swelling ocean, at the seaweed and cuttlefish bones floating in the wash.

Where were the islands?

The long island

They had four bodies to bury and Rees trussed like a roasting hog. He was screaming threats, so Michiel put a gag in his mouth and one of the Frenchies pissed on his head. That shut him up.

It was a tainted victory, for they had the preacher back with them. He sat by the fire, shoveling haunches of roasted cat into his mouth.

Finally Michiel squatted down and snatched the roasted joint out of the pastor's hand. There was grease on his chin, and his jowls hung loose like saddlebags.

'Is Hendrika still alive?' Michiel said.

'I did all I could.'

'That wasn't my question.'

'I tried to protect her, but they pinned me down. It took four of them to do it.'

Michiel heard Rees shrieking and protesting through the gag.

'*Vrouwe* Noorstrandt says you married her off to one of the *jonkers*.'

The pastor licked his lips. He looked trapped.

'She consented to this?'

'Of course.'

'Is the pastor telling the truth?' Christiaan said to Rees. 'She still lives?'

Rees nodded, wide-eyed.

The pastor stared at Rees. 'We should do that one to death. He was one of them that murdered my family.' His lower lip started to quiver.

Michiel looked across the lagoon. It was a shame that that bastard undermerchant had got away from them. Fontaine had told him what he had said to them on the beach. That silver-tongued devil could persuade the angels themselves to a night in hell.

Now he understood why the *muyters* wanted the raft. They were going to try to steal their rescue ship. He and his men would have to make sure they got there first.

The *Zandaam*

Ambroise stood on the deck, his fists white knuckled around the rail. For two days the storm had kept them here, all anchors out. He cursed into the wind. The words carried away on the tempest. It was as if God Himself conspired against him, making him wait for his judgment day.

Evarts held out the eyeglass. 'There are the reefs again,' he said.

Ambroise took it from him and stared at the foam of another breakwater. The *Utrecht* must have somehow passed through this maze that night. The only way they would find her now would be to enter the same foul ground.

He told Evarts what he wanted him to do.

Evarts shook his head. 'It's too dangerous.'

'For a month now, we have been back and forth around these latitudes and seen no sign of the wreck,' Ambroise said. 'I say the *Utrecht* is inside these reefs and we should proceed from landward to pass inside. There is a broad channel here if we proceed with circumspection.'

'If we lose the *Zandaam*...'

'We shall not lose the *Zandaam* if we approach as I say. But if we do not do this my way, we shall be old men with grey beards and still find ourselves under sail.'

An argument ensued. But Ambroise stood his ground. He had nothing left to lose.

The low island

Stonecutter leaped off the raft and ploughed through the shallows ahead of the others. Blood dripped from the end of his fingers.

Hendrika ran down to the beach to meet him. 'Where's my father?' she said

Stonecutter walked straight up to her and sent her sprawling into the brush. The rest of the men stormed up the beach. They were shouting and cursing, blaming each other for what had happened. How could they be defeated by a rabble with pikes made out of flotsam?

Christiaan went into his tent and reached for the ceramic bottle he had left on his driftwood table. He finished it in one gulp, the fine French brandy dribbling through his beard.

The *Zandaam*

There was an eerie silence on the ship as they made their passage. Even the sailors seemed to hold their breath. The only sound was the leadsman shouting the depths as they inched through. In these waters, huge waves would sometimes rear up from nowhere. If a comber came at them now, it would dash them onto the rocks and punch the mainmast through the hull.

But the weather held. They passed the claws of the reef and found thirty fathoms of good water.

'There it is,' Ambroise breathed and passed the glass to Barents.

'I don't know, *Heer* Commander. I cannot be sure it is the place.'

'I am sure,' he said. 'There is the high island we saw from the wreck.' He knew that Barents thought he was being fanciful; that he was seeing only what he wished to see. But he was certain.

The sun was sinking behind the distant storm clouds, throwing the islands into dark relief. They could not make a landing tonight. They would have to wait until morning.

The low island

They sat around a small fire, occasionally jumping to their feet to shout recriminations at each other. Their kingdom had crumbled away to a tiny cay of saltbush and coral slate.

Their nerves were frayed. There were murmurs of conscience pricking even at men like Stonecutter and Krueger. Before this morning, they had thought they were invincible.

Christiaan knew they needed a quick victory to restore their spirits. They must see blood on the sand again. 'It is just a small reverse,' he told them.

'Not for Rees and Strootman,' Stonecutter said.

'So what do you all think we should do? Hide here with the mutton birds, while they use our women and warn the rescue boat about our plans?'

'We must use the muskets,' Krueger said. 'We'll make short work of them then.'

Joost pointed a finger at Stonecutter. 'You said we didn't need the guns. If we had them with us this morning, this would not have happened.'

'We've no time for recriminations,' Christiaan said, 'Stonecutter, Krueger, go and check the powder and the muskets. Tomorrow we go back to the island. Enough of playing around with them. It's time to finish this.'

CHAPTER 61

There were clear skies, fair weather and flat seas for their day of reckoning. Christiaan strutted down to the beach, dressed in the commander's fine red cloak, with a mutton bird feather in his tall black hat. Krueger and Stonecutter walked behind him. He splashed through the shallows and Joost helped him onto one of the rafts.

The rest of the *muyters* crowded aboard.

Christiaan held up a silk purse from his cloak and took out a gemstone. 'A ruby for the man who kills van Texel!'

The pronouncement was greeted with ragged cheers. It had only taken a little wine and bravado to convince them that yesterday's disgrace would not be repeated.

Krueger took out his sword and tested the edge of the blade. Life was a strange master, Christiaan thought. If not for me, he would be sitting in Batavia Castle right now, with a quill in his hand, copying bills of lading. I have saved him from his own mediocrity.

They pushed away from the beach. There was just a gentle chop on the midway channel as they set the sails and headed west towards the long island. The light on the water hurt the eyes. Christiaan closed his, imagining van Texel's screams as they finally cut him down.

Those bastard soldiers wanted to rob him of his woman and his golden promise. But today he would rid himself of the final rebels in his kingdom, and he would claim his queen.

Two rafts drifted into the arm of the lagoon. Michiel's men were already on their feet, stiff and cold from the freezing night. Their hearts were pumping and they were eager to have the fight finally under way.

Michiel threw himself face down in the bushes that edged the cay's shallow cliffs and watched them come. They had brought their muskets with them this time. He could see the wicks burning.

He felt his men looking at him, waiting for his decision. If they stayed in their hiding places, the *muyters* would land unopposed on the beach and any advantage they had would be lost. If they pelted the undermerchant and his rabble with rocks, as they had the first time, they would make good targets for the muskets.

But Michiel knew there was no choice. Some of his men would die, for sure, but once the *muyters* reached the land they were all dead men anyway. Their poor assortment of makeshift weapons was no match for theirs. It all depended on how much dry powder and musket shot these bastards had left. How much had they used up, slaughtering the provost and the others?

They would soon find out.

Christiaan heard mutterings among his men as they drew closer to the beach. There was no sign of movement. Where were they? The smoke from the soldiers' cook fire drifted on the morning wind. He could smell it.

'Where are the bastards hiding?' Stonecutter said. He leaped off the raft, slipped on the coral and fell headlong into the water.

The *jonkers* were not as impatient. Their bravado had evaporated as quickly as the morning mist. They were more careful when they left the rafts, treading gingerly in the coffee-colored water. They kept their clogs on their feet, as protection against the terrible wadcutter shells buried in the mud. It was hard going.

There was still no sign of Michiel or the soldiers. The strip of beach they had chosen for their landing was no wider than the gallery of the

Utrecht and fringed by limestone cliffs the height of a man's shoulders. They could be a few yards away and still not see them.

'Take your time,' Christiaan said, 'there is plenty here for all of us.' He stayed on the raft and adopted a heroic pose, hands on his hips.

Joost stayed on the boat too, with Krueger and some of the best marksmen, ready with the muskets. They couldn't risk wading through the water and getting their powder wet. Their eyes shone like hungry men before a banquet.

The *jonkers* were making slow progress. Several of them went under, as Stonecutter had done, and emerged from the water streaming blood from coral cuts. One of them went down into a pothole as deep as his armpit and let out a shrill scream, thinking he was about to drown.

Suddenly a dozen of Michiel's soldiers emerged from the bushes, and a hail of rocks arced through the air. A large slab of coral hit Stonecutter on the head, just as he had regained his footing in the shallows. He howled in pain and dropped his sword. He held his hands to his face and blood spurted through his fingers and down his wrist.

The soldiers were ranged right the way along the cliffs. Lumps of coral, some the size of a man's head, rained down on Christiaan's army, and there were cries of fright and outrage as rocks splashed into the water around them. Several of the *jonkers* were already stumbling back to the rafts.

Michiel watched them splashing panicked in the shallows. His own missile hit one man on the head, and he went down on his knees then toppled face first into the water. Not one of his comrades went to help him.

He knew this victory would not be as easy as their first. The *muyters* on the rafts had their muskets primed and raised. There was a ragged volley of gunfire, and one of the Frenchies standing beside him screamed and fell back, clutching at his throat, coughing blood everywhere.

But his boys were battle hardened and up for the fight. Another salvo of rocks splashed into the water, and several more of the *muyters* screamed and went down. The rest crouched in the shallows, too scared to advance or retreat.

Michiel knew it would take Christiaan's men time to reload their muskets. He picked up his pike and shouted the order to attack. He jumped from the low cliff, a dozen of his best fighters following, armed with their homemade pikes and morning star clubs. They charged into the water.

Stonecutter came at him, his face a mask of blood. As he came out of the shallows, he stooped to pick up a sword that one of the *jonkers* had dropped in the sand.

Michiel knew what he would do. He had warned him countless times in their drills on the *Utrecht*. But Stonecutter had the bloodlust in him, and rage made a man careless. As he swung with the cutlass, Michiel ducked down and thrust forward with the pike. He took Stonecutter just under the ribs and the big man's eyes went wide as he realized what had happened.

Michiel jumped to his feet and stepped back out of range. Stonecutter staggered, but he kept coming. He swung again but Michiel danced out of the way.

'I'll see you to hell!' Stonecutter shouted.

There's only one of going to hell this day, Michiel thought. He ran forward inside Stonecutter's guard and thrust with the pike a second time. It took his throat out. He went down in a spray of blood, choking.

Little Bean was shouting, 'We have to get back to the cliffs!'

Michiel had never taken much pleasure in killing. But this time he stood over the stricken man, as he kicked and thrashed, and watched the light go out of his eyes.

'Captain, please!' Little Bean yelled.

He looked up. The *muyters* had reloaded. He turned to run back to the cliff, but he was too late. There was a second volley of musket fire, and another of his Frenchies went down screaming. He and Fontaine grabbed the wounded man and hauled him back up the beach.

As they reached the low cliffs, Michiel felt something hit him hard in the back and his legs gave way under him. He stumbled to his knees.

Little Bean helped him up. 'You've been hit, captain.'

'Take over,' Michiel said. He thought that being shot with a musket ball would hurt more than this. It must be just a minor wound. Two of his men helped him scramble up the cliff and he pitched onto his face.

The *Zandaam*

'Smoke,' Barents said.

Ambroise looked where he was pointing. Now he saw it too. It was the site of the wreck, he was sure of it, though they were approaching from the north this time. The high island off the starboard bow was where he and Schellinger had gone in search of water. The smoke was proof that some had survived.

The *Zandaam* edged forward under shortened sail. Reefs foamed all around them.

'You were right, thanks be to God,' Barents said.

Ambroise allowed himself a pained smile. In silent prayer, they drifted in.

CHAPTER 62

The long island

They laid Michiel face down behind the limestone barricade. Cornelia pulled off his red coat and tunic and washed the wound as best she could. A bowl of bloody water and rags lay beside her.

'It is only a small hole,' she said, 'but the ball is still in there. It went in near the shoulder blade.'

'I can't worry about it now,' he said. 'Go and help the women with the other wounded. I'm all right.'

The fight had been going on for over an hour. Each time the *muyters* came, they beat them back with rocks, pikes and clubs, but at a cost. Already nearly two dozen of his men lay bleeding and groaning from musket wounds. It was a quarter of his entire force.

It was sound tactics. If the *muyters* had enough powder they could pick them off like this all day until there was none of them left to fight.

The sun rose up the sky. He heard the droning of the pastor's voice. He was down on his knees again, praying to the Lord. Well why not, he thought. It had worked before when they were dying of thirst on the low island. Perhaps he would bring them another miracle. But he didn't know why anyone, least of all the good Lord, would want to listen to that bag of wind.

He looked around at Rees, who was lying on the ground, still trussed and gagged. 'Don't you go hoping to be rescued by that lot,' he said. 'Last thing I do before I die, I'm going to cut your throat for you.'

Rees wriggled and squirmed. One of the Frenchies walked over and pissed on him again, for the hell of it.

'What are we going to do?' Fontaine said. He and Little Bean waited, as if Michiel had an answer for them. But he had no more tricks. It all depended on whether the *muyters* would run out of powder before he ran out of men to fight them.

Christiaan's inkpot army had paddled away from the beach, preparing powder and shot for another sortie.

The Frenchie with the musket ball in his throat had finally finished with his dying. Blood had congealed like jelly around his neck wound, and flies were swarming over this unexpected feast. His body was unsettling the men. Not all of them had been in a proper battle before.

Another of the wounded men was screaming, and his keening was fraying all their nerves. It was a belly wound; the worst kind.

'If we retreat,' Fontaine said, 'then we can ambush them as they come through the brush after us. They don't all have muskets.'

'But then they will find the raft,' Michiel said. He coughed up a clot of blood. 'It's the raft they want. Once they have it, they could abandon us here again.'

The pastor kept up his prayers of supplication. I think God has forgotten us this time, Michiel thought. He doubted that they could hold them off for more than a few hours.

'Look!' someone shouted. 'Sail!' A ship was creeping into the lagoon from the west.

Michiel smiled grimly. Well how about that. The pastor has his miracle a second time.

'We're saved!' the pastor shouted.

'Not yet,' Fontaine said.

Michiel stumbled to his feet. He staggered and almost fell. Little Bean grabbed his arm. 'I'm all right,' he said. 'We have to get to the raft.'

He headed inland. The raft was hidden on the other side of the island. A dozen men leaped to their feet and went after him.

The *Zandaam*

As they came closer to the long island, the smoke they had seen just after dawn disappeared, adding to Ambroise's frustration.

'The wreck is further to the south,' Barents said. 'The island where we landed the people is much smaller than that one.'

'Yet the smoke came from here. I'm sure of it,' Ambroise said. Surely the people had seen their sails? So why had they not kept the beacon burning? He experienced the first gnawing of unease.

'But we landed the people on the smaller island.'

'The lagoon is too shallow for us to navigate,' Everts said. 'We must turn about and come in again, from another direction.'

'No, we will go and investigate,' Ambroise insisted. 'Break out the scow. We will try the smaller island first, as Barents has said.' He shouted for the soldiers to fetch barrels of water and bread from below in case they found survivors.

They dropped anchor and a boat was lowered over the side. Its mast and sail were quickly hoisted. Ambroise nearly fell into the scuppers in his haste to get aboard. Barents jumped down beside him.

'Hurry,' Ambroise shouted at the crewmen. After three months, a few more minutes would make little difference to the survivors. But it made every bit of difference to him.

CHAPTER 63

The long island

They had hidden the raft in the bush, covered up with loose branches, opposite the northern tip of the seal island. They dragged it from its hiding place and down towards the beach.

The rescue ship was anchored in the lagoon, opposite the low island. The orange, white and blue banner of the royal house of Holland fluttered at the stern. It was the *Zandaam*, Michiel was sure of it.

They pushed the raft into the water and jumped on. Little Bean had the men pole out through the shallows and then set to with their rough-hewn oars. They had to reach the ship before Christiaan and the *muyters*, or their miracle might disappear in front of their eyes.

Michiel lay on his back staring at the sky. It was like he was seeing everything through a darkening tunnel. It was getting harder to breathe.

The low island

Ambroise was first out of the scow, even before she was beached. He waded through the muddy shallows. He saw movement away to his right and turned towards it but it was just a seal, watching him with liquid eyes and warming itself on a rock.

The shelters the people had built were deserted. Was no one left? He found a child's clog on the beach and a discarded ceramic bottle that smelled as if it had once contained brandy.

He took off his hat and ran up the beach, stumbling on the loose coral. He was soon out of breath. Where were they all?

There was a shout from one of the sailors and he looked around. The man was pointing towards the northern tip of the island. A raft had appeared at the headland.

Praise be to God!

The men on the raft were on their feet, shouting and waving their arms in joy at their rescue. Or were they?

'Go back!' he heard one of them shouting. 'Get back to the ship!'

Then he heard a woman's voice behind him. It was Hendrika.

Dear God.

It was not just her physical appearance that was different, though that had changed more than he could have imagined; her skin, burned by the wind, was peeling from her nose and forehead, and her fair hair was bleached almost white by salt and sun and hung loose about her shoulders. It looked so stiff it might have been lacquered. Her dress was just a rag.

But it was her eyes that scared him. They were lifeless, like a fish that had lain all day in the bottom of the boat.

One of the sailors went to help her. She collapsed in his arms.

The men on the raft poled into the lagoon and one of them jumped into the shallows and started to wade in. It was Captain van Texel, though barely recognizable in his rags. His beard was encrusted with salt, and his hair was tangled and straggling around his collar. He had the wild-eyed expression of a man just come from a battle.

'Go back!' he shouted, 'the *muyters* are here. They have two rafts and they will try to seize the yacht!' He swayed on his feet, then fell to his knees and went face first into the water.

Two of the sailors dragged him up onto the beach. There was a bloody hole in the back of his tattered jacket.

He coughed a spray of pink froth. 'The *undermerchant,*' he said. 'He intends to seize your yacht. You have to return and protect it.'

'Look,' Barents said. He pointed at the headland to the north. Two more rafts had appeared, crowded with men, and they were heading straight for the *Zandaam.*

The purposeful passage of the rafts shook Ambroise from his astonishment. 'Get back to the yawl!' he shouted.

Two of the sailors started to pick Michiel up by the arms, but Ambroise ordered them away. 'Leave him,' he said. 'We have to get back to the ship!'

CHAPTER 64

The *Zandaam*

'I should not have left,' Ambroise murmured.

His mind grappled with the enormity of what he had been told, but he did not want to believe it. What I have lost in money and Company goods is bad enough, he thought, but this catastrophe will be spoken of wherever there are Hollanders living. This is the end of my career.

He watched as the awkward beach-built rafts, bristling with armed men, headed towards them across the lagoon. The yawl had sped them quickly back from the beach. The rafts were still hundreds of yards away.

As they drew closer, he could make out the faces of some of the men. He recognized Joost van der Linden. The boy had on a scarlet frockcoat covered in gold braiding. He looked like a court jester.

And there was Christiaan, dressed like a crown prince in one of his own Company coats. What in God's name had gone on here?

When they were in earshot, Christiaan stood up and raised his hand in salute. '*Heer* Commander! Thank God you have returned at last!'

'God be thanked and praised!' Ambroise shouted back. 'But why do you come armed?'

'There has been some trouble among us. We shall tell all when we are aboard.'

By the grace of God, Ambroise thought, you shall not step armed upon this ship, not if what Michiel told me is true.

The *Zandaam's* gunners were ready at the deck's swivel-cannon, and Evart's redcoats had fetched muskets from the ship's small arms locker and had them leveled at the rafts.

Ambroise could smell the burning smoke from the tinderboxes as they lit the fuses. 'Tell your men to throw away their weapons!' he shouted. 'Throw them into the water!'

The rafts made steadily on.

'I recruited these men myself, *Heer* Commander,' Christiaan shouted back. 'I issued them their weapons in the name of the Company for all our safety!'

'Tell them to throw away their weapons or we shall fire on you!'

It was enough. Even from fifty paces distant, he could hear them arguing among themselves, clearly divided on how to proceed. Finally, one of the men – by God, it looked like Krueger - tossed his musket into the water, and the others followed. Joost was last to concede, tossing his cutlass into the waves.

They drew alongside and scrambled up the cleats, to be immediately surrounded by Evart's redcoats, their pikes and swords drawn and at the ready. Christiaan was last to board. Ambroise nodded and two of Evart's men rushed him and forced his arms behind his back, binding them with good manila rope.

'*Heer* Commander,' he protested. 'Why do you treat us this way? We have suffered untold hardships in your absence and thought to be rescued and given succor, not this.'

'Take him below,' Ambroise said. 'We'll have the truth of all this later.' The wave of relief he had felt at discovering that some had survived the wreck had quickly evaporated.

There was to be no redemption after all.

The sun was low in the sky by the time Ambroise was ready to finally interrogate his undermerchant. Christiaan was brought down to the main cabin, bound with ropes.

He was a strange sight. He was dressed like a peacock, but his clothes were at odds with the look and smell of him. He had months of sand and dirt in his hair and his beard.

'Give him wine,' Ambroise said.

One of the redcoats held a ewer of Burgundy under Christiaan's face and he gulped at it like a dog.

Ambroise glanced at Evarts and the clerk, who were sitting silently in the corner. They looked utterly shaken by all they had heard that day.

'Thank God you're here at last,' Christiaan said. 'You have no idea the savagery that took place after you abandoned us.'

'I did not abandon you.'

Christiaan glanced at Evarts. 'Is that what they think in Batavia?'

'You are not here to address Captain Evarts. I am the Commander here and I shall ask the questions.'

Christiaan shrugged, as if the circumstance in which he found himself was no more than a minor inconvenience.

'What have you done here, Christiaan?'

'Only my duty. I have kept order among the people and tried to keep as many of them alive as possible in your regrettable absence.'

'We have spoken to the pastor at some length earlier today. He has told of your rapes and murders.'

Christiaan looked astonished. 'What has that damned pastor accused me of? Does he seek to blame me for what has happened?'

'It is not only the pastor who speaks against you. We have heard evidence from David Krueger and Joost van der Linden. They all say the same thing.'

Yes, they had all confessed; these great high officers of Christiaan's kingdom, his heroes and generals. After what the pastor had told him, he had put van der Linden and Krueger to the question and, praise be to God, they had succumbed quickly to the harsh interrogation. Evarts' provost had employed the water torture; it was grimly suited to their situation, since it required no elaborate equipment.

Ambroise had not enjoyed watching the procedure overmuch, but there had been no choice in the circumstances. It seemed that although the *muyters* had developed a taste for violence, they had no stomach for brutality when it was brought against themselves. With rattling breaths they had soon gasped out their confessions, blaming their wrongdoing squarely on the undermerchant.

Their stories of rape and massacre were hard to credit. Ambroise still did not wish to believe all he had heard.

'May I have a private word with you, Ambroise?' Christiaan said. 'I have things to tell you that should only pass between you and me.'

Ambroise was tempted to agree, for his own sake, but immediately saw the trap Christiaan was laying. If there were any hint of conspiracy between him and the undermerchant, Governor Coen would take him down with the rest of them.

'Anything you have to say must be said before Captain Evarts and recorded in full,' he said.

'Very well, but you should know it was not I who was to blame here, no matter what they like to tell you. It was that brute Stonecutter and Joost van der Linden, your fine *jonker*! I only tried to preserve my own life. A man may sometimes go along with terrible things in order to save himself, as you have discovered for yourself.'

You bastard, Ambroise thought. 'Do not try to draw comparison between my conduct and yours,' he said. He poured himself a draft of wine. His hands were shaking. 'The clerk, David Krueger, has freely confessed to us that it was your plan to seize any ship sent to the rescue after the foundering of the *Utrecht*. You then intended to turn to a life of piracy.'

'That is an outrageous accusation. Of course they all wish to blame me. They want to save their own necks.'

'They say you ordered the deaths of over two hundred of those that survived the wrecking of the *Utrecht*, many of them women and children.'

'Did any of your witnesses see me kill a single man, woman or child? I pretended to be among them, and when the rescue ship came I planned to give fair warning to prevent them boarding it. What choice did I have? It was that or death. You know what that choice is like, don't you, *Heer* Commander?'

He was laboring the point now. So that was to be his defense in front of Governor Coen. At worst, it would bring Ambroise down with him. He felt the perspiration inching down his spine.

But it was true what Christiaan claimed; not one of the witnesses, though they had all named the undermerchant as their leader, had actually accused him of murder.

'You deny these allegations, then?'

'I was the sole voice of reason in this madness.'

'You have witnesses you can bring in your defense?'

Christiaan smiled. '*Vrouwe* Noorstrandt.'

Ambroise licked his lips. 'What has *Vrouwe* Noorstrandt to do with this?'

'She came to me and begged me for my protection, which was freely given.'

'Protection?'

'Conduct your investigation more carefully, *Heer* Commander, and you will find that not only did I do all I could to save the Company property, I also saved her virtue. Something you singularly failed to do.'

Evarts leaned forward. 'We should speak to the others,' he said. 'The women and the other soldiers.'

Ambroise nodded. 'Take him away,' he said. He felt nauseous with guilt.

'But I am innocent!'

'That is yet to be proved.'

'You should thank me that any lived at all.'

The soldiers dragged him out of the cabin. Ambroise could hear him shouting his protests all the way.

CHAPTER 65

The low island

Ambroise did not look well. There were shadows under his eyes, and his face was gaunt from illness. This once handsome man had had all juices squeezed out of him, color and flesh together.

He looked around Christiaan's sailcloth palace. The surprise on his face was plain when he realized that the tapestry that had once hung on the wall of his Great Cabin now covered the opening. The silver ewer that had stood by the stern window of the *Utrecht* was still half full of wine. His priceless Persian carpet lay underfoot, salt-stained and discolored by the coral limestone that had been trodden over it.

He stood half-stooped under the canvas, his hand opening and closing over the hilt of the sword at his waist.

'Would you like to see the seraglio next?' Cornelia said.

'The undermerchant said he tried to protect you.'

'In his way. I think he fancied that I was in love with him.'

'Why would he think such a thing?'

'Commander, I have not had a great experience of life before this voyage, but one thing I have learned is that a man might convince himself of anything if he wishes it badly enough.'

Ambroise nodded. 'And is it true he ordered the murders of all these people?' he said.

'Those with him went along with it eagerly enough.'

'I cannot imagine,' he began, but could not find the right words to finish the thought.

'What happened to Captain Schellinger?' she said.

'They'll hang him, like as not. They can't prove he was one of the *muyters*, but Coen says he lost a Company ship and all the treasure through negligence and they won't forgive him for that. Joost and Krueger will also pay a terrible price for what they've done.' He looked around and shook his head. 'You had a lucky escape.'

'So did you. If it weren't for Michiel and his soldiers, the undermerchant would even now be sailing away on the *Zandaam*.'

'How is the captain?'

'The surgeon is operating on him. Once he has dug for the musket ball, we might know more of his fate.'

'Let us pray for his deliverance.'

She followed Ambroise outside. He stared at the shanties of canvas and coral, and the wreckage of wine barrels and discarded weapons.

'I had no choice but to do what I did,' he said. 'If I had stayed here on the islands, I do not think Schellinger would have come back for us. It was only my presence that led to the salvation of those of you left behind.'

'I do not doubt it.'

'Anyway, how could I have prevented all this? The undermerchant would have killed me the very first night.'

'I understand. I have never thought otherwise.'

There were tears running down his face and his eyes were glassy. 'I am sorry, *vrouwe*,' he said. 'I am so sorry.'

'Ambroise?'

'Every night, I dream about this place. Every single night since the wreck. I just want to go back and do it all again.' He sank to his knees in the sand. The redcoats standing about stared at him in astonishment. One of them crossed himself.

'There was nothing you could have done,' she said. 'You had no choice.'

'Tell that to Coen,' he said. 'Tell that to Holland.'

'I should get back to the ship,' she said. 'I need to be with Captain van Texel.'

'Yes,' he said. 'Yes of course.'

'Will you be all right.'

He stood up and brushed the sand from his breeches. He could not look her in the face.

She made her way down the beach to the yawl.

'Before you go,' he called after her. 'I have some bad news for you.' She turned. 'It is about your husband.'

The *Zandaam*

The surgeon had probed for the musket ball. It had been a bloody business by all accounts. Now Michiel lay in a hammock on the gun deck, his face white as chalk. He was having trouble breathing.

She gripped his hand and his eyes blinked open. 'You did it,' he murmured. 'You survived.'

'You too,' she said.

'I don't know about that.'

'The surgeon said you will certainly leave this world one day, but today is not the day.'

He grimaced. 'What does that butcher know about anything?'

'And you didn't run away this time.'

'There was nowhere to run to.'

She smiled. 'I think we both know that that's a lie.'

He was grey, exhausted. Talking was taking all his strength. But he smiled back and squeezed her hand.

CHAPTER 66

The seal island

It sent a chill up Cornelia's spine when she heard Christiaan raving from the prison of coral slabs they had built to house him. Ambroise had put him on the seal island, for he did not trust him in the hold with the other prisoners.

It was foul weather, grey and cold, and there were whitecaps on the lagoon. She had got soaked through sailing the short distance from the *Zandaam* to the island. Three redcoats escorted her up the shingle beach to the lonely and desolate cell.

'I wish to speak to the undermerchant privately,' she said to the sergeant. He nodded and went to wait outside.

She ducked her head and went in. Rain leaked through the brushwood ceiling that had been thrown over the clinker walls. It was stinking and miserably cold. She heard the rattle of leg chains. Christiaan was crouched in the corner.

When he saw her, he smiled as if he had been expecting her. 'I knew you'd come,' he said. 'You must get me away from here.' His teeth were broken. Some of Michiel's men had done that. It was the limit of the vengeance Ambroise had allowed against him during his imprisonment.

'It won't be easy,' she said.

He stood up, his shoulder against the wall. He was unsteady on his feet. 'You have told them I looked after you, that I treated you well?'

'I have told them everything.' A rush of wind shook the flimsy coral walls. 'Ambroise says you will rot in Hell.'

'There is no Hell, my lady. It is just a device men have invented to keep us from our true desires. But I shall not be leaving this world just yet.'

She took a step closer. 'Tell me.'

'I still have followers on that ship and we are many weeks' sailing from Batavia. Time enough to find the crack in my jailers' souls.' He worked a finger between two of the coral slabs to show her how a whispered promise or an uncommon thought might find its way in.

'Ambroise does not intend for you to go to Batavia. He says he will hang you here on the island.'

'You must not allow it. I demand justice.'

Justice. She stepped closer and put her lips to his ear. 'As you wish.'

Salomon's knife slid in easily. His eyes went wide. She sliced down as hard as she could, and the chains rattled as he reached for her.

She stepped away quickly and watched him crumple to the floor.

Ambroise was summoned urgently from the yacht. When he got to the island, the sergeant ran down the beach to meet him.

'What happened?' he said.

The man began to stammer an excuse. Ambroise pushed him aside and made his way quickly up the sand. He found Cornelia sitting outside the makeshift prison staring out to sea. Her skirts were soaked in blood.

'What did you do?' he said.

'It took a little while,' she said. 'But justice has been done.'

She stood up and walked past him down the beach. Two of the sailors helped her into the yawl.

Ambroise looked at the sergeant who had come up behind him, white-faced and shaking. 'You saw nothing, you heard nothing. Is that understood?'

He turned it over in his mind. He would tell Governor Coen that he hanged him, as he had planned to do. He could hardly tell him the truth. And the truth was such a slimy thing; it twisted and turned in your hands, always changing its shape. You never knew where you were with it.

If he could rescue the silver, he might yet save his career. He had Ruben's vase and the cameo, and if he could bring back most of the coin Governor Coen might yet recommend him for promotion.

'What shall we do with the body?' the sergeant said.

'Just burn it,' he said.

Cornelia stood at the stern of the yawl and watched the low island grow smaller. It was the last time she would ever hear the cry of the mutton birds.

Soon she would return to the society of civilized men and women, if there were such a thing. It seemed to her that goodness was mere affectation. She wondered if she would trust anyone except Michiel ever again.

One day, they said, the Dutch would rule every dark corner of the world and all men would come to know true religion and live in peace.

Well, she thought, I wish the Company and the pastors good luck with that.

END

EPIC ADVENTURE SERIES

Colin Falconer's EPIC ADVENTURE SERIES of historical thrillers draws inspiration from many periods of history. Visit the fabled city of Xanadu, the Aztec temples of Mexico, or the mountain strongholds of the legendary Cathars. Glimpse Julius Caesar in the sweat and press of the Roman forum, ride a war elephant in the army of Alexander the Great, or follow Suleiman the Magnificent into the forbidden palace of his harem.

2000+ five-star reviews.
Translated into 25 languages.
3000+ pages.

'A fantastic read' - Wilbur Smith

The series is available in Kindle eBook or 6x9 inch paperback.at Amazon.com, Amazon.co.uk and Amazon.ca.

A WORD FROM COLIN

Thank you for reading this book. I hope you enjoyed it. It's part of a series of fast paced thrillers that take you all around the world and through many periods of history.

SILK ROAD sees Templar knight, Josseran Sarrazini faced with a formidable task - to ride the treacherous Silk Road to the edge of the known world to forge a crucial allegiance with a people who do not honor his cause, or his God.

LORD OF THE ATLAS finds ex-soldier Harry Delhaze battling the wild bandit armies of ruthless prophet-warlord, Bou Hamra, through the snows of the Atlas Mountains and the baking deserts of the Sahara.

And FEVER COAST is a quest, from the African savannah and the slave markets of Mozambique to the Moghul palaces and British redcoat forts of Carnatic India, that forces Lachlan McKenzie to decide between the life that he always dreamed of and a sworn promise of vengeance.

The books are all stand-alone stories and can be read in any order.

View the whole series here: Epic Adventure Series.

SPECIAL PRICES AND NEW RELEASES

I send monthly newsletters with details on new releases, special offers and other bits of news relating to my books.

Just sign up to my COLIN FALCONER BOOKS mailing list to stay in the loop.

ENJOY THIS BOOK?

You can make a big difference.

Honest reviews of my books help bring them to the attention of other readers.

If you've enjoyed this book I would be very grateful if you could spend a few minutes leaving a review (it can be as short as you like) on the book's Amazon page. You can jump right to the page by clicking below.

Write a book review.

If you've read a few books in the series please would you consider writing a brief series review on the Amazon SERIES PAGE?

Write a series review (scroll to the very bottom of the series page to write your review).

MANY THANKS!

ABOUT THE AUTHOR

Born in London, Colin Falconer started out in advertising, then became a freelance journalist. He worked in radio and television before writing his first novel. He has published over forty books, and is best known for historical adventure thrillers – stories on an epic scale, inspired by his passion for history and travel. His books have been translated into 24 languages.

Colin stays in touch with readers and answers questions on Facebook and via his website www.colinfalconer.org.

AUTHOR'S NOTE

Anyone familiar with West Australian history will know of the ill-starred journey of the VOC *retourschip* Batavia and its foundering off what is now the town of Geraldton in 1629. It was the general inspiration behind this novel.

My thanks to Sue Cox at the WA Maritime Museum for her assistance. Also to Bruce Melrose, who first mapped the Abrolhos from the air. His work greatly assisted the writing of this book.

The Great Cameo is now the chief attraction in the Royal Penningkabinet at Leiden in the Netherlands. The poem that Christiaan recites was a contemporary work *The Anacreontic* by Pieter Corneliszoon Hooft.

Printed in Great Britain
by Amazon

23832110R00199